Bergdorf Boys

Praise for Scott Alexander Hess

"Scott Alexander Hess's *Diary of a Sex Addict* is relentlessly erotic and divinely written."

—Richard Labonte, Bookmarks

"If Dennis Cooper and Chuck Palahniuk had a bastard love child, it would look like Scott Hess's *Diary of a Sex Addict.* It is bareback fiction: raw and dangerous, skin to skin and true. The next morning, we almost regret it. Almost."

—Bryan Borland, author of My Life as Adam

"Hess has the literary talent to make his writing brutally honest and hugely energetic."

—Marten Weber, author of Shayno *and* Benedetto Casanova

Bergdorf Boys

a novel by

Scott Alexander Hess

jms books

BERGDORF BOYS

This novel was originally published in *Ganymede Journal.*

JMS Books LLC
10286 Staples Mill Rd. #221
Glen Allen, VA 23060
www.jms-books.com

ISBN: 9781467907514

Printed in the United States of America

Dedication: For Mary Alice.

Prologue

IT WAS THE day the weather lost its mind.

Neal sighed, considered the sentence as an opener for his new *Pop* magazine column, then continued.

Late May temperatures shot into the upper 90s as a troop of boys dressed as Greek messengers scattered about the city. They each unrolled a hand-painted paper, read it aloud, then pricked a finger and dripped blood into the center of the parchment. Reportedly, some guests winced at the blood, while others began phoning friends to see if they'd snared an invite to Andres Palamos' Oracle Orgy. A few bold and drug-addled recipients asked the soft-skinned messengers what they would do for a wad of cash or a bit of coke. By the end of the day, the pulse of the city's gay heart was aflutter with rumors, resentments and expectations. Competing parties were canceled, hair appointments were made, diamonds were dusted. The countdown began.

Neal grimaced. It would never do. The whole thing felt stale, like the dusty ramblings of an old dowager socialite, not the razor sharp musings of a hip gay editor. He had to 'say' something, not just report. The column had to pop. He shut his eyes, rubbed his temples. At least he had a title. *Bergdorf Boy.*

Chapter 1

THE MEN IN the porno were daring Neal to give up. Every grunt, every smack on the ass, every Romanian groan of pleasure told him to run. He'd been at the Palamos party ten minutes—hiding under a mink blanket in the Jade bedroom. It had started well enough. He'd made it into the mansion confident and ready to mingle. Then, moving from the searing summer heat into the frigid, air conditioned entry hall, he saw the masses of gigantic white teeth, lithe bodies, runway couture outfits, champagne flutes and chattering, fiercely-sharpened tongues, and he felt like a hick Missouri fraud. Suddenly the cute, anchor-detail knit top he'd maxed out his Bergdorf Goodman credit card for seemed very, very last season. He was getting ready to turn heel when he spotted the boy.

A servant likely, wearing a sheer skin-tight white bikini. Barely seventeen, Neal guessed, he was lounging with his ass propped on the edge of a long marble table, one leg draped casually over the tip, his inner thigh open, soft and hairless. The boy was flexing his leg muscles and spreading his thighs ever so slightly. The curved hem of his silken bikini pressed into that crease between the top of his leg and the edge of his crotch. The boy was laughing, turning to smile, as a waiter offered Neal pink-shaded liquor and socialite Trudy Pratte swooped at him. He'd fled to the Jade room.

Upstairs, under the mink blanket, Neal practiced deep breathing. In through the nose, out through the mouth. The Romanian porn actors groaned from the flat screen television, taunting. Sex and alcohol, a perfect pairing since puberty, had finally turned on him. Two months out of rehab, the skin-crawling rawness of being sober had kicked his animal urges into chaotic overdrive. If he wasn't doing yoga, or shopping at Bergdorf Goodman, he was in constant, teen-like hard-on mode. Unfortunately, he couldn't put two flirty words together without a cocktail to lubricate his tongue. The mere sight of a pretty servant boy spun him into a panic. He wanted to leave the party, but he couldn't cop out on his good friend Rovvie. Rovvie had worked like a fiend to get Neal the gig as editor at *Pop* Magazine, the city's premier gay weekly, which his lover Andreas Palamos owned. It was the editor's job to attend fetes like this, and Neal desperately needed the work. The rent was backed up, the credit card bills overdue, Con Edison had sent a turn off notice, and he refused to call his family again for help. Breathing in, breathing out. He felt like he might hyperventilate. Through the shut bedroom door he heard muted voices from downstairs. He imagined the door bursting open, the voices flying at him, attacking. He hated feeling so nervous, so often, with nothing but sex as a possible relief.

Peeking out from under the fur, he eyed his reflection in an elaborate, gold leaf mirror. He turned thirty-one that summer. He wondered if his eyes were sinking in and if he should start tweezing his brows to create a lifting effect. From the mirror's distance, he thought he looked like a child swallowed up by a soft, hairy beast. Strands of his expertly dyed caramel blonde hair sprayed out from the top of the fur, and his compact body curled underneath. It was hot, and his breath—caught in the confines of the cave—reeked of licorice candy and espresso. The Romanian porno was playing fuck-beat music. Neal casually groped himself. The wave of voices from downstairs was getting louder, thornier. He heard the cackle of socialite Trudy Pratte, then a deep, distant scream. One of the porn stars was pitching a climax. He wondered if guests were reading his preview column in *Pop*. Copies of the magazine were scattered about the rooms. He cradled a copy under the mink, reading his tiny teaser again.

Bergdorf Boy here, promising you the sexiest summer on record. Steam heat, men to meet, brassy baskets. Beginning next week, BB will twirl you through it all with a secret peek at hook ups, hang outs, "celeb backroom spottings" and the question on every boy's twittering lips—where is the best pinga in the city, the hottest fashion and the best spot to nab a rich hubby? Until next week. BB.

He snapped the magazine shut. The truth was he had no idea what he was going to write about on a weekly basis. The very idea overwhelmed him. Neal started to rip off the mink just as the bedroom door swung open then shut softly. He lay very still. He heard laughter, two men. He recognized one of the voices—a bar owner and big *Pop* advertiser. Perfect. Editor discovered under blanket, slobbering in fear. Neal shut his eyes. Breathing in, breathing out. If they left the overhead lights off they may not notice him.

"Did you see Trudy Pratte? That ancient sapphire necklace is ridiculous," the first voice said, high-pitched, slurred.

"Shut up. I like her," said the other, steady and mean.

"She came alone. She was supposed to be with Paul, but he disappeared or something," the first said, then belched.

"Hurry up," said the darker voice. "You mean Paul the broker, or Paul the meth addict?"

"Addict Paul," the first shouted from the bathroom, splashing water, then flushing. "I heard he's dead, I think. Was it him? Or maybe he just left town. He's so fake anyway. And sort of fat in the face. "

Neal flinched under the fur. He'd met Paul that spring at a twelve-step meeting, both men barely out of rehab. Paul, a socialite playboy with a hard-core crystal meth addiction, had drifted away after a few meetings. Neal had stayed. He missed Paul. There was a sound from the two men, like a kiss, then a slap on an ass. He pushed at the mink, trying to wedge a hole so he could see. The darker one stood at the door to the bathroom, his hands slung over his head, showing off a tiny tuft of hair on his belly. Neal could see past him into the bathroom where the other man stood at the sink, his pants pushed past his ass as he played with his tank top. Neal glimpsed that curve, that spot where the hem of the man's tight lime green bikini underwear met the supple curve of his plump ass cheek. It was the curves between thigh and crotch, leg and ass, that drove Neal nuts. He was aroused, mesmerized, and the man's underwear were, Neal decided, at least two sizes too small. He pressed at the mink a tad more to see. It fluttered. The tall dark one noticed and moved toward the bed.

"Hey?" the man said.

Neal laid still, eyes shut tight. He'd play drunk. They'd likely tiptoe out. He could hear them whispering, then a laugh. Someone was gently pulling the blanket off him.

"Shit, he's hard," the dark one said.

From the television, the porn actors were grunting. Neal felt one edge of the bed sink, then the other. They must be sitting on either side of him. In his blackness, Neal sensed someone leaning toward him. He smelled scotch. His cock throbbed. There was a snicker and he felt the gentlest touch just below his waist, then the door swung open and a light switched on. Neal sat up feigning sleep, realizing he may have already made an absolute fool of himself half an hour into the party of the summer, at the home of his new boss.

The two men stole away, passing Albert Poke, who posed in the doorway. Over sixty, overweight and famous as the owner of a vintage Rolls Royce, Albert waved a diamond-clad pinkie in the air toward Neal as greeting. As he entered the room he rolled side to side, big hips swiveling, showing off a gold silk shirt open to the navel, bell-bottom sweat pants, and several thousand dollars worth of jewelry. Neal had met Albert at a party. The rumor was that a few years ago Albert had some sort of stroke, tightening some sort of screw in his brain that made him speak in run-on sentences. His thoughts were spiked with nonsense and wisdom. Albert approached, wheezing softly and choosing each word with care, as if he were stringing together a strand of scattered pearls.

"This is…not truly…a Jade room and you know dear one, the Greeks had no room for error, or…was it truth as my dear friend Sylvia promised as she flew the coop, yes, like a bird on a wire you might say, which of course," Albert said, collapsing on the edge of the bed, shutting his eyes to concentrate. "Jade is… a faux Asiatic resemblance to what used to be, in our universal minds, that is. I'm quoting, someone who shan't be quoted."

Albert shook a fat finger glistening with rings that looked as if they would ricochet off into Neal's face at any moment.

"And you, little one, choosing boys over your editorial duties, tsk tsk," Albert said. "Trudy, that wicked one, insists Andreas threw this party to fluff up his flailing little *Pop* magazine. Shouldn't you be hawking the wares?"

Neal had been editor of *Pop* for two weeks. Rovvie had told Albert, Andreas and anyone else who would listen all about Neal's extensive writing talents. He hadn't told them how he and Neal had met: nude and tangled up in a sweaty group scene at the West Side Club bathhouse. Albert was back at the door, one hand on his hip, the other hand poised in the air as if he were holding an invisible tray.

"Are you coming?" Albert said. "I am afraid, oh no, not fear that's too grand a word, but then what are we all so desperately in fear of, when it's only air and water. Touché!"

"I'll catch up," Neal said.

Albert twisted his girth in an elaborate, slow motion turn and swirled his hand upward in three circles as he made his exit. Neal sat on the bed, taking a long look at himself in the gold mirror across the room. He was lean and fit, had a bit of an early summer tan, and his eyes were bright, sober. He wore white skinny jeans and his form-fitting anchor-emblazoned knit blue pullover from Bergdorf Goodman. The shirt had cost him a month's rent. He shut his eyes, guessing what the smart, confident new editor of *Pop* Magazine might say to those fabulous people downstairs. The socialites, the club kids, the filthy rich businessmen like his father. And what would he say to that boy, the servant boy in the white Speedo with the elegant curves. He would say something witty, something substantial, something men say.

Neal fell back again on the bed, then felt a breeze on his cheek, as the bedroom door creaked. He stood up quickly. There was no one, just a glistening speck reflecting up from the soft, cream carpet. He bent and picked up a shimmering diamond ring. Albert's. He'd need to find him and return it. He stared into the ostentatious ring's center which cut up into multiple glassy triangles of light and fire. The thing would probably pay for a full season beach house rental on Fire Island. He pocketed it and stepped into the hallway, moving under a series of small chandeliers which also glinted and twisted light. He stepped past large oil paintings depicting subtly erotic all male fox hunting parties, servant boys stooping at the heels of leather booted, tight-pant wearing gentry. At the head of the stairway, a sweeping curve of marble and wrought iron curled down into the mansion's grand entry hall below. Neal paused, listening to a swell of voices, the clatter of serving trays and a throbbing dance beat. Through it all, he thought he heard his name called. The dance music increased in volume and he turned back to see Rovvie darting up the rear servant's staircase to the third floor. He was barefoot, wearing a skimpy floral kimono. Listening to the ragged cackle of Trudy Pratte, Neal turned and followed Rovvie's path. It somehow looked safer.

Chapter 2

BY THE TIME he reached the third floor landing, Neal had lost sight of Rovvie. He could see, at one end of the hall, a gold door decorated with the outline of a pale blue bird. The infamous "gang banging" gold room. It would open at midnight. Rovvie told Neal he would get a dark blue skeleton key that fitted the lock, a key passed out to favored guests.

He heard voices from the other end of the hall. Andreas' private bedroom suite. The sound of Rovvie's laughter drew him. The hall was lit with small teardrop chandeliers hanging from the ceiling at five foot intervals. The walls were lined with black and white photos of handsome athletes showing off battle scars: a boxer with a black eye, a wrestler with a cracked tooth, a gymnast with a split lip. The last door was barely open. Neal could see through the bedroom into the dressing chamber where Rovvie and Andreas sat talking. Neal hesitated as Andreas reached out and pushed Rovvie's kimono off his shoulder, revealing the boy's elegant back, pale, unblemished; the light hairless curve of his ass; long, long hard legs; and full, wide, manly feet. Neal found both men attractive, but knew it was smart to keep Rovvie in the gay girlfriend category and Andreas as the boss. He knew he should slip away and get down to the party. He lingered.

Andreas stood up and his silk robe slipped open. He was huge, romantically handsome, and dark. He put a pill into Rovvie's mouth, then ran his tongue along the boy's lips, licked his cheek and kissed his neck. Neal took a deep breath and turned away, only to face Caz, Andreas' younger brother and right-hand man. A smaller, plainer version of Andreas, Caz had wide-set eyes, narrow lips and a crew cut. Rovvie said Caz took care of the ugly side of Andreas' business, the darker, violent jobs. Caz smirked at Neal, put his hand on his shoulder and shoved him into the bedroom.

"Somebody here to see you," Caz said.

Neal turned his back on Rovvie's nakedness.

"Come in," Andreas said. "We're all family here."

Neal turned and edged slowly into the large dressing chamber. Caz remained in the bedroom. Andreas sipped his drink.

"Sit down Caz," Andreas said.

Sulking, Caz sat on the edge of the bed as Rovvie reached for Neal's hand and made room for him on a red velvet fainting couch. He squeezed Neal's hand a little too tightly. Two walls of the room were mirrored. An open closet revealed silk dressing gowns on satin hangers. There was a gold plate filled with pills, and a bottle of vodka and glasses. Andreas poured drinks handing a tumbler to Neal, then reached out and pulled Rovvie's foot into his lap. Neal was trembling. He hadn't held a drink in his hand since March. He kept his eyes focused on his own reflection in the mirror, refusing to glance at Rovvie's nakedness. Neal's hand began to sweat.

"Caz come and toast," Andreas said as his brother joined them. "Here's to the success of *Pop* magazine and our new editor."

Neal held the glass to his lips, the pungent bite of the vodka making his eyes water. He quickly feigned a sip and held the glass away. Andreas lifted Rovvie's foot and pressed his lips to the heel, the ball, the soft underside. With his finger, he traced a design. Behind Andreas on a shelf, Neal could see a bowl of liquid, and a long pin-shaped knife.

"Neal, go back to the party," Andreas said.

Rovvie's eyes were shut, but he smiled and waved Neal away. Neal nodded and left. At the bedroom door, he glanced back to see Andreas delicately pressing the small knife into the side of Rovvie's foot.

Chapter 3

WHEN HE GOT downstairs, Neal felt flushed. He wanted to run outside into the heat and flee, but he got caught in a rush of chattering young men pressing through the front door wearing tiny gold Speedos and women's wedge platform beach shoes. Their high asses, soft skin, chiseled cheekbones—it was all too much. He turned to leave when three bullet-like thoughts rushed in: the *Pop* editor must stay; the gold room may be fantastic; the servant boy is looking this way. Indeed, the white bikini servant boy was smiling at him from across the room. Before he could move, the boy was sucked into the crowd.

But we made eye contact, Neal thought.

He sipped a Red Bull and stepped back into a corner, fading as the music drummed a moody, constant beat. He moved further away from the shuffling bodies, as his stomach knotted from too much caffeine. He knew he'd end up at the bathhouse, just like he always did. Trying to look bored, he leaned into the entry hall's wallpaper, which had a raised leafy pattern. He recalled a story where a woman faded into the wallpaper and nobody noticed.

At last, the dreary trance music shifted to up-tempo. He drew another yoga breath. Rovvie said the mansion, which took up a half block on upper Park Avenue, was as spooky as a tomb at night. Sprouting off on both the east and west sides of the entry hall were high archways leading to ballroom-sized spaces cleared of furniture. Neal chose east, where serving boys were strategically scattered, dusted with gold-leaf body paint, crowned with leaves, crotches sheathed. They were all barefoot. Questions had been painted on the young men's shoulders, necks, ankles or cheeks in French, Greek, English, Latin and Italian. Correct answers lead to favors. Most anything asked was granted.

There were ice sculptures of Greek Gods anchored in faux-marble pools. The pools brimmed with warm-jetted water, which would melt the Gods slowly through the night. Neal watched two boys wade into a pool, giggling and pecking at jewels and party favors inserted into the ice sculptures' frozen eyes, feet and bellies. They seemed so confident, those boys, so beautiful. Weaving his way through a dancing trio of Spanish men and a tiny woman having a hysterical coughing fit, Neal caught sight of Annie Fitz, the young, bubbly straight-girl art director of *Pop* Magazine. Knowing her only two weeks, Neal already adored Annie. He breathed easier, happy to see a friend, though a bit appalled at her faux-'60s tie-dye jeans, combat boots, and faded Blondie concert T-shirt. She was chatting with Brandon Blunt.

Brandon was forty and ordinary with narrow eyes, large ears, a pointy bird-like jaw and a lean compact frame. His bank account, and ties to the Blunt Drug Store chain, was anything but ordinary. Brandon's lover Nick Sands—that year's "It-boy" writer for the *New York Times* Style section—stood near him dressed in designer Thom Browne silver cargo shorts and a top-stitched navy jacket with a bright white color peak at the shoulder. He was the nastiest bitch Neal knew. Supposedly, Neal had slept with Nick's boyfriend at a party years ago. Nick never let go of the grudge, despite the fact that he had spun to wild success, while Neal had crashed. Luckily, Nick was pulled away by an obnoxious up-and-coming fashion designer.

As he got close, Neal spotted Trudy Pratte making a beeline for Brandon, gliding forward on kitten heels. After thirty-five, Trudy had replaced her striking beauty with an incredibly taut, girlish gym-body and runway couture outfits. Tonight she was dressed as a jockey—creamy jodhpurs, black hip boots and a silk blouse. She was married to a drunken writer who had been on the short list for the Pulitzer, and whose family owned oil wells. Supposedly, the coupled lived in adjoining but very separate penthouses.

"Brandon darling, I need you a week from Thursday I just invited Duchesse Trandorra and her husband for dinner, both total bores. You have got to finish my table," Trudy said.

At that, a flock of peacocks invaded the room, followed by muscled trainers wearing leather thongs and painted tragedy masks. Just behind them was Albert Poke, who spoke as he approached their group.

"It's certainly an intriguing start dears, but as my friend Sylvia says, what starts may never finish and what finishes is the cooked pudding, isn't that it, or, oh bother," said Albert, belching softly.

Brandon opened his mouth to speak, but stopped, baffled. From the hallway, they heard applause. Rovvie was making his entrance. They all hurried in. At the top of the staircase, Rovvie towered over the crowd, willowy, white-blond shoulder length hair, creamy pearl skin. Neal knew Rovvie was from rural Arkansas, but on the stairs there, with his light pink cheeks, almond shaped fawn eyes and dancer-like curves, he looked like East Coast royalty. A gold swag of cloth had been sewn and fitted around his slim waist. It was beaded with tiny diamonds and a few sapphires, creating the head of a peacock. He wore a short cape that shimmered as he moved, woven leather sandals with gold wings bursting from the sides and carried a shepherd's staff. Neal saw traces of blood on his right foot. Albert clapped, howled and shook his naked belly.

"Now that is an entrance so much like in the day, the '60s that is, not the '70s, which were way too lurid for any of you really," he said.

Andreas trailed Rovvie down the stairs, dressed in a simple black tuxedo, ruffled shirt open revealing a tanned and furry chest.

"What's with the staff?" Trudy asked.

"He's Hermes, the winged Greek messenger," Albert said. "Son to Zeus, herdsman of the dead, the bringer of dreams but of course a cunning thief from birth."

Trudy burst out laughing.

"Well, that simple boy is certainly none of that," she said.

"Don't be so sure, Trudy dear," Albert said, belching again. "Oh dear, bubbles."

Rovvie lilted up and off the final step on the staircase. The glamour faded as his walk became a shuffling limp. Neal made out two Greek letters cut into his right foot. The wound was fresh. The crowd was applauding, and Andreas shaking hands and greeting people as they worked their way toward Neal.

"We are animals," Albert started, though in a tone gentler, more lucid. "The cowboys, the herders, they all do it to keep track of their stock. He branded the boy. The letters are Greek—A.P. Zeus and Hermes indeed."

Neal watched Rovvie approach. His eyes were half-mooned, both bright and dull. Rovvie finally collapsed into the center of the group.

"Ahmmmm flying," he drawled.

He reached out and gripped Neal by the neck, then drew him close and bit his ear.

"I'm so glad you're here," Rovvie said.

Neal and Rovvie shared a close hug as Andreas made small talk with Brandon.

"What did he do to you?" Neal said softly, wanting to pull his friend away, somewhere safe from prying eyes.

Andreas kept Rovvie on a short leash and lately the leash was getting tighter.

"I see you have the keys," said Albert, pointing to the pouch with the gold room keys hanging around Rovvie's waist.

Neal knew Albert's palm would never feel the metal. Palamos wrapped his hand around Rovvie's naked bicep, then pressed his lips to the boy's ear. Rovvie smiled and reached out to Neal, placing a blue key in his palm. Neal noticed Palamos' fingers were digging deeply into Rovvie's arm, issuing a red outline. A thunderous crack quieted the room, followed by shouts and applause, as an ice sculpture crashed in half and collapsed in one of the fountains, spraying jewels. Heels flew. Feet splashed. Annie squealed in delight.

Neal turned back from the spectacle. Rovvie and Andreas had disappeared back into the crowd. Albert and Brandon wandered off for a drink with a chattering Trudy. Neal grabbed Annie and led her toward a bench. They passed a very tall Asian man who was contemplating a question written in Italian on the chest of a serving boy.

"Hestia," the Asian man said to the boy. "She's the virgin Goddess."

The boy curled his plump lips, accepting the answer, then slowly unbuttoned the man's shirt. The man leaned in close, whispering his fantasy. For a second, the color drained from the boy's face and he stopped with the buttons. Recovering, he smiled and licked the man's ear. Neal and Annie rested on the bench beside a pool featuring an ice sculpture of Hades. A school of bug-eyed silver fish swan around the frozen statue. A well-endowed fawn boy passed with a bucket of champagne.

"Is the booze making you crazy?" she said. "You look like you want to bolt."

Neal had revealed his newfound sobriety to Annie, deciding she was a reliable confidante. He nodded, acknowledging that he did want to run, and likely would run soon to the sexual solitude of the Westside Club bathhouse. But as he paused, he realized he'd much rather be at Bergdorf Goodman. He thought of telling Annie about Bergdorf's third floor, its long circling center hallway, the soft murmur of voices from the café, much like his parent's voices, muted, in the kitchen, obscured by the roaring hum of the hallway's attic fan, as he lay in his little bedroom in Missouri. He'd felt safe then. He thought of telling Annie how during his weekly trips to Bergdorf's he fantasized about curling up on a big button leather chaise by the Thom Browne collection, covering himself with cashmere sweaters, and going to sleep. He thought of all this, but instead, he quoted Holly Golightly.

"I got the mean reds, you know, when you're afraid but you don't know what of," Neal said. "That's when I hop in a cab and go to Tiffany's."

Across the room, he spotted Caz, looking very strange, like he'd just stolen a watch or shot someone.

"Nothing bad can happen to you there," Neal said.

Annie looked perplexed, lost to his retro film reference.

"*Breakfast at Tiffany's*," Neal said.

There was a shrill scream then applause from the next room as one of the servant boys waded naked into a pool. Neal smiled at Annie, deciding he would give himself permission to escape the party after an hour. Bergdorf's was closed. The bathhouse was open 24/7.

"Let's get a Red Bull," said Neal, aware that he was carving a hole in his empty stomach.

They left the entry hall and made their way through an ever-growing crowd. An electronic trio was revving up. The male singer, stringy with a shock of red hair, had a nasty growling tone, spitting lyrics about a motorcycle crash. A gorgeous, topless Brazilian girl operated a synthesizer and a teenaged Spanish boy danced and shook a pale wooden instrument. Neal watched the Spanish boy on stage swivel his hips and fall to the floor into a one-armed pushup. He looked genuinely angry. Champagne corks shot endlessly. Across the room, Nick Sands was headed their way with Trudy Pratte on his arm.

"Oh God, not him," Neal said.

Nick and Trudy moved swiftly toward them before Neal could escape. He leaned closer to Annie for support.

"Neal, you finally got back into journalism. *Pop*, what a

funny little magazine to start with," Nick said, eyes scoping the room as he spoke.

"Neal's doing some great things at the magazine," Annie said.

"Tightening up the escort ads?" Nick said. "Cute."

Trudy tossed her head like a mare and laughed.

"Oh you are wicked," she said.

Neal was wilting, lost for a comeback. The party was closing in on him. Coming their way was the white-Speedo servant boy. The timing could not be worse.

"Nothing cute at all. Neal's writing a new column, it's unlike anything I've ever seen before," Annie said. "Anywhere."

Nick's eyes stopped wandering. He gave Neal a hard look.

"Really, a column?" he said.

Neal tried for poker face. He had spoken to Andres and Annie about the promised weekly column, something sexy, but he hadn't come up with a long-term concept. All he'd written was that one brief teaser.

"Do tell," Nick said. "Like nothing ever seen before?"

Neal's mind raced. Sex and fashion is all that came to mind. And the title.

"It's called *Bergdorf Boy*," Neal said.

"I love it," Annie said, far too enthusiastically.

"Maybe a guide to cheap summer drinking spots would be more up your alley," Nick said. "Weren't you a cocktail waiter for a while? And a lush?"

The servant boy had joined their group, but he didn't have a tray. And he was kissing Trudy Pratte on the cheek.

"It's based on personal adventures," Neal said.

Trudy put a hand on Nick's shoulder, interrupting.

"This is my cousin Alfie, he's visiting from Paris," Trudy said. "He thought it was a pool party, isn't that precious?"

This is the moment, Neal thought. The boy was looking at him, lips parted and expectant. Their eyes met.

"I love gay old Paris," Neal said.

"Have you been?" said Nick.

Neal had not, and nasty Nick had guessed as much. Sweat broke out in a thin, ugly line across Neal's brow and he stood speechless, aching for a drink in a dim sleazy bar or a faceless cock at the bathhouse. His stomach churned and growled. Rovvie drifted up to Neal, then Brandon joined the group, wrapping his arms affectionately around Nick's waist. Nick looked up into Brandon's eyes and they seemed to be sharing something for a moment. Neal saw it, a locking of their eyes, a silent communication. It was soft and long, that moment of theirs, and they seemed to be drawing closer to each other without moving and Neal felt the room emptying out. He realized how deeply he envied Nick. That pretty little moment he and his lover had, their intimacy, spiraled Neal into a darkening tunnel which somehow Rovvie seemed to be able to see. Neal's stomach gurgled again.

"Come on, Neal," Rovvie said. "Someone needs a snack."

He squeezed Neal's hand and pulled him back into the party, producing a small digital camera from the pouch around his waist. They moved into the entry hall and Rovvie snapped Neal's picture. As he did, two servant boys, a muscular looking Egyptian and a lean, redheaded teen, stood by Neal, posing. The Egyptian had a question on his firm belly: *Olympic Gods Dwell.*

"Mount Olympus," Neal said.

The Egyptian turned and placed Neal's hand on his belly. He recalled the game rules, answer a question, any wish is granted. Rovvie shoved the camera into Neal's hand, then grabbed both boys and dragged them to the staircase.

"Make me look like a Gawwwwwd," he drawled.

Neal clicked. Rovvie turned and began to crawl up the stairs as a young woman in ridiculously high heels hiked over him. Neal kept shooting. The Egyptian was just ahead, on his butt, coasting backwards up the stairs, waving his arms near Rovvie's face to create a Medusa affect. For the first time that night, Neal was having fun. He kept shooting, as Rovvie crawled and the Egyptian flailed. As they neared the top, they approached a babbling Albert, who had his back to them. Albert turned, colliding with the crawling boys, tottering and for a second looking like he may fall forward and squash Rovvie to a pulp. The adroit Egyptian gave the fat man a push in the opposite direction.

"I'm taking you to the Gold Room, you tense little thannnng," Rovvie said, pulling Neal along.

As they headed upstairs, Neal scanned the pictures on the camera, past a blurry photo of a green haired drag queen and onto something that made him pause. It was Rovvie nude, his hair flying in front of his face.

"Did Andreas take this?" Neal said.

Rovvie sat up as Neal moved onto one more picture. It was off center, and the man's face was obscured, but it was not Andreas. He was dark, well built, nude and sporting an erection. Rovvie grabbed the camera.

"What was that?" Neal said.

"Just playing around," Rovvie said, getting up and heading quickly up the back stairs.

At the top of the stairs, Rovvie turned and took a deep breath, not meeting Neal's gaze. Months back, during a drunken night out, Rovvie had told Neal he was "through" with Andreas. Soon after, Neal went into Rehab, and had forgotten all about it. Now he wondered what his friend may be up to. At the end of the hall, the door to the gold room opened then shut, emitting a rush of music, smoke and voices. Rovvie took his hand and guided him toward the door with the etched blue bird.

"You worry too much," Rovvie said, pulling out his key, unlocking the gold room door, shoving Neal inside, then dashing away.

HIDDEN SOMEWHERE WAS a DJ booth and the source of wild lightning streaks. Neal stood at the entrance to the gold room watching a crack of white leap across the ceiling. Between flashes, in the black, he thought of the desert at night, the hot clean place he dreamed about. Love in a midnight heat, under a slice of moon, his favorite fantasy. There was a lull, as spookhouse black surrounded him, traces of sound floated, and he shut his eyes to see the desert, and his secret lover. Trance music beat in time with a new set of flashes. His eyes adjusted and the sultry mirage folded back into the heat of the party. He looked up at the black ceiling. He felt like he'd been in rooms like this all his life. He'd never been to the desert.

In corners sculpted men and boys stood with candles in their palms, lights that were extinguished if a guest pulled them down to a sofa. There was a long flat glass-topped liquor bar against one wall, with a server wearing a hood, and close by, a metal counter controlled by a huge Greek man dressed as a wrestler. He doled out amphetamines and powder. In a blue flash of light, Neal saw a film star tying up a porn star. Near that, a group of three embraced, slithering up a wall. He was aroused and trembling. The scene was dangerous, titillating.

Neal wandered into the next room, a chamber lined with velvet couches. He sat and watched. One nude bald man lifted another identical nude bald man, likely his twin, over his head, then set the beefy ass on his face. Neal squeezed his eyes shut. He felt dizzy and wanted to leave, but hesitated. He leaned back and felt an odd welling up, a tightness in his jaw, a rush of something unfamiliar and irritating. He was angry and wanted to stop everything and go. He had a weird urge to jump up and pound at the bald twins with his bare fists, to strain with all of his dull, hapless might and destroy them.

There was a hand on his thigh. It was soft, delicate, and he liked it there. He kept his eyes shut. *I will be fine*, he thought. *It's going to be fucking hot.* A rush of sweet-smelling smoke from a sucking cluster in the far corner swept around him. He thought of holding his breath, but realized that was impossible for long, so he pushed his breath out in staccato gasps as if shooing the drug stench away. The hand touched his hip, then went to his shoulder and turned him, guided him, to lie down. There was a skittering of bare feet, a slight moan, and another shot of smoky air. He felt weak, letting the hand guide him onto his stomach. Knees straddled his back. It was quiet. A giggle from afar, then hands on his shoulder blades. The hands were small, but firm. They moved up into his scalp, pushing harder and now adding lips on his ear, nibbling, licking inside. Neal sunk deeper into the sofa, then finally turned over and looked into the eyes of the man above him. The eyes were red slits, and he thought of the quick clip of the devil's eyes in Roman Polanski's film, *Rosemary's Baby*. Ugly demon eyes screwing a nubile Mia Farrow. The guy looked like he'd been high on crystal meth for days.

"Fuck," Neal said loudly, then rolled away and found his way back out of the room, down the stairs and finally, finally away from the party.

Chapter 4

NEAL SAT NAKED in a dark booth, on a hard, thin mattress. Things were moving briskly at the Westside Club bathhouse. There was a French song about boys fucking. He sucked in his breath, puffed out his chest, and studied the curve of his belly. It was tight. A month without white flour had paid off. He pushed his shoulders back, crossed his feet. A part-time job as a sculpture's model last year had given him the strength to hold this pose for at least ten minutes. Ten minutes at the baths equated to about five men passing his booth. On average, he scored a match after three men. He held the pose, guessing at shadows as they approached. A lean silhouette was promising, then fizzled to an ancient Asian. Two men, A-list, scurried past, not glancing at him. He felt a tingling sensation rush up his back, like an end of summer chill. It was crucial to hook up in the first half hour. The adrenalin rush that came with getting naked, lubing up and showing off only lasted about that long.

After thirty minutes, things began to slip. The overhead trance music began to beat a rhythm that became irritating, and the line of men began to repeat themselves—those Neal rejected looked more desperate, and those who rejected him looked sexier and further out of reach. If nothing happened soon, he would have to fight the creeping exhaustion and try not to see the ugly walls of this clapboard booth, the cracks in the concrete floor, the lost and drugged-up looks of loony desperation in the men's faces. He spread his legs, and lowered his standards. An olive skinned man who had been circling was back, and Neal waved him in. The guy had a gut, but wide shoulders and a large cock which bobbed like an anxious eel. Neal reached out to touch him. As the man turned to shut the cabin door, Neal's hand sank into folds of coarse 'gut' skin. He shuddered and mouthed 'sorry man', an end of session standard. He wasn't that desperate yet. A high-energy song called "Crush" came on and Neal watched the man sulk away, then he stepped out into the hall to wander.

The bathhouse was a rat's maze of narrow, drafty hallways weaving in a big square pattern. In the center of the square was a flight of stairs leading to the basement, and smaller cubicles. On the main floor, doors to booths were in one of three positions: shut completely (a fuck match accomplished); slightly ajar, a nude man waving you in or looking away in disgust; or a wide open door. The wide open door occasionally featured a hot and nasty group scene, but most often, it was an older fat man fingering himself, or a submissive lying face down, eyes squeezed shut, ass in the air.

Safe sex placards lined the hallways, and monitors wandered about making sure nothing insane happened in plain sight. At the club's entrance every patron got a towel, lube, a condom. Every thirty minutes a hyped-up young desk clerk took over the overhead speaker, shutting down the trance music, and rattling through the club rules, including no public sex and no drug use. In the short time he'd been working for Andreas, Neal had learned from Rovvie about two hushed up drug overdoses at the bathhouse. Palamos was owner of this and several other clubs throughout the city. He had a ton of political connections, Rovvie said.

In a booth at the end of the hall, Neal saw white, ghostly

teeth. A tongue darted out, snake-like. The teeth crashed up and down, and the face contorted. It was Skelly, an actor/writer friend of Neal's known for his dead-on impression of a chattering skeleton head. Skelly had written and performed a one-man show based on the concept at an experimental theatre downtown. Neal stopped at the booth and air kissed.

"You do that skeleton thing so well," said Neal. "Sorry I missed your last show."

"Don't block the door," said Skelly.

A sculpted Italian guy was stomping their way. Neal stepped back and Skelly tried to look alluring. The man darted back down the hall. Skelly was a riot on stage, but out of shape and with a comb-over hairdo.

"Fuck him," said Skelly.

"Have you heard anything about Paul?" Neal said. "I heard he might be dead."

Skelly screamed. A lean red head coming their way turned heel and fled.

"What is wrong with you?" Neal said. "I overheard it at the Palamos party. It's probably not true."

At the bathhouse, the rules were simple: hot silence, hard looks, fondle your crotch, look disinterested. Never scream.

"I won't be brought down. Get away from my booth you dark cloud," Skelly said.

Neal laughed and walked on. He knew that deep down Skelly hated him. The two had competed for a freelance writing job years ago and Neal had nabbed it. Skelly never forgot it. As he turned down the hall, heading east in the maze, Neal looked back to glimpse Skelly's chomping white teeth, his claim to fame. Skelly would be there all night, finally getting off alone in the group shower room. Neal turned a corner. He felt a little tired, so he leaned against a shut door at the end of the hall, in a dark spot. There was a ceiling fan cranking above, circulating air heavy with sweat, sex and a whiff of amyl nitrate. The breeze felt nice there, with his eyes shut. He drifted for a moment in the breeze, in the dark, and thought again of his parent's attic fan in the hall, how strange and comforting that breeze was, circulating the far off voices from neighboring yards. *That was summer too*, Neal thought, *like this is summer now*. He had always loved summer. He opened his eyes to see a big furry man looking at him with kindness, which was irritating, so he moved on. A few feet up, a cabin door was ajar. A pert looking man was lying on his cot wearing only black dress socks and stylish horn-rimmed glasses. The man had draped a T-shirt over the mounted wall light, to dim the room, and he was reading a book, a slim volume with a pistol on the cover that Neal guessed was an Agatha Christie page-turner. Neal paused to take in the tableau, fascinated and a little shocked, imagining the man would drive away any potential sex suitors with that silly book. As if reading Neal's thoughts, the bespeckled man snapped his eyes away from the page and gave him a long probing look. The man held his steely glare and Neal moved away.

Neal passed a half-open cabin door. An ass in the air. He kept going, then paused and stepped back. It was easy to study the passives before they glanced over their shoulders. From behind, the guy looked perfect. Long lean back, smooth legs, a mess of sweaty black hair falling to his shoulders. What made Neal stop, though, was the ass: a perfect curve up from the nape of the lower back, rising high, higher than any normal ass, almost leaping up, then crashing back down the other side, down to the hairless legs.

Beautiful, Neal thought and with that, the ass rose slightly off the mattress and hovered. He stepped into the booth, feeling that rush of exhilaration, forgetting himself. He felt powerful, a little angry. The ass pressed itself up strong and high. Neal touched it gently. He waited. He slapped it. The mane of black hair swayed. Neal grabbed it, grabbed the ass hard and held it, then he took both hands and held it harder, kneaded into it with his fists, pressed fiercely. Then Neal crawled on top, finally lost, sinking, breathless with a rush of relief, shutting his eyes and glimpsing a long endless stretch of midnight-pitch desert and that fading, illusive lover. He grabbed onto the silken black mane of hair and let go.

AFTERWARD, THEY DIDN'T speak. The ass had huge black eyes, fat red lips. Neal figured him for a South American. As they rested on the narrow mattress, the door creaked open. A blond man peeked in, then darted away. Neal sat up. It looked like Paul. In the dark, the flash of blond looked like Paul. Neal shut his eyes. The ass with the black mane of hair, and an expertly shaved crotch, was snoring lightly.

Neal had seen Paul the first time after rehab at the bathhouse. He'd caught a look at him through an open, gang-bang door. Paul, who was striking with white-blond hair, a year-round tan and eight percent body fat, was lying on a mattress, surrounded by three big men. Neal moved away, embarrassed to see a friend in the nude, but Paul had caught his eye and winked. There was no expression in Paul's face, it was completely still. Just that one, quick, dead little wink. The ass was snoring louder. Neal shifted his weight on the mattress, hoping to stir him. He didn't budge.

"You must be content," Neal said in a whisper. "To sleep so easily."

He laid his hand near him, on the mattress, touching the side of his body just below his armpit. There was warmth and a slight tremble from the snoring. Neal used to hear his father snoring, through the wall. It was a family joke, how loudly he snored. Neal shut his eyes, pressed his hand closer, then rested it on that hollow between the edge of the armpit and the start of the chest. He breathed deeply, then spoke, his lips barely moving.

"Let's run away," Neal said.

The snoring continued, soft and gentle. Neal pulled his hand away, then sat up and grabbed his towel. There was a black leather bag on the ground. He bent, and poked gingerly. There was a hotel room key and a scrap of stationary. Neal reached in and fingered around. He felt a cigarette box, a condom, something wet, then a pen. He jotted his number, added a smiley face, scratched over that, then left. The ass did not stir. He stepped into the hall, which was busy. It would be dawn soon and he hated hailing a cab in the daylight. That first wave of post anonymous sex meltdown was creeping in. It was best to get home, shutter the windows and sleep. Either that or rev up for another sex round. He considered it, then stifled a yawn, and headed to his booth. As he dressed, he wondered if he would regret leaving this quickly. Often, in the cab home, he felt a rush of desire, a longing that overwhelmed him. More than once, he'd gone back to the baths, despite the fact that he had to pay a re-entry fee. Tonight though, he would go, and he would make it home, and he would cook a very large frozen pizza and watch taped television reruns in his tiny, air-conditioned studio apartment. And he would sleep soundly.

Waiting in line to drop his room key, he saw, at the end of the first hallway of booths, a black kid, leaning in, then out of his booth doorway. He was nude, no white towel, just dark black skin and a strange knit hat on his head. He was swaying in and out of his booth, and he was staring at Neal. The kid paused, ran his hand along his chest, and smiled, showing several big gold teeth. He nodded at Neal, then he motioned him over. The key line was crawling. Maybe he could go another round after all. Neal stepped toward the booth and the kid disappeared. He kept moving, a little afraid, then stepped into the doorway. The kid was lying, knees pulled up so his feet touched his ass, hands casually behind his head, weird knit cap and glittering gold teeth. He tilted his head far back, as if drawing Neal on a string toward him. Dawn had already come and gone. Neal stepped in, and shut the booth door.

Chapter 5

HIS NAME WAS Dewalt and he answered his cell phone during sex. The ring tone chanted 'come on muthafucka come on' a lyric edged with a hard rap melody. It rang while he was kissing Neal's thigh. He answered.

"Sup nigga. Chillin kid. No. I ain't. Aw, aait. Fuck him, na 'mean? Not yet. No. Call ya at two. Peace."

Having sex interrupted by a phone call broke the spell, made everything a bit too real. Listening to Dewalt, lying naked next to him on a cot that belonged in an army barracks, Neal suddenly did not feel sophisticated, or sexy, or anything at all. He felt very, very white, very Midwestern. He thought of Cynthia Jones, the only black person he had seen during his childhood in Missouri. She cleaned the house once a week, ate liverwurst sandwiches, was deaf in one ear, and died in his mother's bathroom. Neal had found her there, stiff as a board, one day after school. She had a heart attack. His parents had gone to the funeral but he had not been allowed to attend, because the neighborhood was very dangerous, his mother had said.

Dewalt set his cell phone on the plastic table next to the cot, and laid flat on top of Neal, pressing them both deep into the skinny mattress, attacking Neal's face with his lips. The gold teeth pushed into Neal's cheek. Dewalt reached back onto the table. He was ripping open a condom, then lassoing it onto himself.

"I don't get fucked," Neal said.

Dewalt paused, the condom stretched out to do its work in limbo, then the guy grabbed Neal and began to maneuver the thing over Neal's cock.

"Well then fuck me, white boy."

Dewalt flipped over. It was beautiful, the high curve of it. Neal was nervous, not sure if he could do it well enough, not sure if he even wanted to. Dewalt raised his ass. From his pants pocket lying on the floor, Neal's cell phone rang. He reached for it, glad to have time to decide if he really wanted to fuck this guy. It was his mother.

An insomniac and first-rate golfer, Catherine Tate always called early, refusing to acknowledge that anyone slept past 6 A.M. She also began her calls as if she were in the midst of a conversation.

"Hi honey, so next week, we have a layover on our way to Dublin, so we'd love to see you, can you hear me?" she said.

Dewalt rolled over to stroke Neal's condom-clad cock, which was shriveling.

"Yes. What time?" Neal said.

"Noon. Choose a spot and of course Daddy will treat. I'll check back with you later this week. We're so happy you finally got a real job and all the rest, the rehab thing," she said and hung up abruptly.

Neal set down his phone and sighed a bit too loudly.

"Family or boyfriend?" Dewalt said.

Neal was shocked. This wasn't part of the routine. He didn't chat with bathhouse tricks. A grunt after sex was usually adequate. His image of Dewalt as a big, mean fuckable thug was faltering.

"Lay down kid," Dewalt said, guiding Neal to lie face down

on the cot, then straddling his back. "Don't worry, I aint gonna fuck you."

Dewalt pressed his fingers into Neal's neck. He was strong. He kneaded his shoulders then worked his palms down Neal's back. He slowly worked up and down Neal's spine, then gently massaged his neck and scalp. He pressed his lips to Neal's ear for a second.

"This is what you really want," Dewalt said. "Let go baby."

Neal shuddered, feeling his body let go for the first time that night, that week, that month.

THEY WERE IN the booth all morning. Neal fell asleep briefly, something he'd never done at the bathhouse. Standing now, on the sidewalk outside in the morning sun, Dewalt looked younger than he'd imagined him in the dark.

"How old are you?" Neal said.

"Twenty-nine. Look at you, all fucking sweet and shit. Let me get them digits. I'll text you."

Dewalt's phone rang.

"What up, nigga. I told you two, so fall back and stop calling me. Two is two is two nigga, learn that shit."

Dewalt pressed a button on the phone, pulling up a menu.

"You got them digits for me?"

Neal rattled off his phone number and the guy tilted his head back again, smiled that gold mess, and reached for him. He gave Neal a soft, lingering kiss, then looked him dead in the eye.

"You're sweet. It was really nice, Neal."

Dewalt headed up the sidewalk. Before he hit the corner, he turned back to Neal and stopped. The two men eyed each other. It was hot and Neal was sweating, blinded for a second by the sun, exhausted and lightheaded, suddenly thinking of tar bubbles on blacktop roads in August in Missouri, squashing them with his toes, going swimming or walking the railroad tracks and a first kiss with…who was it? There was nobody back then. Dewalt slowly walked back and stood close to Neal. He put his hand on the back on Neal's neck, smiled, then drew him close for a long, gentle kiss.

"I wanna see you this week," Dewalt said.

Still dazed Neal paused, staring. There was something calming about Dewalt, the way he spoke, walked, stared. He had a steely, steady gaze, and did not look away or drop his eyes. He was also refreshing masculine, unlike most of Neal's fast-talking, joke-dropping, fashion-loving friends.

"Sure," Neal said.

Dewalt smiled and headed off. It was late morning, and the temperature was already tipping past 90. Neal was hot and hungry. He went to the Hollywood Diner on the corner and ordered the Oprah special: two eggs, a waffle, pancakes, bacon, sausage, ham and toast and home fries. He sat in the window and had several cups of coffee. He did not want to move. He wanted to spend the day at the diner. He asked the waitress if she could just leave a pot of coffee, he'd pay for it. She smiled and nodded, looking like she'd had less sleep than he had. Reaching into his pocket to see how much cash he had, he pulled out Albert's glimmering diamond ring. He put it on and held it up to the sunlight.

"Beautiful," the waitress said.

Neal blushed and looked away.

Chapter 6

POP MAGAZINE WAS housed on the second floor of a block-long Chinatown loft. The makeshift editorial office was the first thing visitors faced as they stepped out of the building's rickety service elevator. Formerly used to store reams of paper and industrial ink, the large room had a concrete floor, cathedral ceilings, ornate woodwork and a wall of floor to ceiling windows looking out onto the ever-chaotic Canal Street. Neal had a desk at the far end of the room facing the windows. Annie, head of design, had a series of computer workstations lining one wall. Ralph, a creepy middle-aged man who worked from home and was seldom at the office, ran the escort-and-naked-masseuse advertising department. Andreas had a separate office in the next room near the presses. During a magazine run, the entire place was tangy-smelling with ink and the walls rattled.

Formerly a family-owned operation that made cheap postcards and wedding invitations, Palamos took over the lease and bought out the company and all its equipment to get *Pop* off the ground. Neal was the first full-time editor. The success or failure of the upcoming First Annual Swimsuit Issue would determine his future. That, and his promised *Bergdorf Boy* column. Nick Sands from the New York Times had already sent him an email asking him when the column would debut. Arriving at 10:30 A.M., Neal was the first in the office. There was a Latin hustler sitting on his desk, wearing sheer, skintight white sweat pants, a tank top and huge gold sunglasses. Seeing Neal, the guy ran over and hugged him tightly.

"Can I help you?" Neal said, noticing how large the Latin's ears were.

"You know me Poppi, yes, yes?" the Latin said.

After a second, Neal remembered. They called him Dumbo. He ran weekly ads in the escort section under the name Rocko. The joke was that there was only one thing bigger than his ears.

"*Hablo* english?" Neal said.

"Jes Jes Jes," the guy said. "Swim. I'm for you."

He swung his hips back and forth, making it clear he didn't believe in underwear. He was huge. Word had gotten around that *Pop* was planning its first swimwear fashion issue. Soon, Neal would hear from every Go-Go boy slash aspiring model slash actor in the city. He was determined to reject the onslaught of sexual advances from eager rent-boys who wanted to leap into print work, even if it meant daily dashes to the peep show or jacking off in the restroom. He refused to be caught with his pants down at a job that could actually go somewhere. Plus, there was now a possible date with the mysterious thug-like Dewalt, and a soft, growing hope for something better. He averted his gaze from Dumbo's bouncing crotch, bit his lip a little too hard, then snatched a digital camera. The kid started to whip off his shirt.

"No," Neal said.

He shot a digital picture as Dumbo pushed out his crotch and yanked up his top to show off steely, cocoa-colored abs. Neal stuck a note on the corkboard wall near his desk.

"Gracias," said Neal. "Adios."

The kid frowned, then came up close. He pressed Neal against the corkboard wall, ready to grind.

"I can be in swim, yes?" Dumbo growled.

"Neal, are you okay?" Annie yelled across the room.

Annie was a recent Sarah Laurence graduate whose dream was to publish a book of non-linear "Gertrude Stein" inspired poetry. She always made Neal smile. Graphic design was her survival skill and her quiet, no-nonsense attitude was an asset to the haywire *Pop* magazine office. She was tiny, kept her long auburn hair in an extremely tight ponytail, wore head to toe black and combat boots and ate nothing but granola, tofu and rice cakes. She suffered hellish migraines. Neal discovered she was straight, and a virgin, the first time he asked her to airbrush a crotch on a rent boy ad.

"Make it bigger, like ten or eleven," Neal said.

Annie squinted at her computer screen, studying a super skinny, super young Puerto Rican kid in a thong.

"Isn't that ridiculous?" Annie said.

"Well, I came up against a Vacu-pumped twelve incher last week, so not really," he said.

Annie swung her chair around and gave him a dead-eyed glare.

"I'm not that stupid," she said.

At that point, Neal had realized he knew very little about his co-worker.

"Annie, they do come pretty large you know," he said.

"No, I don't know," she said, blushing, then giggling.

Later, over lunch, she revealed to Neal that she'd only had one boyfriend, found the city intimidating and confessed that she was fascinated and petrified by the concept of a giant cock. Neal promised to take her out clubbing that month and said he'd ask his straight friends about where to meet eligible men. From that point on, they were solid work allies.

Dumbo turned away from Neal and ran to Annie, rattling off something in Spanish as he left. Neal admired Annie's drive and integrity, not easy to maintain when half of their job had to do with airbrushing escort ads and coming up with new ways to say 'Party til ya *Pop*', a phrase their boss had come up with and couldn't hear enough of.

"Andreas wants to approve the swim shoot," Annie said. "I hope I didn't back you into a hole with the column. Nick Sands called twice."

Before Neal could fathom what that catty bitch Nick was up to, Rovvie came through the door, a glowing burst: white silk slacks, a super tight white tank top, flaxen hair, an ivory shoulder bag and a large iced latte. He rushed to Neal.

"You gotta get me out of this one," Rovvie whispered, darting to the window.

Andreas stepped into the office, eyes ablaze.

"I ran ahead to get coffee, Andreas," Rovvie said.

"Shut up," Andreas said, moving steadily toward Neal.

During his two weeks on the job, Neal had experienced Andreas' moods. Always controlled, quiet and soft spoken, there were slight adjustments in the boss' demeanor that signaled danger. Neal's gut told him never to cross the man.

"Did you see Rovvie yesterday?" Andreas said standing in front of Neal, one fist clenched.

In the next room, the clattering roar of the press signaled the morning's first run. Neal had spent the previous day alone in bed and hadn't heard from Rovvie. The grinding wheels of the press gave him a second's breath. Neal glanced over Andrea's shoulder toward Rovvie. Meeting at Bergdorf Goodman's was their default cover up, something Rovvie had set in place at the start of their friendship. Neal couldn't be certain.

"It's a simple question," Andreas said.

"We met at Bergdorf's for coffee," Neal said.

Andreas moved a step closer. Over six feet tall, he loomed. Neal got a whiff of cologne, Tom Ford's Black Orchid, he guessed. He noticed Andreas' chest pressing through his tight knit polo. Annie broke in.

"I know you're busy, Andreas. We can go over the swimsuit

issue whenever you want," she said.

Rovvie sipped his coffee and stared out the window at Canal Street.

"Denny Morgan will shoot the spread. He owes me a favor," Palamos said.

"I love his work," Neal said.

Annie laid out a pile of swimwear images from Chelsea boutiques, all potential advertisers. She tossed out the idea of shooting on the West side Piers, or at Andreas' house on Fire Island. Palamos turned from them as he spoke, giving them his back as he moved toward Rovvie.

"Use the Fire Island beach house and remember why I hired you Neal," he said. "Impress me. And I want to see that column. It sounds interesting."

Andreas kept his back to them as he reached Rovvie, wrapping his arms around the boy's waist and kissing his neck. As Palamos guided Rovvie back through the swinging doors into the pressroom area, Neal felt mildly aroused, and hated himself for it. The longer he knew Rovvie, the more he felt an urge to rescue him. From what, he wasn't exactly sure.

Chapter 7

NEAL HAD BEEN staring at the screen for what felt like decades. Punching at keys, erasing. Deleting sentence after sentence of useless crap. Rereading Nick Sands' email between failed thoughts. *"Can't wait to see what you come up with for your column. Clever, for sure." NS.* A not so veiled challenge. Since getting sober, Neal's brain felt brittle—frail, spinning, ready to break into pieces with the slightest breeze. He ran ideas though his head, and kept coming back to sex. Write what you know and obsess about. Sex and fashion. Sitting, reaching for an idea, he calculated that he'd slept with over two thousand men since moving to the city. He began to type.

After sleeping with two thousand nameless men I've come to realize that anonymous sex is definitely everything it's cracked up to be.

Annie was over his shoulder. He could feel her breath, feel her stepping back.

"Sit down," he said.

"A sex column is good," she said. "Like dating advice for the new era gay boy."

Neal buried his head on the desk and moaned, ignoring Annie's irritating 'ooh no what have I done?' caws and gentle pattings on his back. He had never dated in his life. He had sex.

At the baths, the gym, the steam room, the park bathroom, the last row of a movie theatre, the back of a taxicab, the beach dunes, a deserted diner's booth at dawn, the peep show. He turned to Annie, an idea brewing.

"You know what I did to a guy," he said.

Looking at Annie, he realized he was willing to unearth sacred secrets, his alter ego's dirty jock strap sex-capades, all in the interest of not letting that nasty Nick Sands one-up him.

"I punched him in the nuts," Neal said.

Annie grimaced.

"Not right away. He liked to dance for me, this ritual, and then strip, we'd make out and end it all with nut punching," Neal said.

"That's really strange," Annie said.

"I've got a lot of stories like that."

The service elevator squealed, opened its rusty doors, and spat out Nick Sands. Nick stood brushing off his beige linen single button suit. Under that, a paisley spread-collar shirt. Neal lusted after Nick's Barker Black skull and spade slip-on which he'd seen on Bergdorf Goodman's third floor. It was a black velvet slipper-like shoe with a white skull and cross bones embroidery on the vamp.

"I felt like slumming," Nick said, moving to Neal's desk. "You didn't answer my calls or emails so I got a tetanus shot and hailed a cab."

Annie pressed out her meager chest like a lesbo warrior, but Neal patted her hand and waved her back to her desk. Neal stayed silent, waiting. Nick would never visit the bowels of Chinatown unless he needed something. They'd had little contact over the past few years, only occasional eye roll exchanges at parties. Nick sat on an old stool by Neal's desk.

"How quaint, a bar stool. You always did like the trappings of liquor," Nick said. "You must have a bottle in your top drawer."

"I quit drinking," Neal said, immediately realizing his mistake.

"Really?" Nick said, drawing out the Ls.

The two men eyed each other, Nick pulling out a tiny tube of balm to moisten his lips. Neal could wait as long as needed. Nick was a lot busier than he was.

"So how's the column coming?" Nick said. "Or did you give up on that. Nobody really *reads Pop,* do they?"

"I've finished it. Pick up Friday's issue," Neal said.

There was a squeaky cough from Annie's area. In his head, Neal calculated the timing to that week's press run and the insanity of what he'd just gotten himself into.

"Your personal wanderings?" Nick said. "I take it that means exploring the city's dirty underground. You always seemed so proud of being a slut. Stealing boyfriends, that sort of thing."

Neal stood up and Annie stood with him, in solidarity, at her desk. She looked so tiny, hands on her hips between what looked like a homemade ankle-length prairie skirt and a deep purple tank top featuring a picture of Kermit the Frog.

"Nick, why are you here?" Neal said.

"Research. Charity work," Nick said. "Don't be so paranoid. I'm on my way to Soho."

He stood up, brushed his ass off as if the bar stool had herpes, glanced around the room and turned to go.

"We really should bury the hatchet, Neal," he said. "Meet me for a drink soon at Trapeze. It's a chic little bar on the Upper East Side."

"I know Trapeze," Neal said.

Stepping into the elevator Nick gave the place a final glance.

"Of course you know Trapeze. They probably run an ad in that sweet little '*Pop* a cocktail' section. Did you come up with that one, or did little 'Annie Get Your Gun' over there," he said as the doors snapped shut.

Neal laid his head on his desk. Now he had a column to write, in addition to planning a swimsuit issue, both which would likely be trashed by every bitchy fag in the city, beginning with Nick Sands. Andreas' voice crackled over a desk intercom and Neal snapped back to life.

"Come in my office," the voice said.

"That thing is so creepy. Who uses intercoms? It's so '80s, like using a beeper or something," Annie said, then covered her mouth, realizing the boss could be listening on the other end.

Neal picked up a pad and headed toward the printing press area and Andreas' office. The press area was silent, the middle-aged straight men that ran it on a coffee break. He paused and looked at the huge metal contraptions. Big mechanical things always frightened him. As a kid, he'd been forced to work summers at his father's successful restaurant equipment company in Missouri. He'd spent hot afternoons in the back warehouse, surrounded by towering meat saws that needed to be squirted down with a hose and scrubbed. They were used and had grisly bits of old meat stuck in their sharp slicing jaws. His brothers, both who had gone into the family business and had the Jaguars to prove it, tried to get him to 'put some muscle into it' and attack those steel monsters. He refused and eventually got fired.

Heading to Andreas' office, he had an instinct he might be getting fired again. He was a good writer, but had never been a magazine editor. Maybe Andres smelled his fear, and after his flighty behavior at the party, the end may be in sight. Neal took a breath, and went into the office. The room was large and fairly empty. A long elegant desk, a small leather sofa, and a bar. Caz sat on the sofa, Andreas at his desk. Neal stood awkwardly waiting for instruction. Andreas indicated the sofa.

"Shut the door," Andreas said.

Neal moved slowly to the sofa, overcome with gloom. The ax was falling. He wondered if he could get another two weeks pay out of Andreas. Caz, legs spread wide, didn't move, making Neal sit near the edge of the sofa.

"Let's have a drink," Andreas said, stepping to the bar.

"I'm all right," Neal said.

"He don't drink," Caz said, downing a bottle of beer. "I saw you at the party. Nothing but those fucking Red Bulls."

Andreas turned to Neal and studied him.

"I can use a sober man around me," Andreas said.

Neal's shoulders fell. This was sounding better. Avoiding the view of Caz's still wide-open legs, he focused on work. He hadn't done a budget for the swimsuit issue. He'd been too worried about his column.

"Do you know where Rovvie went?" Andreas said.

The bubble burst.

"No," Neal said.

Andreas stood up and gave his back to the two men on the sofa. Caz sighed and pulled his legs tight, then spread them wide again, over and over, like an impatient child. He caught Neal staring at his crotch and smiled, glanced at Andreas' back, then rested his hand in his lap.

"I want you to keep an eye on Rovvie," Andreas said, still facing away. "Let's make it a part of your job."

Neal froze. He'd been pulled into this relationship drama from Rovvie's end. Now he was being asked to be a double spy.

"He's my friend, Andreas," Neal said.

"Exactly. We want what's best for him. We don't want him getting in with the wrong type," Andreas said. "Be smart, Neal."

Caz grunted, his hand still in his lap, and turned to Neal. At a loss for words, thoughts of debt and honor colliding, Neal began to wonder what type of liquor Andreas had poured into his cut glass tumbler, what was in the pretty bottles lining that bar, and how big Caz's cock was. He needed to get out of the office. His stress level was skyrocketing. He thought of yoga, but couldn't remember whether to breathe in or out first.

"I think we understand each other," Andreas said, ending the interview. "Keep up the good work."

Neal stood quickly, anxious to get away from Caz's crotch and Andreas' piercing stare. He hurried out, back to his desk, to the comfort of Annie's prairie skirt, and the stress of his waiting column. He had no idea where Rovvie was and hoped he never found out. He sat, he wrote, he doodled, he fretted. Finally, it came.

BB Column 1 / Draft

Bergdorf Boy here, ready to reveal every nasty little gay secret this big city has to offer, starting with the fact that I've had sex with over 2000 men. Scandalous? Not really. Grab an ounce of honesty and your iPhone calculator and think about it. Include the men in the steam room, the quickie at the baths, that one-nighter last Saturday. The figures add up, boys. Before I go on: these are not the rants of a hapless nymph. Inspired by my naughty guardian angel, that trail blazing pop novel icon of the 1960s Jacqueline Susann, each week I'm going to give the man-lover inside of you permission to step into your most reckless fantasy—along with a few very fresh, very hot fashion tips from my inspiration, Bergdorf Goodman. Because what's life without sex and fashion?

For my virgin column, let's get steamy and dive into: A major orgy at that glam Chelsea sex club – I mean gym – owned by one washed up muscle runt whose ancient wife still runs club-kid theme parties in Soho. Last week at said gym, nobody blinked or hid their asses as the steam room door swung, the air swirled, and your own BB spied a total of nine men licking their chops. The steam room itself, NYC's tiniest at barely 8X8, had that stuffed-in-a-phone-booth feeling and two of the largest schlongs BB has seen in ages. The 20-something scruffy bearded boy (dancer Harry from Splash Bar) was nearly ten plus. Too bad that rod was being hogged by a slobbering, just off a binge late 30s' cock-hound, who also happens to write restaurant reviews for NY Magazine. That queen's got an appetite. Ready to suffocate from bouncing balls and swirling steam, BB had a rushing thought. Truth be told, that steam room is one of the most famous quickie sex spots in the city. So, why does that runt of the gym owner (and all of the city's gay gym managers) still make a shameful show of throwing out a member for naughty steam behavior at least once a month. If you build it, they will cum. I say shame, shame on their hypocritical, homophobic asses. Boys will be boys. Get over it.

This week's tidbits: Check out the Libertine ruffle tuxedo shirt on Bergdorf's third floor. The red and blue trim is amazing and for $650 it's a steal. And lastly, BB's trick of the week: A quickie from Manhunt, this cutie wore a Speedo and goggles and had a high-pitched moan like a dolphin in heat. Straddling me, Flipper thrust his head back, screamed—and *spurted blood. He had a nosebleed. Squeezing his nostrils halted the flow. The kicker. Once it all stopped, he wanted to pick up where we left off. Nuts! Believe it, girls. BB never lies. Until next week. BB.*

Chapter 8

DONE WITH THE column, and a bit riled up by reliving all the steamy memories, Neal decided to hit the gym to clear his head. It was in the cab on his way that he made the disastrous call to Dewalt. He got voicemail and tried to make it sound like a thank you call for a great night, but in the midst of it, talking into dead air, Neal had a flight of paranoia. He suddenly decided he was making no sense so he started talking faster, then laughed and sighed, hoping to make a joke, but after a long pause, he just hung up, his stress level sky rocketing. He rushed through the aromatherapy entrance of the tarty, testosterone-packed "DBoy" gym. The place was a proving ground for pumped-up queens sporting Sally Hershberger haircuts and D&G gym gear. Prior to his *Pop* paycheck, he'd worked out at the YMCA.

Skipping his leg and ass workout, Neal headed straight to the steam room, telling himself he was fact checking for that week's column. Unlike the bathhouse, which required a few hours and a forty-dollar cover, steam at the city's gayest gym was an absolute quick fix. No matter what they said, how long they'd been married, who they dated or what they looked like, every gay man in Manhattan jacked off at least once on a sticky steam room bench. It was mid afternoon so it would be the actor-dancer out of work crowd, or the Euro tourist who'd seen the gym listed as a 'hot pickup' spot in a guidebook. Since rehab, Neal had sex in the steam room at least twice a week to calm his nerves. He stepped barefoot and towel-clad past a line of deep green-tiled shower stalls to a glass doorway. He thrust back his chest, and stepped into the room, an oversized walk-in closet really, all white tile, one dim light attached to the wall, wet bodies barely visible through a swirl of vapor. The action was in full swing and the place was jammed. There were slat-wood benches on two adjacent walls, filled. Several men were pressed against the wall which held the shrouded light. The steam was at a peak, soon to shut off and dissipate. This was the best time for sex. The room was thick with mist, hot and overpowering heat, faces obscured, hands grabbing and cocks bobbing. As was common gay practice, one older voyeur stood on guard near the entrance, in case a new gym monitor (not yet on the take) was making rounds.

Neal stood against the wall and a hand groped him. Nearby, a dark-haired fellow was on his knees, and beyond him, a cluster of bodies was engaging. He let the stranger manipulate him, thinking briefly of Dewalt, fantasizing about his gold-toothed smile, his hard black ass, while the hand became too aggressive. He pushed it away.

The glass door was shrouded with steam, but for a moment, a hand pressed, then pulled away, leaving a wide palm print and a sketchy glimpse into the shower stall area, which was empty. As the steam slowed, a pearl of sweat slipped down the top of the door. Neal thought it looked like a thin teardrop. He moved toward a gnarly little cluster, pushing through the hot air. As he stepped closer, through the steam, he saw a lean body and wide shocked eyes. It was Nick Sands. Twice in one day. Uncanny.

As Neal turned, Nick stood up quickly and gave him an angry glare. Neal darted out of the steam room, still nagged by a slow fading image of Dewalt. He went to his locker. He'd seen Nick only occasionally on the gym floor. He had always grudgingly imagined Nick happy in love, and he realized now that the fantasy was important to him. Neal paused, recalling that long hug Nick and his lover Brandon had shared at the party. His perfect couple picture burst into dizzy little flames. From his locker, his phone rang.

"What's up, kd?" said Dewalt over the phone.

Neal's chest tightened, his breath stopped. He was still a trifle hard from the steam room.

"Hold on, I'm just leaving a store," Neal said.

Covering the phone, he took a deep breath, cursing himself for lying.

"So you shopping? You like that right, I hate shopping, hold on," Dewalt said.

Neal was sweaty and trembling. He wondered where Dewalt could be. Another voice said, "Go on shorty," then a third, "Peace."

"My boys, getting out. Got your message. You funny, anybody ever tell you that?" Dewalt said.

Neal stood up, realizing he would be walking if he was leaving a store. He stepped up and down in his towel imitating movement. A Botox-faced fellow with a deep tan gave him a look on his way to the showers.

"I hate leaving phone messages. I text a lot," said Neal.

"You wanna come over for dinner?" Dewalt said.

Neal stood still and covered his mouth with his free hand.

"All right," Neal said quietly. "I'd like to see you."

There was a sound on the other end of the phone, like a grunt or a sigh, just a sound of breath inhaling, exhaling. Then silence.

"Come on then. I'll text you my address," Dewalt said, hanging up.

Toweling dry, Neal headed back to the shower stalls to rinse but paused when he saw Nick Sands standing alone at the sink, staring into the mirror, looking flushed, exasperated and a little sad. Neal caught a hint of desperation, and had a flash to college, his first year, when he and Nick had briefly been friends. Over a six-pack, Nick had told him about a lost boyhood flame, and wept openly. Nick turned and saw Neal. He stiffened his shoulders and shifted back to the mirror.

"Why did you come to my office?" Neal said.

Nick spun, his eyes narrowing, and Neal again saw a tiny whiff of something needy, and also a little diabolical.

"These walls have ears. More will be revealed when we have that drink," Nick said, then scooted off to his locker.

Neal headed to the shower. He was excited to see Dewalt, and happy for this long day to wind down. As he lathered, he wondered what lay beneath the façade of Nick Sands.

Chapter 9

NEAL STOOD IN the center of his tiny studio, imagining his worst nightmare of Harlem. Heavy-set black women in polka dot dresses and wide Sunday hats preaching religion; ebony thugs with jeans hanging past their knees, itching to slice Neal's lily-white faggot throat. He'd vowed never to travel past 42nd Street but tonight, to have dinner with gold-toothed Dewalt, he was venturing to 145th.

He thought Dewalt would back out, change his mind. Dinner with a bathhouse hook-up was far-fetched, and besides, Neal had never dated a black man, or an Asian man or a Puerto Rican or…anyone other than a white man. The truth was, he'd barely 'dated' anyone. He often had dinner and sex, a movie and sex, or, just sex. Second dates were rare. Tonight would be a change. His rehab counselor Manny said sobering up would open up new horizons. The truth was he liked Dewalt. He was the weirdest, toughest guy he'd ever met and sort of funny. And he had a really big cock. He doubted it would go anywhere but what the hell. He also realized that, despite his attempts at being liberal, cosmo and sophisticated, the residue of a sheltered, all-white, limited-thinking suburb upbringing kept him caged. This was a chance to step out of the cracker box.

Neal lay back on the wood floor. The window air conditioner was working overtime in the late day heat. He could see his entire apartment: a kitchenette crammed against the far wall, two large windows looking out onto 9th Avenue, a small white pull-out sofa bed, and a tiny ivory desk and chair. He'd bought a pair of retail-style clothing racks that served as a closet, these pressed against the largest wall. He'd tacked up images from European fashion magazines featuring models dressed as matadors, skinny boys in short shorts and caps, and a fur layout. He quipped to friends that it was his 'salon'.

When family visited they shot him long, sad looks suggesting he move to a nicer area like Queens to rent something larger. Out of towners never got the city/size thing: space relative to location. His neighborhood, Hell's Kitchen, was trendy and blooming with gays. Dirty delis had been replaced with chic soap shops and linen boutiques. Three gay bars had opened in the past year, and an Asian dessert and *sake* hut was moving in a block away. He sat up and scrutinized a rack of jeans. Wear something to fit in, he decided, or at least that doesn't scream Midwestern bone-white homo with a penchant for chocolate. All his pants were skinny. In an obsessive fashion fit, he'd even had his oldest boot cut jeans lean-tailored. Would a combat boot butch it up? An Armani leather lace up? He sat back on the floor, wanting to masturbate. He thought of skipping the Dewalt dinner and hitting the bathhouse. Sex was Neal's tonic, and right now, he needed a double. He wondered if he would ever be ready to give up anonymous sex, and the layers of anxiety it took care of, neatly, reliably.

He lay back, shut his eyes and thought about the surprise of Dewalt's ass. That smooth, uplifting fuckable ass that swallowed Neal's cock so sweetly and gave him a chance to explore topdom. Because of his size, he was forever taken for a submissive bottom. Neal however, did not get fucked. One closeted, pig-skin-tossing hulk had rammed it up his ass in college, despite his protests. Neal had punched the guy in the gut, then reeled back and fisted him in the cheek (aiming for the eyeball). The guy had gone cross-eyed in surprise and hit the deck.

Neal got up and yanked on the darkest shade of Levis he owned, paired it with a white T-shirt and high-top tennis shoes, then glanced in the mirror. He had cab money if he needed to make a quick getaway. For a second, he thought of hunting the streets for a bottle of pepper spray in case Harlem lived up to his worst Midwestern-inspired fears. He thought again. It was a date, not a military maneuver.

Chapter 10

THE SUBWAY LEFT Neal on a clean, well-lit corner just past dusk. It was a hot, clear night, with a full moon. The block at 145th Street sloped steeply down toward 8th Avenue. A luxury Condo, The Langston, sat primly next to a Starbucks, then a New York Sports Club. A stone staircase swept down into a park with a public pool and rows of flowering cherry blossom trees. A petite blonde woman chatted on her cell phone, yanking a Yorkshire Terrier on a silvery leash. A super-thin black girl laid her hand on the shoulder of a teenaged boy with an overdone Afro and pale blue shorts. The boy with the Afro held a bouquet of peonies. Neal laughed at his pepper spray moment. New York Magazine was right, Harlem was up and coming.

At the bottom of the hill, he turned the corner toward 150th Street, and paused. As if the moon had dissolved, and all light had faded, the street suddenly became the Harlem of Neal's fear. The buildings were dark, bleak. A tenement had a row of windows boarded up, and on the top floor one smashed pane had a torn red curtain flapping. He kept walking, stiffly, quickly, passing a deli at 146th Street, door wide open, bulletproof glass and a drawer for cash. A Middle Eastern man waved and winked at him from behind the glass. A shuttered storefront promised to cash checks and redeemed food stamps at 147th Street. Four young black men sat on a stoop, laughing. Neal was now at an equal distance between the subway and Dewalt's place. At 150th, he saw the Dunbar apartments. It was a block-long red brick complex with a series of arched entrances, lined by flowering trees. A plaque announced the place was a historical landmark built in 1928 and named for Renaissance Harlem poet Paul Laurence Dunbar.

Neal darted into the first archway, glancing over his shoulder at the young men on the stoop to see if they had followed. They were talking loudly, slapping each other's backs. The center of the Dunbar complex was a massive courtyard. A central sidewalk ran the length of it, offering pink and purple bushes on either side, and in the center a concrete play area alive now with screaming children. He stopped in the courtyard to check Dewalt's building number and as he looked up, he saw the children swooping toward him. They surrounded him, six of them, tiny bird-like tots. They joined hands making a circle with Neal at the center. They rocked and sang.

"Come on mister, try to break through," said a small boy with a shaved head and a huge purple shirt covering tiny blue jeans.

Neal remembered ring around the rosy as a kid. Or was it red rover red rover let someone come over? He froze, not knowing whether to light-heartedly bust through the children's ring of arms, or go for a stern look and tell them to step away. He was afraid that if he skipped through the tiny link of interlocked arms he'd knock one of the smaller kids down. A chin scraped, a tooth chipped, blood and then angry older brothers, rusty knives, gun shots, a spot on the news at eleven. Sassy gay editor slaughtered.

He walked to the edge of the ring and smiled.

"All right. I have to go now," he said.

The children looked disappointed, then an older boy, maybe aged seven, stepped out of the ring toward Neal and asked him to bend down. Reluctantly, Neal did.

The boy gently touched Neal's hair.

"Hey, you have yellow hair."

The tot turned to the rest of the set.

"He's got yellow hair."

The children shrieked with laughter and surrounded Neal, grabbing for his expertly dyed, chestnut blonde, salon coiffed hair.

"Yellow hair, yellow hair."

They were yanking strands, pulling. One child rested her head on Neal's shoulder and shrieked with laughter, another ran his hands roughly up into the grain of his scalp.

"Okay. Enough now. I have to go," Neal said, straightening.

Rattled, he skulked away to the delighted laughter of the children, and their dying taunts of yellow yellow yellow hair. Maybe he'd started a trendy new game.

DEWALT LIVED AT the top of a six-floor walk-up. A throbbing, vile chant was playing as Neal climbed the stairs. It got louder, then assaulted Neal as Dewalt opened the door.

'Wasup all you niggas in da house'

Dewalt was topless, wearing a pair of white boxers and an orange oven mitt, his gold teeth glistening. He smiled, then grabbed Neal and kissed him, a wet, long sloppy mouth kiss in the hallway of the building. Neal imagined angry, homophobic neighbors, or those religious hat-wearing Sunday woman. This date, he decided, was likely to be a disaster though he was enjoying the salty taste of Dewalt's tongue and the metal tang from his gold teeth.

Keeping his mouth on Neal's, Dewalt pulled him into the apartment, then swung the door shut, notched three locks, and pushed Neal against the wall. He licked his cheek, his ear and went again for his mouth; long, deep, aggressive.

Rap music pounded.

"Hey," Dewalt said. "Come on in.

'Check da junk in da trunk yo mothafucka'

With his oven-mitt covered hand, he pulled Neal into the apartment.

The living room had two big windows looking out onto the courtyard. Neal could see the children playing. A smooth, dark leather sofa, a pair of oatmeal colored fabric chairs. On the wall, a mahogany antique table, and a series of black and white prints of a familiar looking black prizefighter. The living room led though an archway into a large eat-in dining room, which was unheard of in Manhattan (other than in true luxury apartments). An oval dark wood dining table, set for dinner, stood near a large window. The kitchen was off the dining room and fed around back to the living room then down a hall to a bedroom, and a bath.

The music pounded. Dewalt pulled Neal toward the bedroom.

"Could you turn down the music?" Neal said.

"Come on kid," Dewalt said, grabbing Neal around the waist, kissing him again, and lifting him off the floor, humping him to the beat of the music.

"No, really," Neal said.

Dewalt slid him to his feet.

"What?"

'Come on and shoot da bitch'

"This place is great, but the music, can you just…" Neal said.

Dewalt smiled.

"Sure."

Dewalt turned off the rap. In the quiet, Neal could hear the distant screams of the children. He wondered if Dewalt had heard the yellow hair taunts. Neal felt awkward, more uncomfortable now with the silence then he had with the audacious rap. He sat on the sofa, glanced toward the window out at the courtyard just to look like he was doing something.

Dewalt came back, oven mitt gone, two glasses of wine.

"You like wine?" he said.

Neal shot to his feet. Then he sat down again.

"I don't drink," Neal said.

"At all?" Dewalt said.

Neal nodded. Dewalt stood still for a moment, then flashed a smile, the gold teeth.

"No beer either? I got juice, you like juice?"

Neal brightened and settled back. The distant screams of the children were fading, replaced with haphazard shouts from women calling them in for the night, gathering their chicks. As he waited, he noticed the softness in the linen curtain which fronted the living room's main window. A stripe of shadow from a courtyard light edged across its center, and as the night grew darker, he thought the curtain, long, flapping and rich, looked milky and cool. He never imagined Dewalt having such beautiful drapes, and with that, his date called him to the table for dinner. Two fat, bloody steaks lay on two lean china plates, crowded next to French Fries and a large wedge of tomato. Neal sat at the table, stiffly. The napkins were pale blue, the silverware had duotone dots. Dewalt stood by his chair.

"Go on now."

Like an obedient child, Neal cut into the steak and ate. There was a slight smoky flavor, and a touch of something spicy. Delicious. He went for another jab.

Dewalt sat down, sucking down his wine. He watched Neal.

"Kitchens my ground, ya know. Loved cooking as a kid. Then, got off, ya know. Got messy, ya know what I'm saying?" he said.

Half way through his steak, Neal paused, and Dewalt started to eat. He began with the tomato.

"So you got messy?" Neal said.

"I ran around for awhile, did some shit with my boys. You know what I'm saying?" Dewalt said.

Neal didn't know what he was saying, but recognized the slang. Still, he had to stifle an urge to ask more questions, to blurt out, 'No, I really don't know what you're saying at all. What is the shit? Is that good shit or bad shit or just shit?"

"So what do you do?" Neal said.

Dewalt finished his tomato, and eyed his steak.

"Is this too rare? I love rare. It's ok?" he said.

Neal nodded.

"Construction. It's steady work. Good in summer. You gonna like dessert, you like Carmel? You gonna like it if you like Carmel," Dewalt said, eating quickly now, ravenously, like some hunger-lever had flipped.

Neal watched him devour the meat. Dewalt gripped his utensils hard, like tools, and cut roughly, shoving fat bits of food into his mouth. The muscles in his arms strained. He looked a little beastly and dumb, which Neal liked.

"You work out a lot," Neal said, immediately regretting the question.

"No. The job's it, ya know, heavy lifting. I keep in shape," he said.

Dewalt tipped up his face up, chewing ferociously on the last of the meat. He gave Neal a good long stare, then licked the end of his fork.

"You know how fucking sweet you look right now?" he said.

The linen curtain behind Neal blew forward with a breeze, as evening spread and the room got a tiny bit darker. Dewalt stood up. His white boxer shorts were tenting. It was bobbing, pulsing up, then down, through his boxers. Dewalt set down his fork and leaned his palms on the edge of the table.

"So you like my place?" he said.

It was rubbing against the edge of the table, resting on the wood. Dewalt leaned further into the table and pressed his crotch so it grazed the china plate. Left over juice from the steak touched lightly onto the front hem of his shorts.

"I do," said Neal.

Dewalt pressed further into the plate. His boxers were getting wet.

"Stay the night," Dewalt said.

"I have to work or I would," Neal said.

"I'm up at five. I'll feed you. Turkish coffee. You ever had it? Sweet and mad strong," Dewalt said, coming around the side of the table toward Neal.

The courtyard had gone silent, the breeze was picking up. Dewalt stood at Neal's chair. The front of his white boxers was stained brown with meat juice. The outline of it, full and reaching, pressed toward Neal.

"You gotta stay, you get that?" Dewalt said.

He leaned down and kissed Neal gently. Dewalt tasted of steak, his tongue tangy. He was exploring the insides of Neal's cheeks, side to side. He placed one hand, warmly, on Neal's shoulder, the other in his hair. The kiss kept going, as Dewalt lifted Neal from his seat and murmured something unintelligible. Neal suddenly wanted to get rough with Dewalt, to yank his head back, to push him down and start to fuck, to treat him like a dumb beast, a nameless nasty thugfuck, but he felt himself unwillingly falling into Dewalt's rhythm, a slow, awkward mingling dance. Dewalt was holding him now, still exploring his mouth, his teeth, lips. He had both hands around Neal's back, then slid them down to his ass, pressing his fingers past the band of his jeans, touching.

"Get 'em off," Neal said.

Neal was dizzy, out of breath. There was no overhead light in the dining room and as night came, the room grew darker. Neal wanted to push forward, but Dewalt moved away from his mouth and knelt, he untied Neal's sneakers, took them off; unbuttoned his jeans, slid them over soft white feet. He ran his mouth up Neal's legs, brushing his crotch, back to his mouth.

"Lift me," Neal said.

Dewalt stepped back, his skin was wet, sweaty. It glistened in the dark. His shoulders were lean, tight. He nuzzled his face into Neal's stomach, then swept him up, grunting, swept him up across his forearms and pulled him toward his chest. Dewalt swung around and headed to the bedroom. Neal leaned his head into Dewalt's shoulder. He felt tiny, frightened. The bedroom was dark.

"Turn on the light," Neal said.

The switch flipped, and two steel bedside lamps glowed. The room was masculine, all mahogany, shuttered windows, a pile of dirty clothes, a jock strap on the floor near the window. Dewalt set Neal gently onto the bed. Neal sunk down, gazed up, as his date stood still, staring, then slowly pushed off his stained white boxes, letting them linger mid-thigh. He loosened himself, sighed and shutting his eyes, roughly pushed the shorts to the floor and stepping forward and onto the bed, on top of Neal.

He ground into him, his wet skin slicking over Neal's legs, their stomachs pressing close together. Dewalt's moves were urgent. He licked at Neal's chest, bit his nipple, then yanked Neal's arms and pressed them over his head. He buried his face and breathed hard on Neal's ear, whispering.

"I wanna fuck you now, good," he said.

Neal pressed hard upward, into him, wrapping his arms around Dewalt's back and squeezing him, holding him steady while he found the man's mouth and tongue. He reached down and held tight onto the ass, which was clenching with every grind, and he wanted to slap it, to punish him, hurt him, make him less.

"You my boy, yeah, got that, now, my boy's here," Dewalt said, grinding, kissing.

Neal pressed up into him harder, squeezed his back, then shook, holding back a rush of far off, wandering tears that chose to push through, now, at the wrong time, now with the light on, trapped under Dewalt.

"All right," Neal said, as his eyes clouded, and he failed to stifle a sob.

He buried his face in Dewalt's chest and concentrated on their breathing, together, and didn't care anymore what happened, who fucked who, how it all came out. Dewalt was murmuring in his ear, pressing into his belly, lost in the soft rush of his skin, shooting on Neal's center, whispering.

"It's good," Dewalt said.

Neal pulled himself up a little, holding onto Dewalt's shoulders, pulling himself out of the whole thing, in the jerky movement, upward, toward his date's cheek, he shot too, on Dewalt's belly, mingling, both of them, mingling.

THEY SLEPT WITH the light on. Neal woke, late into the night, and switched it off but before he did, he noticed the curve of Dewalt's body, lying still on top of the sheet, knees up, arms pulled in. There was a small tattoo on Dewalt's inner bicep, and a scar. He killed the light, got in bed and as his eyes adjusted, he crept close and studied the map of Dewalt's body. He trailed a finger along his right arm. The tattoo, hidden on the inner bicep was a skull, with a drop of blood oozing out of one eye. Below, on his forearm, a jagged scar had healed. Neal pressed his hand to the man's shoulder, testing. Dewalt didn't budge, sound asleep. In the dark, now with a heart of moonlight laying some light into the room Neal lifted his date's arm and saw another healed cut on the inside of Dewalt's hand. He held the hand up and noticed how long and jagged the scar was, like a life line. He lay Dewalt's arm down and trailed a finger over his sleeping chest. His breath was easy. In bed as dawn came, Neal felt something unraveling. He'd never noticed a man in bed, never noticed so closely and never, ever waited so patiently for anyone to wake up. He finally fell toward sleep, remembering, all at once, the narrow cot he'd slept on at the bathhouse, the voices in that hall, and his bedroom in Missouri, the snores of his father up that hall and outside the pink curtained window, sprinklers shooting at night, and children he never knew screaming taunts far down a tar-ravaged street.

Chapter 11

NEAL WOKE TO a strong, spicy aroma. He was disoriented, unsure where he was. He'd kicked the sheet off the bed and woken cuddling a pair of stained white shorts. He heard the shower running, and a man singing. As he woke, his head cleared. Dewalt was bellowing in the shower, some rhyming rap rhythm. Neal made his way toward the aroma. The living room was incredibly sunny. On the dining table was a steaming copper pot with a chipped wooden handle. A petite white coffee cup sat next to the pot. Turkish coffee. He sniffed it. Madly fragrant, woody, stiff. Like some over the top Middle Eastern cologne. He poured the thick, muddy liquid into the cup and sipped.

"You like it? Strong shit, right?" Dewalt stood in the doorway to the bathroom, wet and dripping.

"I have a new addiction," Neal said, taking another slug of the outrageous coffee.

Dewalt walked to the table and rested his hands on Neal's shoulders, then bent down for a kiss.

"You better put something on or I'll never get to work," Neal said.

Dewalt laid his lips on the top of Neal's head, then rested his cheek there, breathing. Neal felt the heat, as water beads dripped. Dewalt pulled away and went to the bedroom.

"The train's express," Dewalt shouted. "You'll be downtown fast."

The dining room was also very sunny with two large windows. The place was becoming warm with the morning heat. Neal shut his eyes, drank the muddy Turkish coffee, felt exotic and foreign. Dewalt returned, dressed in jeans, construction boots, a white T-shirt.

"I've always wanted to go to Egypt," Neal said. "Drink Turkish coffee on the Nile."

Dewalt went to the kitchen, clanged pots.

"You serious?" he said, cracking eggs. "I've been saving for two years now to go there. I got a bunch of books. That Pharaoh shit is so fucking old. And I'm into tattoos, symbols and signs. Mad shit. All started in Egypt."

Neal could see him cooking, hovering over a frying pan of eggs, leaning back in his big cracked up and dusty construction boots. He noticed how very broad Dewalt's shoulders were, in contrast to his small waist.

"I'm terrible at saving. But every few years I get a part of my trust from my father. They give me bits of my inheritance as a gift to save on some sort of tax. Next time, I might use it for Egypt," Neal said.

"So we'll go together," Dewalt said, bringing in breakfast.

Neal took the plate of eggs, blushing. Dewalt had said it so easily. We'll go together. For a split second, Neal had thought the same thing, but swatted the instinct away. We'll go together. We just met, but, we'll go together. To Egypt. Sure. He looked up at Dewalt as he sat across from him.

"You're sort of spontaneous," Neal said. "I think a lot."

Dewalt salted his eggs, poured a ton of sugar into his coffee.

"Think what?" Dewalt said.

"I think everything to death. Always," Neal said. "See, now I'm over-thinking how I think things to death."

Dewalt was still pouring sugar. He saw Neal watching him.

"I like it sweet, what can I say," Dewalt said.

At that, Dewalt set down the sugar, took a big gulp of coffee, then stood quickly and went to Neal. He lifted him up out of his chair, lifted him up over his head, then brought him down for a kiss. Then he set Neal back down in his chair and went back to finish his coffee.

"I wanted it, I went for it. How you like that, kid?" Dewalt said. "I'm not a patient man."

Neal started to laugh, tried to drink his coffee, looked at Dewalt, then laughed harder. From the bedroom, he heard his cell phone ringing. He dashed for it, thinking it could be Annie letting him know she was out sick. He snatched the phone out of his pants in time.

"Neal, it's Mom, did I get you at a good time?" she said.

Walking back toward the dining room, Neal was silent.

"Honey, it's Mom. Hello?" she said.

"I'm here Mom," he said, sitting across from Dewalt.

"We will be there this week, for our stop over on the way to Dublin. Did you pick a restaurant for lunch?" she said.

Neal tried to remember his work commitments surrounding the swimsuit shoot.

"Honey, where are you?' she said.

"I'm at a friend's," he said.

"At this hour?" she said. "What friend?"

"His name is Dewalt," he said. "This week is good. We'll go to High 8 restaurant at 53rd and 6th Avenue. Call me from the airport."

"All right. Bring your friend along if you like," she said, and hung up quickly.

Neal set down the phone. Dewalt smiled.

"More coffee," he said.

"My mom. She invited you to lunch," Neal said. "Isn't that spontaneous."

Dewalt looked into Neal's eyes.

"Is she like you?" he said. "Did she give you those blue eyes?"

"I'm not at all like her. Why don't you come to lunch and see," Neal said.

"Sure," Dewalt said and went for more coffee. "Then we'll get a travel brochure about Egypt."

Neal sat back, not caring if he was late for work. His parents had never met anyone he'd dated. They'd barely met any of his friends. But this week, they were meeting Dewalt. And for once, Neal wasn't going to think about it. He would just let it happen.

Chapter 12

THE HUGE, DILAPIDATED air conditioning unit at *Pop*'s Chinatown office had broken down again. Mammoth industrial floor fans hammered the hot air from all angles of the loft. Every window in the place was open. The fans circulated scents of peanut oil and Chinese spices from the take-out joints below. It was noon and Neal was waiting for the first wave of swimsuit models. At Andreas' insistence, and to align with photographer Denny Matthews schedule, they were shooting on Fire Island that weekend. They were also starting with the stable of escorts that advertised in *Pop* weekly. If nothing panned out, Neal could move on to more legitimate models. Waiting, looking sharp in a short sleeved Brook's Brothers button-up shirt and narrow Seersucker pants, Neal thought of Dewalt and smiled. He wondered if he would really make it to lunch with his parents. The whole thing made him nervous, but he hoped Dewalt came. His own big, hot hunky brute. His own big black toughie to swagger in and shake his father's hand. He hoped his parents were shocked.

Three of the escorts arrived at the same time. They stood in the center of the room, staring at Neal first, then eyeing each other with disdain. Before Neal could begin his 'no drugs on the set' speech, the tallest one, a Swede with a white blond crew cut and a sneer, began to undress. Neal felt he should clap his hands, or shout something about no nudity required, but rapidly, the other two—an over-muscled Latino and a cut-up, lean Italian with bad skin, began to strip. They moved frantically, as if they were contestants in a relay race caught off guard by the shot of the starting pistol. The Swede fell behind while trying to yank a tiny pair of briefs down over his supple ass. The Latin, who wore nothing under his jeans, leapt ahead for a moment, but literally toppled over pulling off his boots. The Italian, who was sweating more than the others, began to grunt, stopping to mop his brow with each piece of removed clothing before he folded it and set it on the floor. In record time they stood nude in front of Neal, refusing to glance at one another's cocks, each striking a ridiculous version of a runway pose. Neal stood up, attempting to take control. He stepped out in front of his desk and folded his hands. He was hoping the tie and seersucker dress pants screamed authority.

"Why don't you each grab a swim suit? There won't be any nudity so, well, just suit up," Neal said.

The Swede went for a floral bikini, the Latin a sheer square cut, but the Italian stepped toward Neal, frowning and biting his nails. Close up, the man looked older than the other two, close to thirty, and his eyes were tiny and red. His ribs were showing. He was trembling.

"I'm not auditioning. I've done runway. A lot," he said, spitting the last 'T' at Neal. "My cock is bigger than theirs that's why I…I mean come on man, I'm right for this. It's a bar rag. I'm a professional model. I can't just…"

Before Neal could speak, the Italian turned heel and stomped back to his clothes folded on the floor, muttering and twitching. He dressed quickly.

"I'm over this shit. I don't need this sort of low class crap," he said, his voice getting softer and softer as he dressed, then he darted out.

The other two models stood bulging out of their suits, ignoring the exiting competition. Neal shot a few digitals. The Swede looked pretty good. He thanked them both and got their numbers. As they left, an incredibly pale, tall and very freckled red head came in the door and waved to Neal.

"I'm Toby," he said in a Southern accent worlds thicker than Rovvie's.

Neal nodded. His cell phone rang. It was Dewalt. His heart raced.

"You busy tonight?" Dewalt said.

Toby stopped in front of Neal's desk, spread his feet apart and rested his palms on the desk. He mouthed, "I'm a Broadway dancer," with lips that had seen too many shots of collagen for a man so young. Neal turned away from the sea of freckles.

"I'm meeting Rovvie for coffee at five but free after that," he said softly.

"Come over when you're done," Dewalt said. "I been thinking about you."

Neal's entire body tingled. He wanted to run up to Harlem that minute.

"I'll be there around seven," Neal said.

"Great," Dewalt said and hung up.

Toby had stepped back out to the center of the office floor.

"I've only been in the city two weeks. Can you believe that?" he said. "I live in Annie's building and she was so sweet to send me your way. This is such a great opportunity."

The kid was adorable, untouched. It might be nice to have a pale country boy in the shoot. Neal smiled, and as if cued, Toby slid down into a split then bolted up and did a very accomplished flip. He smiled at Neal, as if the whole thing were an Olympic try out.

"I wanted you to know how flexible I can be," he said, all freckles and glistening sweat.

Neal took Toby's photo, got his number and waited for the next escort. He was pleasantly surprised at the initial turnout. It might be tough to choose only a few.

Chapter 13

THE BERGDORF GOODMAN men's store glimmered at 58th Street and Fifth Avenue, all black marble, glass and gold. It was Neal's habit to stand outside, savoring every moment before he leapt down his own little rabbit hole of glamour. The store's front windows reminded him of a fantastical gentleman's dressing room—a hand-carved bench holding one fine leather loafer, a five-foot brass scissors, a tuxedo shirt draped over a sugar cane wood chair backed with ostrich feathers. He had stumbled across the store one Sunday morning two years ago. It was the day after he'd dissolved a cocaine-fueled, six-week fling with Wilhelm (muscled ass, bad skin, angry). He'd wandered in, dazed from a lack of sleep, and was swept away by the store's beauty and elegance. He never took the elevator, rather lazily climbed the curling back staircase past lushly framed etchings of Fleet Street and Charing Cross, London. Bergdorf's was, he decided, the deserted country home of an eccentric royal, and the third floor belonged to him. Three was circular, littered with fine antiques and petite designer "chambers" (the Jil Sander Room, the Michael Bastian lounge). A single bone white cashmere sweater hung on a satin hanger; a rabbit hair scarf rested on a mahogany side table. The store was never crowded, the sales help invisible. Neal stopped to admire a silk striped side chair across from the Thom Browne chamber. Some day he'd have a home with a chair exactly like that. He wondered what Dewalt would think of it. Across the room was an ornate, floor to ceiling mirror with three silk scarves draped across the top. In front of the mirror was a narrow table lined with resort swimwear. He stopped, glanced around to make sure he was alone, then shot a few digital pictures. He would never get the store to lend him the dashing little square cuts and bikinis for the *Pop* shoot, but he could steal inspiration. He suddenly remembered Albert's diamond ring, and that he hadn't yet returned it. Might as well use it in the shoot. The old man obviously wasn't missing it.

Around the bend, tucked in a corner, was Bar III Cafe. The café's front façade was a ceiling height, curved wall of twenty-four square windows framed in mahogany and looking into the chic restaurant. During his first visit, Neal decided the cafe was the dining car of a foreign train, shuttling him from New York to the Orient or Russia or even Egypt. Inside the café, the main window wall was lined with two-seater booths. There was a thick, marble-top circular slab in the café's center with a blooming wild flower exhibit and stools for four. Above it hung a huge, masculine octagonal light fixture. A granite cocktail and espresso bar stretched the length of the other wall. The café was packed at lunch and for late afternoon coffee boosts, but died out after five and was nearly empty now. Neal took a booth against the window wall.

Across the room at the bar a blond man in a pinstriped suit and massive square sunglasses was reading a script. He looked like an actor. Keifer Sutherland? So far that year he'd spied Susan Sarandon, Colin Farrell, Joan Rivers and the Duchess of York, the one who made weight watcher commercials, at Bar III. He ordered a double espresso, flipped open his notebook and started to write. He wanted to harvest ideas for his next *Pop* column. If he had a backlog of ideas, maybe he wouldn't feel so nervous about the whole weekly undertaking. He'd heard about a chic Chelsea spa where, supposedly, one beefy attendant offered facials "with release". He considered visiting the spa, and also possibly mentioning a reality show celebrity on a meth binge he'd spotted at a downtown peep show. He sipped his espresso and wrote about the café and Keifer, and how he loved the store and then he stopped, pen poised, feeling reckless yet lost. He thought of Dewalt, and suddenly wondered where the night could be headed. He felt excited, intrigued, and tried a new column angle.

What is a 21-century gay date? Doesn't it really come down to one of two greedy goals: great frivolous fuck or future husband? If you are on a hubby hunt, isn't that a scam? Can we gay men really keep our pingas in our pants for any extended period of time? The most committed couple I know, "J" a former shop boy and "C" a successful surgeon living in a glam condo, still hunt down an occasional three-way, and each go on regular solo hunts to squeeze out a bit of relief in the steam room. Is that commitment?

Rovvie entered and rushed to the booth, out of breath, as if he were being pursued. Neal shut his notebook. Rovvie was all shades of pink: flushed cheeks, high-cut pink tennis shorts, bubble gum polo. He sat, waved to the waitress lingering in shadow.

"I need me a stiff drink. I'm nervous as awww shit," he said.

Very thin, very pale, very blonde, the waitress dropped menus and waited. Neal wondered why Rovvie was letting his Southern drawl worm its way back out into the open. A few months ago, he'd pleaded with Neal to help him find a speech therapist to make him sound "high class" to please Andreas.

"Gimlet," Rovvie said. "Thanks darling."

Neal ordered another espresso.

"So what's the emergency," Rovvie said. "About *Pop*? I can't wait to read your new column."

Neal considered how much to reveal about his unsettling meeting with the boss. He owed allegiance to Rovvie. They were friends and Rovvie had gotten him the job at *Pop* to begin with. His friend's inability to be discreet concerned him. Rovvie had a fiery, southern-fried temper. The wispy waitress brought their drinks.

"Andreas called me into his office," Neal said. "He wants me to keep an eye on you."

Rovvie downed his gimlet. He glanced away from Neal and there was a moment of calm. Neal saw something unexpectedly soft. Rovvie seemed to be drifting away and Neal had a sudden instinct to hold him.

"Are you going to leave Andreas?" Neal said.

Rovvie snapped back. He gave Neal a hard, steady glare.

"Who told you that?" he said.

"You did last winter. We were drunk," Neal said. "And you never told me why you have naked pictures in your phone."

Again, Rovvie glanced away. Neal thought he looked suddenly intelligent, like he was solving a math equation, or a difficult riddle. He also looked older, and melancholy, sitting there, in his cheerful form fitting pink clothing, slender fingers grabbing tight onto a Bergdorf Goodman gimlet glass, refusing to acknowledge Neal, for the moment at least. Rovvie was, in truth, his only good friend in the city. He'd had a host of drinking buddies, fuck buddies, even online chat buddies, but few in the flesh friends to actually talk to. Rovvie was flighty and selfish, but he was there. Neal deeply regretted what he'd just said.

"I can always find a job. I'm here for you Rovvie, and I have no right to judge you," Neal said, reaching out for his friend's hand. "Andres is an ass."

Rovvie's palm uncurled and let Neal's in and as they touched, he recalled the first time they'd seen one another, naked at the bathhouse orgy, and how their eyes had met and they'd both smiled and shared a moment acknowledging the insanity and messiness and utter loneliness of what a group orgy really is all about. Rovvie waved for another gimlet.

As Rovvie sipped his drink, and let his hand lie limply on

the table, Neal again considered his column and tried to conjure what it was he wanted to write about. He gave Rovvie a look and glimpsed the depth of his friend's running and the lengths he was willing to go to keep running away from Neal's probes, toward Andreas' money. He saw how similar he and Rovvie were and also how he had been racing frantically toward something unnamed since he got to the city, and how underneath it all he wanted to slow down a little, slow down and sit quietly with someone, someone like Dewalt.

Chapter 14

IN THE CAB up to Harlem, Neal watched the changing landscape. The sidewalk cafes and savvy boutiques dissolved after 96th Street, and by 110th Street the avenue grew dimmer with fewer street lamps and stretches of deteriorating public housing complexes. The heat had people swarming on stoops and street corners, blaring music, drinking beer, cracking open fire hydrants. The cab had no air conditioning, so Neal had rolled the window down. At 145th Street, an obese teenaged black girl was screaming, climbing a hill west, flipping her head back to shout at an unseen lover.

"...Cause your mama shoulda had the abortion, you fucking homo you ain't even got no dick you stupid bitch," she said, ascending the hill, puffing like a locomotive, sweating in the night heat, which was holding steady at 98°.

As the cab moved away, Neal heard distance shouts of queer bitch, fag, fucker. He wondered if she'd caught her man in the arms of a boy. Was he on the down low, had he fathered her child? They stopped at 150th Street and Neal got out and entered the Dunbar complex. Dewalt was near the door to his building with a tall, skinny man. From a nearby window, a wordless, pounding base battered out a rap rhythm. There was the smell of pot smoke. Dewalt saw Neal and waved, giving his skinny friend a ritualistic farewell handshake. The man, late twenties, oversized baseball cap with a glittering "SUP!" splattered across the front, jeans hanging low, nodded and laughed as he passed Neal. Dewalt guided Neal into the building, and once in the hall, pulled him close for a kiss. Neal resisted.

"Why didn't you introduce me?" Neal said.

Dewalt stepped back, made a grunting noise and turned away, heading up the stairs. Neal hesitated, then followed. They were silent climbing the six flights. Dewalt was quicker and reached the top before Neal. He entered the apartment and left the door ajar. On the landing, Neal stood alone, suddenly wondering if he should leave. For a moment, he was aware that he was in Harlem, in a dark hallway, with a man he barely knew. He moved forward and tentatively pushed the door open.

The apartment was dim, just a light from the kitchen. It looked duller and dirtier than the first time he'd been there. There was no laid out table, no welcoming scent of grilling steak. A gym bag lie open on the living room floor, a stray sneaker was upended on the sofa, a copy of *Pop* magazine sat on the side table with a beer can squatting on top of it. The place was stifling and hot. Dewalt sat on the sofa, arms crossed. Neal waited.

"I'm getting the bedroom cool, the AC's in there. I got a fan somewhere here," Dewalt said.

Neal didn't move, just stood awkwardly.

"So my homey, you wanted to meet him, that's it?" Dewalt said.

Neal took a step further into the room.

"It's polite," Neal said.

Dewalt moaned loudly, then beat one hand on his skull. He stood up and puffed, then came at Neal like he was going to hit him. He swept Neal up, held him in his arms and squeezed him, then carried him into the bedroom, grunting and moaning like an angry beast all the way. The bedroom was a messy disaster but a little cooler. He threw Neal on the bed.

"I don't know how to do this shit, kid," Dewalt said. "I

ain't done this. What do you want, the truth or what? You want to know this shit?"

Neal sat up. He realized he'd never done this shit either. He'd never dated anyone with intention. And he realized, lying on Dewalt's unmade bed, surrounded by stacks of hip hop magazines, two empty bags of Ruffle potato chips, and a series of dirty, mismatched socks, that he did have intention. He wanted more with this one. He really liked Dewalt. And for once, it wasn't just the hot sex or his cock or his hard gorgeous ass or the fact that he could help Neal's career in some half-assed, dreamy way. It was the man, Dewalt, with an attitude that was alien to Neal, an absolute foreignness in how he saw the world and also, a deep, soft, muffled sweetness.

"I guess truth is good," Neal said.

Dewalt yelped loudly, shouting a version of 'Oh man' but with a long series of N's at the end. Then he undressed, muttering, ripping off his shirt, pants, underwear, socks. He jumped onto the bed, naked, jumped up and down like a child, his leg muscles popping. Then he fell down next to Neal.

"Aw ait, here we go," Dewalt said. "I dealt for awhile. But I quit now."

Neal sat up. He didn't expect that. He thought the guy at the door was a secret trick.

"Dealt what?" he said.

"Nothing mad, stupid. Pot, coke. Mostly in clubs, some local stuff," Dewalt said, not looking at him. "But it's done. The construction job is real."

Neal wanted to ask him when he last dealt, how much money did he make, how long did he do it, did he still do drugs, but he hesitated. It was going too fast. This was their second date. He was sober nearly three months and was dating a drug dealer?

"So the guy at the door?" said Neal.

"Bender. Old buddy. Still dealing. We don't hang much for real, but he lives around here. So, that's it," Dewalt said. "Can I get a kiss?"

Neal paused. He heard something from inside his head, a whimper, like an animal under the sheets, something caught just outside the window. There was an utter stillness, and he felt his lips forming a sentence, telling himself to get out, that this wasn't all right. He couldn't risk his sobriety. You will get up and go now, forever, because that is the right thing to do. Dewalt took the pause and Neal's vacant look as a yes, and leaned into him, gently, pressing his lips to Neal's soft mouth, touching his forehead and lightly kissing his cheek. Neal saw himself getting up, not looking back and leaving, he saw this as he shut his eyes and spread his arms out to his sides, resting one still sweaty cheek on the pillow. Dewalt was whispering something into his ear. Neal kept his eyes shut as he saw himself leaving the room, saw himself descend the stairs, saw himself go to sleep alone in his apartment. He saw this as he gave into the absolutely terrifying feeling of Dewalt on top of him, holding him back, kissing his mouth with a hard, ravenous desire. Neal felt his eyelids fluttering, and saw blinking snaps of Dewalt's face, teeth, eyes as he reached for a fear to save him, and he reached finally for a familiar anger and loneliness to comfort him. There was nothing there. Just Dewalt.

Chapter 15

NEAL'S MOTHER AND father had called, opting for late afternoon drinks instead of lunch.

"Plane delays. Daddy needs a few drinks, he's such a boy you know," she said. "Bulls and Bears, at the Waldorf, meet us in the bar. Oh, the bar, is that allowed with the new group you go to? The rehab thing?"

Neal slumped at his desk, shutting his eyes.

"It's fine mother, we will see you there," he said.

"We, you're bringing a group?" she said, the sound of jet engines blotting every other word. "I'm…to…hang…we're… uggage…bye."

Neal called Dewalt and told him about the venue change. Annie was collecting swimwear and clothes for the Fire Island shoot. They would go the next morning.

"Are we doing a photo of you for the first column?" Annie said. "And I need the text for layout we're going to press."

"Read this, then tell me if I should sign my name to it," Neal said, giving her a print of the first column about the steam room, which he'd tweaked a bit.

Annie grabbed the page gleefully. As she finished, she looked a bit pale, and didn't seem to want to look away from the paper. Remembering Annie was a virgin, Neal felt like a derelict older brother who'd just spilled the contents of his porn drawer.

"Is this really you?" Annie said.

"Yes. I jazzed it up a little," Neal said. "Let's skip the photo. Nobody needs to know it's me. At least until it succeeds."

"I feel like Rebecca of Sunnybrook Farm, but I think it's great," she said.

Neal wasn't convinced, but it was too late now. Maybe his next column about dating would be sharper.

"I'm meeting my parents, I'll check back with you later to make sure we're all set for tomorrow," he said, heading out.

"Can I bring someone with me to Fire Island?" she said.

Neal stopped. Annie the virgin hadn't had a date since she'd been working at *Pop*.

"You met someone?" Neal said.

Launching into a giggle fit, Annie turned red and ran to him like a school chum.

"Yes, yes yes," she said. "I took your advice, about getting out there and he's so sweet. He's a singer."

"Bring him," Neal said.

Annie let out a high-pitched squeal. As he left, he glanced with admiration back at her, hunched over the computer, hair pulled in a tight ponytail, wearing another of her homespun skirts and floral print tops. She was a doing a knock-up job turning around the overall design of *Pop*. He regretted he couldn't tell his parents about the upcoming swimsuit issue, the column, his tiny bit of success. They'd never get it.

NEAL MADE HIS way slowly through Grand Central Station, buffeted by the anxious rush of travelers and the rumble of trains meeting platforms. The Waldorf was a few blocks away.

While he felt a bit nervous, he expected minimal drama. His parents had a way of making meetings like this pleasantly flat, like a necessary but dull charity cocktail party. They would not be bothered by their son's black gay lover, because nothing of the sort would be verbally acknowledged and therefore it did not exist. The Tate family did not dwell on uncouth, tasteless, or unnecessary details. Drinks at The Waldorf would be very civilized, Neal was sure of it. It was how things always had been, and always would be.

He took a moment, tilting his head back to take in the station's massive domed ceiling decorated with the star patterns of the zodiac as seen in a nighttime sky. For a moment, he thought of his family home in Missouri, of lying on the blacktop looking at the stars and gripping the constellation book his father had given him. A big-hipped blonde woman in a Chanel suit brushed roughly past him. He picked up his pace. He didn't want to be late, or leave Dewalt alone to face them.

DEWALT WAS WAITING, sitting in a big leather booth at the Waldorf's Bulls & Bears bar when Neal arrived. It was late afternoon and the place was buzzing with business suits, and out of towners. The room was dim, all dark wood, dark leather, high banquette seating, old world men's club. Neal—in his ankle length dark wash skinny jeans, pink V-neck T-shirt and chunky Roman sandals—felt a bit too impish. Dewalt smiled, gold teeth gleaming. He had on a button-down blue shirt and dark jeans. Respectable. Dewalt stood as Neal approached, then grabbed him for a hug and lip kiss. Neal looked around. Nobody seemed to notice. He sat in the booth, leaving the two outside facing chairs for his parents. Dewalt was drinking a beer. Neal wondered if he ever did drugs. He gave up dealing but that didn't mean he didn't flare up a pipe on a night out with the boys. His mother's voice shifted his attention.

Catherine Tate came into the lounge wearing an elegant pantsuit, a hat and gloves. She was lithe and fit from the lady's golf and tennis leagues. She had a long, narrow face, sharp green eyes, deep red hair and very small ears featuring very large pearls. She was an impeccable dresser, and a strict Irish Catholic. His father, Francis Tate, followed, drifting yards behind her. He'd stopped at the edge of the main bar, chewing a toothpick, studying the room. His black hair was cut short and spotted grey. He wore an expensive brown suit and leather lace ups (his wife did all the shopping). He was handsome, though round faced with a rash of freckles across his forehead. Narrow lips gave him a slightly peevish profile. He nodded at Neal, not moving, as if he meant to spend the visit hovering nearby. As his mother approached the table Neal saw a faint glimmer in her finely pencil-lined eyes as she noticed Dewalt. It was not shock, more intrigue, the intrigue of a safely distant scandal or a heard-about car wreck. As she reached the table that glimmer faded, replaced by a pleasant smile. The cocktail party had begun. She met Neal's stiff hug. Dewalt stood and shook her hand, as Neal blurted an introduction and Catherine turned back, looking for her husband.

"Where is that man?" she said, gloved hand waving him over. "This is just lovely. Here comes Dad."

Neal's jaw tightened as his father, Francis Tate, slowly approached. Dad ran Missouri's largest restaurant equipment company. His father had addressed the idea of Neal's going into the lucrative family business only once.

"Oil and water son, you and this company" his father had said before Neal left for college, not looking up from a balance sheet. "You'd hate the work. You'll have your inheritance money once we're gone. And there's a bit of a trust for now. That's what I did all this for."

His father approached, shook hands, then sat across from Neal and Dewalt. The waiter, a middle aged black man dressed in a work tuxedo handed them drink menus. Catherine, avoiding any eye contact, went for white wine, Neal a diet coke.

"Martini," his father said looking up at Dewalt. "What about you?"

He gave Dewalt a long, wandering glance.

"You look like a scotch man, am I right?" Francis said.

Neal's mother took off her gloves, speaking in hushed tones.

"I don't think they drink, Francis. Like your sister Stella, God bless her," she said, crossing herself, then kissing a diamond studded rosary hidden under her silk top.

"I don't drink, but Dewalt does," Neal said.

"Scotch sounds good," Dewalt said.

"Makers Mark," said Neal's father.

Neal was shocked. His father was usually silent at these little meetings. He often spent his time jotting financial figures on a napkin while Neal and his mother chatted about fashion.

"What do you do?" Francis said to Dewalt.

"Construction," Dewalt said.

"Tough work. Especially in winter. I was a brick layer one winter. Brutal shit," Francis said.

"Language Francis," Catherine said, smiling, checking her watch.

"I didn't know you were a brick layer," Neal said, sipping his coke, feeling things sliding away from him.

"Your father did all sorts of things when we were courting. But what about you, tell us about this new job," Catherine said, looking directly at Neal for the first time since she sat down.

Dewalt rested his arm across Neal's shoulder, naturally, in a friendly way. Neal began to sweat. Catherine studied her perfectly manicured nails. Francis glanced toward the window. Drinks arrived. Dewalt sipped the scotch.

"Good stuff," Dewalt said.

"So the job, tell us all about it," said Catherine, still analyzing her nails.

His father glanced up. Neal was in the hot seat. He'd always kept some type of job—waiter, proofreader, foot model, or that short, disastrously drunken stint as a go-go boy. Through the years, he'd managed to scrape up the rent, at times reluctantly borrowing money from his parents. That was a habit he vowed to give up now that he was sober.

"I'm the editor at a small magazine," Neal said.

"What's the magazine," Francis said. "Anything we heard of?"

Neal took a long drink of his soda. He tried to meet his father's stare.

"It's a lifestyle weekly," he said.

Francis nodded, dropped his eyes, sighing. Dewalt squeezed Neal's shoulder.

"You're doing a fashion thing, right? Swimsuits?" Dewalt said.

Neal nodded. Francis drained his drink and smiled.

"Another round? " Francis said.

"I'll get this one. I think that waiter went on his break," Dewalt said, getting up and heading to the bar before anyone could argue.

"Nice guy," Francis said.

Neal's head was swimming. Suddenly his father—Mr. tight-lipped, keep to himself, arrogant fuckhead—was all supportive buddy boy.

"He's not like your other friends, " Catherine said, lowering her voice again and speaking quickly. "I mean not just that he's black but he's so, well, I don't know where did you meet him? I didn't know people still put gold caps on their teeth."

"Leave the boy alone, Catherine," Francis said. "Don't fuss."

Neal hated when his father stood up for him. It made him feel small, fey, completely absolutely and entirely useless. Dewalt returned with the drinks, including another scotch for himself. Neal calculated: a beer, two scotches. Was he drunk yet? Dewalt and Francis sat back, while Catherine outlined their upcoming Ireland tour, "Zest of Shamrock".

"I'm off to the ladies room. We have to go soon," Catherine said, sounding relieved.

She excused herself and left the booth. The three men sat

quietly. Francis reached across the table and pressed a bill into Neal's hand.

"You boys go out and celebrate that new job of yours Neal. Good luck," he said.

Neal, as always, took the cash, wishing he didn't need to.

"Nice talking with you," Dewalt said, reaching out his broad hand for a shake.

Francis hesitated, then slowly reached out and gripped Dewalt's hand. The two maintained eye contact, shaking hands firmly as if they'd just sealed a business deal. As Catherine returned, and the group made small talk, said good luck, safe trip, Neal felt himself shrinking, perplexed by what had just happened. As they all rose to go, Neal quickly checked the bill he held folded in his sweaty palm. A hundred. Decent. An overdue Bergdorf Goodman credit card payment. If he freed up a little credit, he could get the Libertine ruffle tuxedo shirt. He shoved it in the pocket of his skinny jeans and followed Dewalt out of the bar.

"LET'S GO TO my place," Neal said.

He said it out of anger, or frustration, or some attempt to regain control of what he considered an unsettling meeting. He quickly realized it was a mistake as Dewalt nodded yes. They'd never been to Neal's tiny studio apartment, always gone to Dewalt's house. Dewalt was smiling, surely a little high. Neal was suffocating in the sweltering heat, trying to figure out a way to suggest they go to Harlem.

"I've been waiting for you to ask," Dewalt said.

There was no turning back as they crossed Eighth Avenue, a block from his house. He tried to remember if he'd taken the trash out, if there was anything to drink in the house, if any stray phone numbers from old tricks were stuck to the refrigerator. They climbed the four flights, then Neal struggled with the two locks and showed Dewalt in.

Dead flowers in a vase, the pull-out sofa open, but other than that not bad. No dirty underwear, no dishes in the sink. Neal bent over to force the bed back into its sofa tomb so they could move through the place, but Dewalt stopped him, pulling him into the twisted green striped sheets. Neal gave in, laying his head on Dewalt's chest.

"Your dad's cool," Dewalt said.

Neal sat up.

"You must be drunk," he said.

"It takes a lot more than that," Dewalt said.

Neal struggled out of Dewalt's grip, toppled out of the pull-out sofa and went to the sink against the wall in the kitchenette. He poured a glass of water.

"I know how fathers can be," Dewalt said.

"No you don't. Not him," Neal said.

Dewalt sat on the edge of the sofa bed. Neal finished his water and looked at Dewalt.

"Everybody likes him. Great guy. Big success. Man's man," Neal said. "And he's never said anything to me that's not nice, I guess. It's how he looks at me."

Neal paused and looked down.

"He hates me," he said softly.

Neal looked at Dewalt and shuddered. He hadn't said that before, he hadn't said 'hate' but he realized he always thought it. Dewalt stood up and went to Neal. He opened his arms and pulled Neal close. He smelled of scotch. His hands were rough on Neal's cheek. He pulled him closer and whispered. Neal shut his eyes and burrowed his face.

"I want you to come with me to Fire Island tomorrow," Neal said. "I'm sick of being alone."

"Sure," Dewalt said, then softly, very softly. "I love you, Neal."

Neal looked up at him, at his deep, soft eyes.

"You ever rode the Cyclone?" Dewalt said, grinning.

Chapter 16

THE SUBWAY WAS chugging up and over the Manhattan Bridge and the muddy East River into Brooklyn, before it crept back underground on its way to Coney Island. Dewalt was giddy, like a kid, excited to introduce Neal to the last, decaying bit of New York sideshow grandeur.

"We'd hit it in the summer, me and Boney," Dewalt said. "Got me into tattoos and shit. You gonna love dis shit."

Neal realized he'd often spoken of himself, but never asked Dewalt about his past.

"Did you ever go with your family?" Neal said.

Dewalt stood up, leaning against the grimy train's window and looking out at the last glimpse of the water before they slid down into the underground darkness. As they went underground, he sat near Neal.

"I was raised by my Aunt, Big Lou," he said. "My mom died when I was really young. Lou was the shit. You'll meet her someday."

Somewhat terrified of the idea of meeting Big Lou, or any of the Harlem gang, Neal went quiet, not wanting to imagine the great differences in their childhoods. They rode the rest of the way quietly, Dewalt occasionally squeezing Neal's knee and smiling broadly, as if he could barely take the suspense. Neal had heard about Coney Island, heard that it was trashy, greasy and scary. The ghetto of amusement parks and beaches. Once at a party, a young girl had confessed to swimming at the Coney Island beach and the fashionista crowd had screamed in horror, stunned that she hadn't dropped dead from some nasty water disease. As the train halted, he realized they would be visiting one another's favorite beach spots, Dewalt's Coney Island, Neal's Fire Island, within hours of one other.

The street outside of the subway had a third-world feeling to it, Neal thought. There were ugly store fronts selling ghastly furniture, a boarded-up transient hotel, and a noisy bumper car ride playing hard-driving rap music. Dewalt rushed forward into Coney Island proper. Off the main drag, several side streets lead into different quadrants of the park, also known as Astroland. Each street lead past screeching amusement rides and game booths, ending at the boardwalk and ocean. There was a pink, electric feeling to the place. Swirling, angry looking metal monsters were spinning, voices screaming, little people strapped into chairs, jolting them in circles and one ride, the Zipper, literally twisted its captors upside down. It all made Neal dizzy. The neon blues, lavenders and hot whites illuminating the rides were, however, sort of pretty, Neal thought. Dewalt took them up Surf Street and stopped at the first attraction, the Coney Island Circus Sideshow. A gangly man with a Mohawk and multiple piercings barked over a microphone.

"Ten-in-one circus sideshow. They're here, they're real and they're alive. Freaks, wonders. Be amazed," he said, winking at Neal and holding up a welcoming fist to Dewalt.

The sideshow building itself looked like an old warehouse with big murals all over the front heralding the exhibits: a twisted shockmeister who ate fire and glass; lady Serpentina, a snake charmer and contortionist; a two headed baby; Danny

Vomit; and Bob, the human tattoo canvas. Dewalt took Neal up to the skinny Mohawk man, who was sitting in a makeshift ticket booth.

"Wat up my man?" he said, high-fiving Dewalt.

Dewalt pulled out money for tickets but the guy scoffed.

"Get in there mofo," he said.

Dewalt ushered Neal in to a dimly lit area. It reminded him of the inside of a circus tent, though in reality it was a warehouse. It felt cool inside, compared to the lingering evening heat. A small group sat on bleachers as a fragile, very young-looking man swallowed fire as twanging instrumental music played. Off to one side was a black curtain. Dewalt took Neal toward the bleachers and they sat in the back. The very thin young man gulping fire finished, though a sickening scent of lighter fluid lingered. Next up was Danny Vomit. Neal shut his eyes, thinking how lovely it would be at Bergdorf Goodman. The store would be empty, close to closing time. He could linger, try on sandals and Gucci tennis shorts. Dewalt nudged him.

"You're gonna love this," he said.

Danny stood center stage. He was lanky and bald with a huge handlebar mustache. He was wearing a suit and bow tie, and holding a hammer and a huge nail. An energetic wash of campy music came up as Danny grinned, leaned his head back, then delicately placed the giant nail into his nose and began to pound it in.

"Yeah, get it in there Danny," Dewalt yelled, along with a few other rowdy patrons.

"You know him?" Neal said, keeping his eyes on the floor, unable to watch the spectacle.

"A few of 'em, yeah," Dewalt said, still clapping.

The hammering went on. Neal studied the concrete floor, still thinking of sandals, swimwear, sweetly ruffled shirts. Armani, Gucci, Sander. Finally the nailing was over, and Danny revved up a chainsaw, announcing that he was going to toss and catch it in the air.

"Dear God?" Neal said.

Dewalt gave him a hug, then pulled away as a devilish looking woman Neal recognized from the front mural as Serpentina saw Dewalt and came at them. She ignored Neal, but leaned into Dewalt, hugging him in a sensual way. She was, Neal guessed, over six foot, all long legs and wild, curly waist length hair. She wore a black bustier and heavy red sparkle eye makeup. Despite Dewalt's mild protests, she was not releasing her grip on him. Neal wondered if she held her pet snakes so tightly to her robust bosom. She was whispering something in Dewalt's ear, and then stuck her tongue there. Dewalt pushed her away, laughing.

"Missy, this is Neal," Dewalt said.

Missy gave Neal a tight hug, pulling away quickly.

"Wow, you are really holding so tight, honey it's OK," she said, her huge glittering red eyes opening wider.

Dewalt looked awkwardly from Missy to Neal. The sound of Danny's raging chainsaws finally shut off as the crowd applauded.

"I know Missy from way back," he said. "You want to see the two-headed baby?"

Missy was watching Neal, her huge black eyes frightening, her lips deep black, hiding a smile that Neal decided was as fanged as the serpents she tamed. Neal wondered if she had given birth to the show's two-headed baby.

"Would you mind if we went for a Diet Coke," Neal said. "It's hot in here."

Missy's lips curled into a wicked snarl and she grabbed Dewalt's arm.

"You holding?" she said.

"I quit the shit Missy, I'm a tourist," Dewalt said, taking Neal by the hand and leading him straight out of the warehouse before Missy could protest.

In front, near the Mohawk ticket man, Neal felt like he might vomit, and at the same time wondered if Danny had that in store as a finale. It felt incredibly hot, there was no breeze, the moon was fiery, and the constant swirl of rides in the near distance, along with a smell of rancid frying meat was too much. Mohawk man began to laugh, trying to speak through his piggish chortles.

"Pussy," he finally got out. "Sideshow virgin pussy man."

Dewalt took Neal further up Surf Street, stopping to buy him a soda. They continued to the boardwalk and a bench facing the ocean. Neal gladly took a seat, sipping his coke and sucking in the salt-tainted air. In the dark, the beach looked almost pearly gray, the sand lit softly in the moonlight, and the cresting curl of waves almost clean.

"You all right?" Dewalt said, wrapping his arm across the top of the bench and Neal's shoulder.

Neal was quiet. He just wanted his head to stop aching. He was in a familiar "brain" spot, a spot where his fears sank. When he felt threatened and conflicted—wanting to connect to Dewalt, but more deeply, wanting to run away in disgust—when he felt both, he became calm, did not speak, and experienced all the feelings good and bad sinking at once. The fear, in some way, became so large and heavy, that instead of rising, expressing, it simply sunk far, far down below his gut. He sat, as if caged, blotting out the man at his side and the strange sickly scent of burning meat and cotton candy, and waited until he could get away from here. He felt very much like a child.

"What did that woman think you were holding?" Neal said.

"I guess it's gotta come out," Dewalt said. "You ever done heroine?"

Neal sat up, feeling Dewalt's arm across his shoulder.

"No," he said.

"I used to scratch myself, like one spot, it'd itch so bad. I'd get a steak knife, ya know the cutting knife edge, and scratch, wake up all cut and shit," Dewalt said. "I dealt it awhile too. Missy was a regular. I quit all that shit now, really Neal. I'm done. But it still comes at ya, you know?"

Neal turned to look at Dewalt, the tiny slice of a moon

lighting the edge of his black cheek, his lips reaching up and around the side of his face, the side of his eye elegant and smooth ending at a knick at the nip of his lower temple. He thought Dewalt looked beautiful, sitting so still, speaking so softly, so honestly. He knew what Dewalt meant, how it all comes at you, how it haunts you, how things you did that you are too ashamed to ever admit to yourself, that they seem clear late, late at night and you spend so much time tying them up and shoving them in boxes and smacking them down.

"After dealing I did some scams," Dewalt said. "Hit department stores, cut out the wires and wore the clothes out. I could do two thousand a week. Sold it all to a fat blonde bitch in Queens, Miss Marney. She ran a restaurant and bought the stuff in back, in the kitchen. I did some time, that's what got me off all that. It's not me now."

Dewalt turned and held out his arm to Neal. A tiny cross tattoo was etched on his forearm, faded.

"That's my prison tattoo," he said. "I was lucky. Only eight months."

Neal held Dewalt's arm and looked at the tiny, worn-out little cross. All this revelation, this revealing, took away that desire to run, and made him want to crawl up into Dewalt, to get closer, to get on his lap and feel every bit of him. He put his lips to the cross and looked up to meet Dewalt's lips which were rough and salty like the nearby sea waves. He fell into the kiss, tasting it, and thinking, always thinking, of Missy and jail and his own secrets, his own dread and how good the kiss felt and what he ought to say, how he ought to reveal his own drinking and sex struggles with Dewalt, now, here in this shitty little place. He would open up to him now. The screaming men broke the spell.

They were fat, white and drunk, holding bottles of beer. Neal couldn't figure out their ages. They had that beat up, grizzled look of men who live on cigarettes, Twinkies and liquor. One had a big tattoo of an American flag on his arm. He came forward ready to pounce. Dewalt stood quickly, and Neal waited just behind him, thinking they should run back to the safety of the park.

"Nice tattoo," Dewalt said.

The comment seemed to throw the fat man off, to halt him. His friend, a little more unsteady, lingered behind him. The man eyed Dewalt, then spit and came back alive.

"Shut your mouth faggot," the man said.

The fat man's friend laughed like a movie hillbilly, snorting to accent his giggles. Neal's body shook as if with a feverish chill. He'd never been in a fight. Those instances when a passing car or a stray group shouted gay bashing insults, he'd always quickened his pace and found safety, content that he was being smart and avoiding harm from ignorant, dangerous derelicts.

"Mind your business," Dewalt said.

Dewalt's shoulders were tensing, Neal could see a transformation. Dewalt's arms dangled loose at his sides, but the top part of his body, the neck and even his head, seemed to be centering and becoming stiff. The boardwalk was empty, save for three young girls near a beer booth a block away. There were no direct lights, just the distant neon, and a sliver moon and the reflective ocean waves. Not too far off, the Zipper flipped riders upside down, the pink and blue machines twirled, and the Mohawk man hawked. Neal estimated it was only a block's run back there.

"You have a good night," Dewalt said, then turned and took Neal's hand.

Neal froze. Dewalt was squeezing his hand tight, trying to pull him forward, directly in front of and past the men.

"Fuck you, nigger queer," the fat man said, smashing his beer bottle on the edge of a bench and coming at Dewalt.

Neal screamed, high and girlish, without thinking, then he covered his mouth. The other fat man was shouting at his friend to stop. Dewalt had released Neal's hand and was moving to meet the fat man. The girls at the beer booth had turned to watch, and one of them started to move then stopped. The fat man swung the jagged bottle in the air, poised, ready to slice right into the little cross on Dewalt's lean forearm. The bottle never landed. Dewalt seemed to pause and think in the brief moment of the bottle hanging high, then he bent over and rammed his head into the fat man's gut, grasping the fleshy sides of his body and literally throwing him to the ground. The cut bottle rolled away and the fat man smacked his head, curling up in a ball, muttering. His friend knelt at his side and Dewalt grabbed Neal's hand again, taking him swiftly down the boardwalk, past the three gawking girls and toward the Cyclone. They paused at the edge of the street leading back in the park and toward the huge wooden roller coaster, lit in bright white lights trimmed in red. Neal's head was completely clear. Dewalt was checking the boardwalk to make sure no one followed them. Neal thought of all the bullies he'd experienced in his life, and the fact that he'd never spoken up for himself. He wasn't afraid. He was incredibly turned on, and wanted to feel Dewalt fucking him, right there, by the ocean, naked in the rough sand. He wanted to be totally connected with this tough ex-convict, former drug dealing, shoplifting mofo who just rammed his head into a big assholes homophobic belly.

"You okay?" Dewalt said.

For the first time since they'd met Neal didn't wait to be touched, taken, held or kissed. He didn't check around to see who was watching, or wonder what the exact right move would be. He just grabbed Dewalt, there for all to see, he pulled his face to him and he kissed him, then he shoved his tongue into Dewalt's ear. Dewalt pulled away laughing, rubbing a finger over his ear, rubbing a hand over Neal's head.

"I think you ready for the Cyclone now, kid," Dewalt said.

The moved swiftly to the ride, climbing the stairs to the top. They sat in the front seat of the beat-up looking coaster, a scrappy red bar flat across their chests. The ascent was slow, creaking, and the higher they went, the more beautiful Coney Island appeared. Neal could see the white capped ocean waves crashing below, the expanse of the park, subdued from above, all lights and sparkles, reaching up toward the night sky which had a few faded stars hanging high. As they reached the peak, Dewalt started to scream and laugh, and at that dizzying top, looking down into the steepest slope Neal had ever seen, straight down, into the pit of hell, Neal sucked in his breath, hanging there in that moment before the rattling old car soared over the top and bulleted straight down. In that moment he thought for the second time that night that he was going to perish, and for the second time that night, he was glad to be at Dewalt's side.

Chapter 17

NEAL SAW FIRE Island as a tiny bit of sand, sex and fluff bobbing far enough away from the city to give it an otherworldly vibe. People swam nude, had impromptu parties on the decks of their creaking plank houses, and late into the night a wooded area known as the "meat rack" stank of sweat, coconut oil and sex. Sitting on the upper deck of the ferryboat from Sayville to the island, Neal followed the nose of the boat as it struck out into the blackness, steering straight into a broad tangle of summer stars. The boat churned through black water, sea foam splashing, a rising screech of crickets and tree frogs overwhelming any stray chatter. His group—Rovvie, Dewalt, Annie and her date Laird—were unusually quiet. They'd taken over the back section of the boat's upper deck. Dewalt sat at Neal's side, one hand resting lazily on his thigh. He wondered how they'd all get along and if Rovvie would cut Dewalt some slack and be gentle, as opposed to probing mercilessly. Most of the men on the boat were white, gay and at least striving to be elegant. Sitting close to Dewalt, Neal took in a slightly murky body odor and noticed a wide rip in his date's boardshorts, a hole in the front of his sneakers. He was glad they were arriving in the dark.

In the distance, the lights of the tiny island shone, setting off its two distinct areas. To the right was Cherry Grove (lesbians, aging show queens, laid back artists); to the left, the Pines (preening gay boys, New York-centric celebrities, new money). The two sections were divided by the winding, wooded 'meat rack'. The island bloomed in the 1960's as a gay-lib hangout, then morphed through the decades to become both a status weekend spot (out celebrities mixing with big gay money). The scene was deceptive, Neal knew, with beauty a constant trump card. The sculpted boy in the D&G swimsuit could, in reality, be a waiter who'd scrimped all winter to land a one-eighth share in a house of ten. He could also be an oil heir making a pit stop en route to the South of France. Neal had never 'done' an entire island summer, just visited friends who were part of the weekend share scene.

Andreas' house was in the Pines. It sat empty most of the season, save for one or two big parties. If Andreas had time off in the summer months, he spent it at his house in chic, old-moneyed South Hampton. He could entertain his straight business associates there. Off the ferry, they crept through the small crowd across the landing dock and into the Pines proper. Rovvie lead the way, past the lively two-level Sip and Twirl disco where shirtless model boys hung off the upper deck, martini glasses in hand. Neal's group took the main plank path toward the beach house. Annie had a huge ugly piece of rolling luggage which bounced over the slats, and her date Laird carried a guitar. The kid was cute in a nerdy wannabe-subway-singer sort of way. Tall and skinny, Alaska pale, long ratty hair, freckles. Rovvie caught Neal studying the boy as they moved along and tapped his shoulder.

"Tall, probably has a giant cock. Go Annie," Rovvie said.

Neal took Dewalt's hand. Dewalt had only brought a small plastic bag stuffed with a toothbrush and underwear. Rovvie and Neal had small, chic leather duffle bags. He wished he'd shoved Dewalt's bag into his duffle.

The island had a series of plank boardwalks stretching and

intersecting through the beach houses. There were no street lamps, no cars, one grocery store and a few bars and restaurants near the ferry. The jutting walks were not clearly marked and maneuvering at night was madness. Neal offered his cell phone as a source of light as they wove down paths, deeper into the island. The houses, ranging from knotty, charming wood plank miniatures to sprawling modern double-deckers with elaborate pools, all had names: Xanadu, Seascape, Mama Rose. Half way down the ocean side walkway, they landed at Tycoon. Rovvie fished out keys. The two-story house was empty, dim. The place had been decorated sparsely and modernly. A few key pieces of elegant furniture faced a glass wall looking out onto a long rectangular pool. Beyond that, the beach. Andreas and Caz were arriving in the morning with photographer Denny Matthews and the models. They'd stayed behind to wait for that week's issue of *Pop* to finish printing. They were bringing a few hundred copies to the island. The issue had Neal's first column. He was keeping his expectations low for its success, and had not mentioned it to Dewalt. He was secretly hoping Dewalt never read it. Neal guided the group in as Rovvie threw his duffle on the sofa.

"Everybody grab a room. Andreas and I are in the first one on the left. There's a big bedroom in back and two upstairs," Rovvie said. "I'm going dancing, anybody wanna go?"

"Sure," Annie said, glancing at her date, who had slept and spoken few words throughout the trip thus far.

"Awesome," said Laird in a voice far deeper and richer than anyone expected.

Neal took Dewalt to explore the back of the house. They found the rear room. It faced the ocean and was done simply with a dark wood slat headboard bed, two end tables and a private bath. Dewalt threw his plastic bag on the floor and sat back on the bed.

"You didn't say they were slamming rich," he said.

Neal wondered if he should unpack his extensive line of skin care products, reveal his neatly folded designer underwear or his collection of seven swimsuits, five square-cut, two bikinis. He'd never been to the island with a date and always been drunk from the moment his toes hit the sand. He'd always spent a good deal of his time in the sex-drenched meat rack. Dewalt yanked him onto the bed.

"You never stop," Dewalt said.

"What?" Neal said.

Dewalt gently ran his finger along Neal's forehead, back and forth slowly.

"Up here," Dewalt said.

He kissed Neal's forehead.

"Yeah," Neal said, drifting.

The touch was gentle, lulling and Neal could feel a slight roughness from Dewalt's callused finger, trailing across then back over his forehead. He imagined the finger sinking into his thoughts, smoothing them out, calming the chaos that Neal lived with and often hated. Dewalt stopped, and pressed his palm on Neal's hot cheek.

"Let's see the ocean. I only been to shitty Orchard Beach," Dewalt said.

Eyes shut, Neal nodded, not really wanting to stop feeling Dewalt's fingers and hand.

"Come on," Dewalt said, taking charge.

A NARROW PLANK path jutted from the edge of Palamos' house toward the ocean. The city's extreme heat was replaced with a breeze and the ocean's spray. The beach was deserted. It was after 2 A.M. The Sip and Twirl dance club near the ferry dock would be packed. Stopping for a moment, Neal took in the enormity of the space around him—the limitless expanse of the star-cluttered sky sweeping down to meet the ocean. Dewalt ran ahead to the ocean's black edge as Neal lay back in the sand. He knew the big dipper, but the others were vague patterns. As a boy, he'd lie on the driveway of his parent's home in Missouri and tried to figure out which constellation was which. There was a belt, twins, an ox. His father had given him an astronomy map, but never had the time to explain it, and the designs had made no sense to Neal. He'd thrown it away. Behind him, something rustled in the grassy dunes which separated the beach from the boardwalk and the homes. Deer from the island's Sunken Forest area were known to clip up to the boardwalk, hunting for food. He turned back, watching Dewalt run toward him, big, wet bare feet kicking through the sand.

"It's huge out there man," Dewalt said.

They lay back in the sand, Dewalt twining his sand crusted feet with Neal's. It felt gritty, and Neal wanted to pull away, find a towel and clean things up, but he stopped himself. He pointed up at a massive cup in the sky.

"Big Dipper right? Or Little?" he said.

Dewalt raised a hand like a painter with a brush.

"Big. But look over there," he said.

Dewalt sat up, and went behind Neal. He pressed his hands to Neal's temple and guided his face East, then leaned down toward him.

"See that triangle there," he said. "It's a swan. You see?"

Neal let his head be guided. He'd never heard of a swan shape, but as Dewalt lifted a hand and traced over and over, in front of him, a pattern, Neal could begin to see a tail and wings and even a head.

"Called Deneb. Big fucking star that's got enough light to make like sixty-thousand suns," Dewalt said. "I read that. Always remembered that one."

"You read about that?" Neal said, trying not to sound shocked.

"Stars and tattoos. Mad shit. It's what got me into Egypt. They used the stars when they built the pyramids. Fucking hot shit. We gotta go see Egypt, right?" Dewalt said.

Neal considered it, traveling to the far reaches of the world with this man at his side. With the rush of the ocean waves, under the stars, it all seemed possible. He sat up and had an urge to swim, to swim naked, something he hadn't done since he was a boy.

"You want to get in," Neal said. "We could skinny dip?"

Dewalt sat back in the sand.

"Shit, I can't swim," he said.

Neal stood up and started to undress. He wanted to take Dewalt into the water.

"We'll stay in the shallows. It's safe. Hold onto me," Neal said.

He stripped quickly and Dewalt stood up slowly, hesitating, then also stripped. Neal held out his hand, small against Dewalt's, which was big and callused. As they moved to the water's edge, lit by a thin summer moon, Neal had a wave of fear. The water licked his toes. He hesitated, recalling warnings about rip tides, swimming at night. The waves, dark save for the barely visible white waves caps, looked foreboding. He took a deep breath, then pulled Dewalt closer to the surf. A wave knocked at their ankles and Dewalt let out a wild hoot, like an Indian on the warpath.

"Shit oh shit," Dewalt shouted.

The beach was silent but for the crashing waves. Dewalt grabbed Neal around the waist and held him so tightly that he lost his breath for a second. They waded in very slowly. A new wave smacked their thighs and Dewalt let out another bellow. Neal stopped as the water sprayed at his waist. He pressed close to Dewalt and kissed him, tasting salt. Dewalt bit at Neal's lip and started to laugh as the ocean roared.

"Back, that's it, back," he said.

Dewalt broke away and ran to safety, standing on the sand watching Neal in the water. Neal waved in the dark, then moved further out and dove under, feeling the utter blackness deep down, trying to peer through the ocean up at the moon, then finally surfacing, and swimming back to the shallow water. He stared back toward Dewalt, who was small and dim. He got out and ran to him. They lay on their backs, Neal's back gritty with sand. He had no urge to brush it off.

"I had to take swim lessons all summer. I hated it, but guess it was good," Neal said.

"Shit," Dewalt muttered.

Neal detected a tone of distaste, which surprised him. He tried to think of a way into a next line, but Dewalt took care of it.

"I'd see you on TV, those white kids that swim all summer at some fucking club," Dewalt said. "I delivered shit all day. Hot as fuck."

Neal sat up, sand drifting off his back with a breeze. Dewalt sat up too, looking at him a little harshly. Neal felt a twinge of fear, and a sudden sinking feeling that the last few moments they had shared were fake, and would be swept away with the tide.

"Yeah, you a spoiled brat I know, cute little shit," Dewalt said, and pushed Neal roughly into the sand, then climbed astride his chest. "You just want to lie around and make me do the work. Big nasty man for you."

He straddled Neal's chest with his wide black legs, reigning over Neal like a boy-king wrestling the weak kid to submission. He sat there, smiling, turned on, happy, then folded his arms and started to laugh. Staring up at him, Neal felt at once frightened and taken care of, and beyond Dewalt, Neal could make out the swan constellation, the wide collection of stars taking flight. He shut his eyes and waited for whatever might come next. There was a wind, a bit of sand scalding his face, then that hand, those fingers again, trailing across his forehead, and then hard lips, and a full surrendered body crushing them together into a deep wet sand imprint.

Chapter 18

MALICE SHOWED UP at 7 A.M. and woke Neal and Dewalt from a deep sleep. He stood at the end of the bed, yanking on Neal's foot until he came alive.

"She's arrived to do her magic, so up up up my darling," Malice said. "I didn't know She had a man-friend?"

A well-manicured, middle-aged visual artist, Malice (real name Michael) was committed to calling all of the male population 'she'. The pronoun game (she's a mess, did you see her hair?) was an occasional bit of camp most gay men engaged in at one point or another, but Malice had made it a way of life. He did it without reservation, and no one was safe, be they gay, straight or otherwise. Somehow, he always got away with it. Neal roused, while Dewalt yanked the covers back over his head. Malice was done up for the shoot: white hot pants, a silk top knotted at the waist, platform flip-flops and a straw hat. A respected portrait painter with midlevel success (he had a few key celebrity clients including Elton John), Malice had spent his first ten years in the city as a downtown drag performer and raging heroin addict. He'd put down the needle in the '90s and focused on art. Neal had met him at a twelve-step recovery meeting soon after rehab, and they'd had lunch a few times.

Malice was spending two weeks on the island and had agreed to art-direct the shoot. He also set them up with their location, the infamous Belvedere Guest House. From the kitchen, there was a shattering scream. Dewalt sat up.

"Oh my biscuits, this is gorgeous," the voice said.

It was Toby, one of the three models, Southern twang and over the top enthusiasm intact.

"Let's see what She lured out here," Malice said, winking at Dewalt as he left. "And nice to meet you. She is choco-gorrrgeous, lover."

Malice's audible gasp from the kitchen told Neal he'd made the right model choices. Dewalt sat up.

"What the fuck was that?" he said.

THE BELVEDERE GUEST House was in the Grove. They cut through the meat rack to get there. A wooded area with shrouding trees and winding paths, the rack divided the gay muscled Pines from the laid back lesbian Grove. The shoot photographer, Denny Matthews, was meeting them at the Belvedere with Andreas and Caz. Neal and Dewalt lead the caravan through the woods, carrying a bag stuffed with swimwear. Neal had decided on a mix of models. Toby, ingénue, pale skin, lean, wild rash of freckles; Apollo, thick muscled, swarthy looks, huge cock, hard snarl; and 'C', tall beautiful Swede, blonde crew cut, killer ass, divine definition. The group was overtaken by Malice, who decided on an impromptu tour for the younger set.

"Stop and look," Malice said, pointing in the distance to a tiny slat bridge that covered a dip in the path. "You are crossing the Judy Garland memorial bridge."

Toby, who had decided to go barefoot, stepped toward the bridge for a closer look.

"She was in *The Wizard of Oz* right?" he said.

Malice snarled.

"Dear God, another legend forgotten," he said. "She was so much more tragic than you could ever hope to be."

Pulling up the rear were Annie and Laird. The two were a perfect pair: Annie in black jeans, dykey combat boots and a wrinkled Curt Cobain T-shirt; Laird in knee-torn jeans, a long-sleeve tie-dye button-up shirt and magic marker decorated sneakers with holes where his big toes popped out. Neal had high hopes for Annie's virginal coming-out. The three models were grumbling, the Swede asking Toby why they hadn't taken a water taxi over to the Grove. Neal wasn't sure if Apollo spoke English.

As they crossed the Judy Garland bridge, Dewalt stopped, looking for a plaque.

"So somebody built this or what?" Dewalt said.

Malice rolled his eyes and pinched Rovvie's arm as they reached the other side of the bridge. The duo stood under a lean little tree, eyeing Dewalt. Neal had already moved ahead of the pack but paused. Annie and Laird still lingered behind everyone. Dewalt stood dead center on the bridge.

"She's a bit out of her league isn't She," he said. "Poor thing."

Dewalt held still, then stalked across the bridge toward Malice. Rovvie moved away, up the path to Neal's side. Malice stood his ground near the little tree, pushing his narrow chest out as if he had huge breasts to shield himself.

"You talking to me?" Dewalt said.

Putting his hands on his hips, alone now under the tree, Malice stepped back ever so tentatively, his back to the bark.

"She's a bit uptight, yes?" he said loudly to the group. "We're not in Harlem, dear."

At that, Dewalt grabbed Malice's thin white arm.

"Listen, she's a he, so cut that shit out, and if you got something to say bring it," Dewalt said.

Malice lamely tried to yank his arm free, but Dewalt held tight. Neal stepped up and Annie made her way quickly across the bridge with Laird.

"She's a brute," Malice said. "Neal, tell Her. We are not in the projects."

Dewalt squeezed Malice's arm tightly, getting ready to speak, or strike. Malice went pale, looking genuinely alarmed, seeking Neal.

"I am not one of Her nigga thugs," Malice said. "Release me."

At this everyone froze, and in a swift move, Dewalt threw Malice ass first into a pile of leaves, releasing a mighty grunt as he did it.

"Listen, you mothafucka—" Dewalt said as Annie swept in, Neal just behind her.

Standing between a screeching Malice and a fired-up Dewalt, Annie stood, hands on hips, face deep red, huffing and puffing and taking charge.

"Stop it, just stop it," she said very loudly, though with a voice incapable of anything without a touch of syrup. "Malice apologize."

Then to Dewalt.

"He's just a crazy bitch, you don't need to..." she said, pausing. "I'm sorry, Dewalt."

Dewalt was breathing deeply, but calmed as Annie reached out and gently touched his arm, and Neal came to his side. Malice, helped by Rovvie, stood up. Dewalt stepped back.

"All right, all right," Malice said in a voice twisting up an octave. "She's a bitch, and a drama queen and by that I mean me. Let's start over shall we. Truce?"

Dewalt shook his head, gave Malice an up and down then kept moving. Neal gave Malice a light punch in the arm, then moved ahead too, followed by Annie and the rest. Neal was at a loss of what to say to Dewalt. The whole thing was a blur. As they emerged from the wooded tangle, back onto the slatted walk jutting into the Grove, they were met by a coal-eyed, large antlered buck. The deer stood still, not flinching, lifting its head and observing the caravan. The group froze. Rovvie moved toward the animal slowly, then reached out his hand and caressed the deer's nose. He leaned his face close, and whispered something. The buck took in the touch, then turned and wandered off down the path. Malice thrust his hands on his hips.

"What in the world did She say to the animal?" he said, approaching Rovvie. "Dear God, don't those things have ticks?"

Dewalt stepped up.

"It was the shit, man, you nuts?" he said to Malice, then reaching out to smack fists with Rovvie.

The group was silent, Dewalt standing there fist in limbo, Rovvie baffled, stepping back with a hint of fear. For a moment, Neal noticed how his date's knee length board shorts, plain white T-shirt and high-top tennis shoes clashed with his clan's crisp tennis shorts, designer sunglasses and Bergdorf beach hats. Dewalt withdrew his fist, shrugged and stomped forward, now leading the crowd. Neal caught up as they all silently headed to the Belvedere.

Chapter 19

THE BELVEDERE GUEST House was a big overstuffed relic on the Bay side of Cherry Grove. Completely out of place amongst the knotty little cottages and slick glass-walled beach house, it was built in the late 1950's by John Eberhardt (of the Eberhardt pencil dynasty) with an eye to Austrian High Baroque. More a film set than a home, every inch of the decaying gothic mansion was over the top: an elaborate wrought-iron gated entrance lead past a lavish mirrored fountain, bawdy Greek statues, masses of purple lavender and lattice fence work ending at a huge set of wooden double doors. The inside was a cluttered mess of gold leafing, dusty chandeliers, beautifully detailed wall murals and a maze of hallways, skinny spiral staircases and ornate antiques. The back sections of the mansion were toned down, and not open to guests. This area had a set of floor to ceiling windows looking out onto the bay and stretching the entire length of the house. A huge dining room, complete with mahogany table and petite antique side chairs, connected through an archway to a large living room which was uncharacteristically sparse and elegant. A fainting couch, an ornately carved side table and a few Caravaggio knock-off oil paintings was all the room held. Despite its campy film set glory, the place had become a glorified "clothing optional" guest house that drew both elderly out-of-towners looking for a thrill and gold-digging young hustlers looking for a fuck-buck. Malice, who knew the owner, had set them up in the off limits back section of the house for their shoot. Apollo kept winking at everyone and pointing upstairs, indicating his familiarity with the place.

It was 10 A.M. and The Belvedere was quiet. The photographer, Denny Matthews, would arrive with his hair and makeup crew soon to begin set-ups along with Andreas and Caz. Neal heard the sound of shattering glass. It was a small vase, a cheap knock-off that Toby had tipped while doing a "Gawd I can't believe I'm here" pirouette.

"For Christ's sake save the ballet and get into a swimsuit," said Malice, quickly sweeping away the evidence and taking charge.

Toby was dripping blood from a tiny gash where his arm had collided with the glass. Neal ran for first aid, and returned to find Dewalt gingerly pressing a rag into the gash. The cut was small and stopped bleeding with a little pressure. Neal brought the three models together with Malice and Annie so they could all discuss the shoot.

"You are country gentlemen, straight from a swim in the ocean, caught in that moment before dressing for an elegant dinner," said Neal, having rehearsed the speech to prepare. "We're going to drape you on the fainting couch, near the window in pairs, at the dining table feeding one another. We will use both evening clothes and swimwear, mixed. Think Tennessee Williams' *Suddenly Last Summer* meets Fassbinder's *Querelle.*

He finished the speech with a flourish of his arms. Blank stares from the models. Neal immediately had second thoughts, now in the moment of shooting, suddenly afraid the whole thing would fall completely flat.

"Just do what we tell you and don't break anything else," Malice said.

Malice gave him an overdone wink and a set of snaps, then twirled away at the sound of the front door and Denny Matthews' booming, cigarette-gutted voice.

DENNY HAD MADE a gay splash in the '90s with a series of black and white male beach nudes and a follow-up coffee table book entitled *Manscape*. It was at the peak of the circuit party explosion, and he'd captured a moment of hunky muscular abandon. That moment petered out quickly, making way for skinny-boy chic. The recent anniversary re-issuance of *Manscape* (with an introduction by Bruce Villanch) kept Denny's name vaguely familiar. Denny, however, had never gotten over that first flame of fame. He was under the illusion that he was an A-lister the likes of Bruce Weber or Herb Ritz. Smoking non-stop, Denny introduced his crew and let Neal know that Andreas and Caz had gone to the beach house after dropping copies of that week's *Pop* Magazine at the bars and restaurants. Neal had a rush of exhilaration, knowing his column was now out amongst the queens to be devoured, and possibly spit out with disgust.

"How about the blond first," Denny said lighting up. "The Swedish-looking hottie. And someone get me a bottle of good scotch."

Neal's face dropped.

"Don't worry, She's not a lush, She sips," Malice said.

While Malice went for a bottle, Neal ran his shoot set-up ideas by Denny. The photographer listened closely, nodding, smoking, then kneeling on the floor to frame a shot. They agreed on the first set up.

"Love the ideas," Denny said. "Get them in hair and makeup. You've got a good eye, Ned. "

"It's Neal."

Malice spun up with a bottle of scotch and a very cute tray of glasses, ice bucket and tongs. He started pouring drinks, handing one first to Denny, then one to each of the models.

"Can we hold off on cocktails for the models until they finish," Neal said.

Toby, already stripped down to a thong, downed his drink quickly. The others waited.

"It loosens them up, I'll swing the whip if I have to, honey," Denny said, laughing very loudly, like a cackling old witch. "Drink up girls. I want you loose and nasty."

Malice poured himself a shot, refilled Toby's glass, and started ordering the models around, directing them to their outfits. Dewalt stepped up briefly with a Red Bull.

"Thought you might want this," he said, then gave Neal a gentle kiss as he retreated to a corner to watch.

The first shot set the tone. The Swede wore a snug gold bikini, a white tuxedo shirt fully unbuttoned, black nearly-to-the-knee dress socks and a cap toe lace up shoe. He was staring straight into the camera, head cocked slightly back, framed by an ornate, floor to ceiling doorway into the dining room. Behind him, out of focus, the Italian and Toby were intertwined, like pieces of sculpture, lying nude on the long mahogany table. Neal checked out the digitals as Denny shot. He knew it was risky, his 'gentry caught with their pants down' concept but Denny was adding a lurid sexuality that gave the shoot a *Pop* inspired zest. Big-bulged muscle-heads on the beach was a safer concept but this issue had to make a statement, and the first shot sparkled. As they set up the second shot, Dewalt hung back, chatting with Rovvie. Neal kept an eye on the two. Rovvie was laughing, flashing those big perfect teeth of his, leaning in to touch Dewalt's arm. Annie nudged him. She and Laird stood smiling, each holding up bathing suits.

"The navy or the floral?" she said.

Neal chose three matching navy drawstring square cuts with white trim. Malice wanted to match the suits with white buck lace ups and plaid sport coats. Denny thought it was too much. Neal glanced at a huddling Rovvie and Dewalt. Rovvie knew a lot of his deepest secrets. What if Rovvie mentioned details from Neal's messy past, his three day crack binge, horrible credit, inability to hold a job. Of course Dewalt may not even care, but it was the sort of thing Neal would rather explain himself, and much later in the relationship. Rovvie was sipping a big cocktail. Once drunk, his friend had absolutely no boundaries. Rovvie had his hand on Dewalt's knee. Neal was desperate to run and check on the duo, but Denny was getting impatient.

"A sport coat on just one, the Swede," Neal said. "The other two in swimwear."

The idea sparked both Malice and Denny and they shouted at all three models.

"I want one nude," Denny said.

Toby jumped forward, holding another glass of scotch. He pulled off his trunks and moved nude toward Denny on his long dancer's legs. The photographer smacked the kid's ass, cutting loose with another one of his ragged, witchy laughs.

"That's the spirit honey, but She needs a fluffer," Denny said.

Annie giggled and followed them with an armful of clothing. Neal turned back to Dewalt. Rovvie and Dewalt were drifting out of the house. Dewalt mouthed 'be back soon' and Neal nervously turned to the next set up. He took several yoga breaths in and out and realized he had to trust Dewalt and focus on the shoot.

The models had loosened up, and the pairing of swimwear with elegant eveningwear was bringing Neal's vision to life. He was feeling increasingly confident. Laird had disappeared but Annie was on top of things, sorting the outfits, tracking clothing credits and helping hair and makeup as they sprayed, coiffed and spritzed the boys. After a half dozen set-ups, Denny announced a short break, then moved to a back corner of the living room, followed by a chattering Toby and Apollo. The Swede wandered outside talking on his cell phone. Alone, sucking on a Red Bull, near the entryway to the living room, Neal noticed Toby, Denny and Apollo huddling. He was pretty sure they were snorting coke. He respected Denny's work, but really didn't want to deal with drugs on his set. He wished Dewalt was around. Before he could go to them, they separated, Toby stepping away. The moment seemed to have passed.

"It's going great honey," Denny shouted, giving Neal a thumbs up from across the room as he swirled his scotch.

Neal nodded, turning to go, but paused, noticing Toby and Apollo, against the far wall, slowly embracing. Denny had turned back to them, and was snapping impromptu pictures. They were far across the wide living room, but Neal could see they were making out more intensely, and Apollo was pushing his trunks gently down a bit. Neal glanced around. Everyone was on break. Dewalt was still nowhere to be seen. He turned back to the little group, forgetting his role as Editor, forgetting his rules on the set, feeling like a lecherous voyeur. He was becoming increasingly turned on, incredibly agitated, as Apollo leaned back, and Toby went to his knees, Denny all the time shooting pictures and occasionally breaking in with a dark witch cackle. Neal's mind was a wash. His cock was pulsing and he wanted to move over to the group, join in, acting out one of his many porn set fantasies. He could see Toby now pressing his head into Apollo's crotch. Malice's hand on his shoulder broke the moment.

"Christ, She always does this," Malice said, then shouted across the room. "All right Denny, you fucking whore, let's get back to fashion. And save the coke for the wrap party, bitch, before one of those kids passes out. Remember the Undergear shoot?"

Malice turned and spoke softly to Neal.

"A bleach blonde heroine-chic twink boy threw up in the middle of a shot," he said. "Messy, messy, messy."

Denny spun, glared at Malice, then threw his head back and cut loose with the loudest, most guttural laugh of the day. Toby and Apollo broke it up, and Annie returned with Laird on her arm and the next set of outfits. Neal breathed easier, wishing he knew where Dewalt and Rovvie had disappeared to, but turning his full attention to the shoot.

Chapter 20

THE SHOOT—THREE hours and 350 shots—was a raging success, according to Annie. Denny Matthews was talking about using a few pictures in his follow-up book to *Manscape*, aptly titled *Manscape2*. Malice insisted the spread would rocket *Pop* into a new hemisphere.

"This is the best layout She has ever done, it's Men's Vogue with hard-ons," Malice said, swirling a pink straw in a huge frozen cocktail.

They had tromped back to the beach house after the shoot to be greeted by two houseboys, a heavy-set cook named Gretta and Andreas and Caz. The boys, both dark skinned, big lipped and lean, had chairs, umbrellas and a small tent to create a makeshift bar on the beach. Andreas and Caz handed out copies of the new *Pop*, and guided the group to the shore. Rovvie was missing in action. Andreas gave Neal a glance and waved him over as the houseboys set things up on the sand.

"The column is good, keep it up," he said. "I take it Rovvie will be back soon."

The sky was clear, but the temperature had dropped and

the waves were enormous and green with an onslaught of floating seaweed, indicating a coming storm.

"He's on his way," Neal said, trying to sound confident.

Andreas and Caz begged off, heading back to the house to deal with *Pop* business.

"Bring it honey, bring it," Malice said into his cell phone, then hung up. "Candy Pinkerton is doing a thing for her TV show. There's press all over the island this weekend. She's coming to our little house party with her models and film crew."

Candy Pickerton was a model turned reality television star with a 'modeling agency' show on the Oxygen network. Neal loved the ballsy, super-Botoxed broad, who years back had labeled herself America's first supermodel. He and Dewalt sat in striped beach chairs under a broad creamy canvas umbrella. Neal wore the first of his seven suits, a Burberry-striped square cut he'd bought on sale at Bergdorf's last year. Dewalt wore board shorts past the knee and the knit cap he'd sported the first time Neal had spotted him at the bathhouse. He was reading a hip-hop magazine and sipping a beer. Malice and Denny were to his right in dark-tone Armani bikinis and big square sunglasses. The three models had disappeared into the water. Annie and Laird were behind them, dressed in ugly cut off shorts and T-shirts, slathered with sunscreen.

Neal watched the waves and took a deep breath, then turned to look at Dewalt. Dewalt was nodding off as the breeze picked up. He had nestled his dark toes into the bright sand. There was a tattoo Neal hadn't noticed on Dewalt's ankle. An eyeball. He wondered if it was Egyptian, or tied to the solar system. The chatter of his friends was sucked into the crashing of the waves as he trailed up Dewalt's legs to his belly. His stomach was very smooth, though up toward his chest Neal could make out little nicks, cuts, scars. His chin showed stubble and his wide, full lips were parted, a gold tooth peeking out. Dewalt reached out and swatted at something, but kept his eyes shut as he settled back again. The bottle of beer near him titled slightly and drizzled into the sand. The colorful knit cap contrasted Dewalt's soft forehead. Neal sunk into the arc of Dewalt's cheek, the lulling sound of his breath. He sighed and let his eyes flutter, then noticed a big white foot near Dewalt's head. Laird.

"Dude, know where we can score weed?" Laird said.

Dewalt roused briefly. Laird, looking bone thin and very pale with gooey sunscreen not quite rubbed into his snow-white skin, was hugging himself in the sultry wind, as if he were cold. Neal stayed silent, wondering if Dewalt had any drugs with him. He had neatly shelved fears of his boyfriend's former drug dealing, hoping it would neatly fade away. Dewalt shrugged, and rolled on his side, as the ever-eavesdropping Malice fluttered toward Laird.

"Darling, we can get anything, but pot is so old school, why don't you try something a bit more mod," Malice said, guiding Laird back to Annie.

As Malice looped his arm through Laird's and guided him to the umbrella where Annie sat waiting, Neal saw Rovvie in the distance. He was shirtless, barefoot, wearing the same powder blue shorts from that morning's photo shoot. There was someone at his side, someone taller, broader and darker than Rovvie. A chill ran up Neal's back as the first set of fat white clouds blocked the sun and a strong, stinging wind had Malice screeching and beach umbrellas tumbling. As Rovvie got closer, Neal gave him a long steady look, but his friend kept his eyes cast down. Dewalt was napping. Neal stood and headed down the beach toward the approaching Rovvie who waved weakly. The man next to him—built, red Speedo, huge basket—kept a stern face then stopped, and turned back the other direction. Rovvie approached alone.

"Hey girrrl," Rovvie drawled.

Rovvie kept walking, moving quickly to join the group ahead. Recalling the blurred shot of the man with an erection he'd seen on Rovvie's camera, Neal grabbed his arm to stall him, but Rovvie moved on. Checking that Dewalt was still dozing, Neal gripped Rovvie's hand tightly and pulled him down toward the waves. The water had gone clear blue again, the seaweed swept back out with the tide, but the undertow looked vicious, the fall of the break thunderous.

"Who was that?" Neal said, shouting over the ocean.

Rovvie kicked at the sand.

"Nobody important," Rovvie said.

"Andreas is not a stupid man," Neal said. "You have to be smart. Is that the guy you have a naked picture of?"

They drifted up the beach, away from the water. Rovvie laughed, then sighed heavily. In the distance, Neal noticed a cluster of men who had set up an elaborate site with bright red canvas umbrellas, matching lipstick-bright beach chairs, small gleaming metal tables for drinks, and a flapping piece of red canvas with an insignia featuring a big pair of pursed red lips. As they got close, Neal realized it was Nick Sands, his boyfriend Brandon and a few other men, probably writers. Several of them had copies of *Pop* in their hands. Neal froze, wanting to turn back but Nick spotted him. He'd surely read the column. Neal walked cautiously forward through the sand. Nick stood and moved toward him. Nick was tall and immaculately fit, not an ounce of fat. Neal took in a breath, hoping to disguise any bit of waist flab pulsing out from the sides of his year-old square cut. Nick was wearing the latest jungle print, cuffed trunk from Gucci and in his hand was a copy of *Pop*. Neal was glad to be walking next to Rovvie. His friend was strikingly attractive. He steeled himself as Nick greeted him with air kisses.

"Twice in a week, what a delight," Nick said.

Neal was silent, hoping for a quick exchange, though making a mental note of the fact that he'd actually seen Nick three times that week, if they counted the steam room encounter. There was a long pause. He wished Rovvie would say something.

"Like nothing ever before, that was what that sweet little country girl you work with said about your column," Nick said. "This must be her first publishing job."

Nick was looking straight into Neal's eyes. The sounds of the surf, the voices of Nick's friends faded as the sun beat mercilessly and the wind picked up. Neal knew what was coming. Nick finally had him exactly where he wanted him, on the meat block, naked and ready to be slaughtered. Nick would snap Neal's neck, here on the beach, with an audience. Nick of the New York Times Style Section, Nick with the millionaire boyfriend, Nick with no body fat. Neal had nothing to say, he just wanted to get it over. Two of Nick's friends, basketball tall blonde twins who looked just past puberty, were approaching, also holding *Pop.* Neal felt like a peasant being thrown to the beasts in a Roman gladiator arena. He prepared to be devoured slowly with bitchy finesse.

"You know what Truman Capote said about Jackie Susann," Nick said. "She doesn't write, she types."

The twins flounced over, giving Rovvie a full up and down.

"Hey, you own *Pop,* right," the first twin said, squinting in the sun at Rovvie.

"My husband does," Rovvie said.

Neal thought of turning and running, through the sand, back to Dewalt, fleeing like a terrified lamb.

"This new column is fierce, girl, I can't believe someone finally outed the steam room," the other twin said. "I hope it's every week. I'm buying that Libertine shirt at Bergdorf's."

"Tell him, he wrote it," Rovvie said, smiling broadly, then to Nick. "Jackie Susann typed her way to fame and fortune girrrrrl. *Valley of the Dolls* is a classic."

Nick opened his mouth to speak, but the twin's screams stopped him.

"Oh my God, I love you," the first twin said, wrapping his arms around Neal's neck. "I think I've had sex with like a thousand men. It's like you read my mind."

"That would be a short book," Nick said, and turned away, back to his camp.

Oblivious to Nick's comment, the twins invited Neal and

Rovvie to their blanket, but Neal declined, turning back to his own patch of sand and Dewalt. As they moved up the beach, Neal couldn't help but smile, and was hoping Nick was boring a hole in his back with an envious glare. He momentarily forgot all about Rovvie's bulgy friend, or his fears about Dewalt reading his column. He felt, for a moment, like a successful and content man. A columnist, a real writer.

Chapter 21

THE DROPS WERE huge. Perfect pear-shaped wallops of water spaced strangely far apart. The hail, they said, would come later. The erratic dive in the temperature had brought a storm system that promised to compare to dark, violent summer afternoon thunderstorms Neal recalled from his Missouri youth. The island had gone dim with the sweep of clouds, and the warm winds and patter of the rain added energy to Andreas' upcoming house party. The inclement weather brought everyone in and kept them in, so the festivities began earlier than planned. The servant boys and Gretta bustled about preparing food, setting up trays of martini glasses and two makeshift bars in the main room, cleaning under and around the clusters of people. Malice had already taken charge of the music and was playing an eclectic mix including something called "Shut the Fuck Up" by rap artist Big B. The singer repeated his own name in the song, nearly as often as he said the work fuck.

In their bedroom, Neal surveyed his outfit choices, wondering if the song was a nod to Dewalt. Dewalt, still in board shorts, lounged in bed, singing along with the music. With a new string of lyrics, he hopped up onto the bed, shouting along.

"I'm Big B and you mother fucking haters out there lick my nuts," Dewalt said.

Neal turned to watch as Dewalt flopped back down onto the bed.

"They say shut the fuck up a lot in that song?" Neal said.

"Big B. Angry mo-fo raight?" Dewalt said. "Come here kid."

Anxious at his lack of outfit choices—he had not prepared for a party—Neal took a break and lay next to Dewalt. Listening to the rap, he took a breath. Dewalt stroked Neal's hair, humming with the increasingly violent lyrics. From far off on the beach, a crack of thunder echoed. Neal felt soothed there, in Dewalt's arms, enjoying the touch, being close without sex. For a moment he tried to recall his last anonymous episode. It was the brief steam room visit. Maybe that urgency, the nervous need for constant fucking would lift. Granted, he and Dewalt had a lot of sex, but it was more than that. For now, he didn't feel that racing, trembling angst to get it, find it, grab it. The gym, the steam room, the baths, the streets, the constant rush to escape life and devour men's bodies. He wondered if he could make it through a visit to the gym without the requisite blowjob in the steam room. He wondered if he should tell Dewalt about his drunken, slutty past. They had yet to discuss his column. Dewalt was resting his warm palm on Neal's forehead. Finally the 'shut the fuck up' song ended. There was a momentary lull.

"That kid, Laird, he's doing ecstasy tonight," Dewalt said. "He asked if I wanted any. You're no drugs right?"

Neal started to shift upward in the bed, but Dewalt held him down, his palm still pressed on Neal's forehead.

"You want to tell me about it?" Dewalt said.

"What," Neal said, struggling to not pull away.

"Why you freak about partying," Dewalt said. "What's up with that? I told you my messy shit. Come on Neal. I did heroin. It can't be that bad."

Neal took a deep breath. Dewalt was slowly running a finger

along Neal's forehead, back and forth. From the living room, Malice had flowed the music into REM's ballad, "Nightswimming."

"Take your time," Dewalt said.

Neal felt his shoulders falling, his mind emptying. The REM song had been one he'd listened to alone, over and over, a few summers back, drunk on the beach here at the island. The singer had a soft but ragged voice, with only a piano behind him, the lyrics all about memory, loss and to Neal, sudden revelations. It was suddenly too much. The questions, the music, that song. He wanted to run, but Neal didn't get up.

Neal took a breath, and found he couldn't speak. He couldn't quite put it into words, what had happened for him since he quit drinking. His throat was tight and he felt a rush of something long buried, maybe back in Missouri, in his little pink bedroom, from the hallway, on the back porch, in the woods, maybe.

That line, Neal remembered, that line over and over, the waves and a bright moon last summer on the beach and he'd wept, drunk and stoned and alone. He remembered now, he'd wept and wished someone had come to find him, then he'd passed out. He'd woke, disgusted, under a blazing morning sun, hung-over, with sand in his mouth. He shuddered now, his forehead under Dewalt's coaxing hand. The callus of it, the darkness of it, the slow soft drifting of the man's fingers crossing side to side, like guidance.

"You can tell me anything, it's all right," Dewalt said softly.

"It's been so long, I don't know," Neal started.

His words choked, and he couldn't continue. He felt afraid, the rush of emotion was fast and he didn't want to freak Dewalt out, but it kept coming. That damn song. If it would just end.

"It's been hard," Neal said, then broke.

He wept, not soft low weeping at a movie, or even calm sad weeping at a funeral, but a hard, ragged ripping cry. He sobbed and turned his face into Dewalt's naked chest, and buried his face, and wanted to run. This was too soon. But Dewalt held him tighter and tighter and kept making those soft whisper-like noises, repeating 'I'm here,' and that made it worse, and that song kept at him, slicing at Neal until he finally let go and shook, harder and longer and Dewalt held him roughly and they rocked until the music changed, and from the beach they heard screams of laughter as the first sharp pelts of hail landed.

Chapter 22

THE HAIL TERRIFIED half the gay island, including Candy Pickerton. Rumors spun about hurricane winds and rip tides. Neal's group was hanging out in the beach house living room. Malice, dressed as a French sailor, was serving strong martinis garnished with mango. Andreas and Caz lingered in the kitchen going over *Pop's* distribution figures. They were the only two wearing navy blue business suits. Toby and Apollo were dancing close, still in Speedos. Neal and Dewalt had just secured a pair of bar stools at the edge of the living room when the front door burst open with a rush of spotlights. Candy—wearing a gold one-piece swimsuit, gold sparkle Christian Louboutin stilettos and a gold chocker—swept in with four bikini-clad boys and a film crew of two. Behind her was Trudy Pratte, overdressed in a Balenciaga swaged charmeuse skirt and pearl-encrusted top.

"Denny Matthews, you nasty fuck, get over here," Candy screamed.

As Candy smacked lips and mingled, Trudy scoped, looking at bit crestfallen to be unfashionably early. The door swung again, and a group of ten filed in, cooling Trudy's nerves. A house party down the boardwalk had just ended, so troops were traveling in clusters over to Andreas', battling through the storm. The house was quickly filling with pretty boys, rich, silver-haired daddies, a group of elegant Brazilian women and a few stray scraggly-haired artists on summer retreat. It was barely sunset. Gretta and the houseboys were frantic keeping the bar and food tables stocked. Candy's cameramen with their blinding lights kicked up the chaos level, as another little group of collegiate men swirled in, screaming about the storm. The hail clattering on the roof, wind rushing in through the open glass doorway out to the pool, and Malice's increasingly loud trance music mix and martini hand outs, pushed it all, Neal felt, toward insanity. He sipped a Red Bull and stayed close to Dewalt, who had passed on Laird's ecstasy offer and told Neal he'd 'keep it cool'. What 'keep it cool' meant Neal didn't know, but they'd lain in bed for an hour cuddling after Neal's crying jag and he felt he could trust Dewalt. He hadn't seen Dewalt drunk, or taking drugs, though he had no idea what he did on his own or with his Harlem "bros." The bottom line was that Neal felt safe with Dewalt. Dewalt squeezed his hand as Annie approached. She was wearing an odd, thrift store style floor length floral dress and ballet slippers. Her eyes glistened.

"Neal darrrrling," she said.

Neal gave her hug as she whispered in his ear.

"I took this pill with Laird and I feel fantastic. I think it's time," Annie said. "He's the one."

Neal took Annie by the shoulders and looked into her eyes.

"Are you sure?" Neal said.

From behind, Laird wrapped his hands around Annie's waist and pulled her out into the center of the living room where people were dancing. Laird was barefoot, topless, wearing a pair of knee-length cut-off shorts. He looked cute, in a super-skinny, nerdy straight boy way.

"She'll be okay," Dewalt said.

Annie had her hands around Laird's waist and was leaning her head back, shaking her hair out of its ponytail and swaying to the music. She looked nearly like a woman. Neal recalled how he lost his gay "adult" virginity (sucking off neighbor boys in tents did not count). He was seventeen, drunk, in the parking lot of Faces, the local late-night disco. Faces, with its three floors, loose door policy, drag shows and leather lounge, was the only club that stayed open until dawn. It was a bridge trip over the muddy Mississippi River in East St. Louis, perched at the edge of a dangerous and decayed strip of bombed-out ghetto housing projects.

The man was tall and thin, seemed very old at the time, and had a very ordinary cock. Neal had wanted to get it over with, to experience sex with a man not a boy. He'd drunkenly insisted they do it in the parking lot instead of driving to the man's house. The guy had shot down his throat, and Neal had gagged, turned away then thrown up cum and beer. Glamorous. He hoped Annie had a better first.

Neal turned to watch Candy Pickerton get up on a chair to dance and just beyond her he spotted Nick Sands and his lover Brandon, swirling big martini glasses. He did not look forward to Nick's personal view of his new column. Clapping her hands and quieting the crowd, Candy launched into a speech from her perch.

"Listen you bitches, a shout out to Andreas for this fab-fuckilicious party," she said, holding up a copy of *Pop* as the crowd applauded. "And don't we love this nasty new column. I demand to be quoted next week. Lovvvvvvve it, bitches."

Neal caught Nick's eye as Candy finished up. He and Brandon were headed across the crowded floor. Neal leaned into Dewalt. He regretted not having brought more clothing. He'd gone with jeans, flips flops and the anchor detail knit polo he'd worn at Andreas' May party. Nick was wearing a Thom Browne pinstripe short, knee length socks, leather sneakers and a short sleeve nipped collar shirt with a bow tie. Straight off the runway. En route, he was stopped by Trudy Pratte who literally yanked him down onto a sofa as Brandon escaped to the bar. Trudy was leaning in and speaking directly into Nick's ear. Nick was trying to stand, but Trudy kept tugging at him to sit. Finally, Nick burst free, grabbed Brandon and headed Neal's way.

"That shirt's cute on you, Neal, I remember it from the Palamos party in May," Nick said.

Nick stared at Dewalt, waiting.

"This is my boyfriend Dewalt," Neal said, realizing he'd never introduced his date in public that way.

Brandon and Dewalt shook hands and Nick took the moment to pull Neal to him. His breath smelled of gin and Neal realized this was not likely Nick's first martini of the evening.

"I gotta talk to you alone, you owe me one," Nick said.

While he felt he owed Nick nothing, he was intrigued. Leaving Dewalt with Brandon, who was rattling on about a stock he was wild about, Neal indicated the back patio. Nick followed as Candy stepped down from her perch, insisting one of her TV show 'model' boys get up and strip for the cameras. A willowy, very pale boy in a pink Speedo stood on the table looking awkward and a little tipsy.

"Give us some skin, bitch," Candy screamed.

The patio had a slight overhang. Bits of hail blew at them. The pool water, lit from below, was twisting and churning with the wind and dots of the hail's onslaught. They were alone.

"It's sex," Nick said, his words slurring.

Neal turned to face Nick and caught a fleeting look of desperation.

"Everyone I know is an addictive gossip," Nick said. "That sow Trudy Pratte is already starting to sniff out a scandal. I need someone to..."

A strong wind blew bits of hail at Neal's cheek. He'd wait for the punch line. He didn't trust Nick and was waiting to hear what this was really all about. He expected Candy Pickerton's cameramen to swarm them and scream "Candy's Candid Camera" at any second. He wondered if Nick was concerned about the steam room encounter.

"Brandon's been talking to people," Nick said, lowering his voice as if the patio were bugged. "He wants to try S&M."

Neal hesitated. Nick sounded authentic. Could it be, after all these years, he truly was reaching out.

"Why ask me?" Neal said.

"Because you've always been a total slut, afraid of nothing," Nick said. "I can't afford to rock the boat. Brandon is very particular about what he wants. I really don't have much money of my own."

Neal glanced inside. The crowd was chanting "strip" and the model boy was swaying his skinny hips, reluctantly pushing down his Speedo. Through the glass doorway, which was tinted and slightly beveled, the whole thing looked barbaric.

Nick stepped toward the pool into the slowly dying hail.

"Do you remember what you said to me?" Nick said. "The night I broke it off with Charles?"

Neal did not. Charles was the coke-dealing boyfriend that Nick had accused Neal of sleeping with. Neal had no memory of the drunken night. Another black out.

"You both were so stoned and stupid. But it was my apartment so I wouldn't leave," Nick said, dipping a hand into the pool and running it gently across the dancing water.

"You made Charles say it, you kept laughing, I guess he'd told you my secret and you kept hitting him across the stomach so he would repeat it to me," Nick said. "It wasn't enough I caught you two."

Neal wracked his brain, pulling up a vague, lost catalogue of drunken nights, nasty things he'd done to and with people.

"Nick cries when he gets fucked, like a boy, he cries," Nick said. "I never knew why you found that so funny."

The pool water was moving more gently now and the storm seemed to be passing, as a sickle moon slid out for a moment. Neal moved to the pool's edge. Nick looked truly desperate. He had the life Neal dreamed of, yet he was anxious over some dumb S&M

thing. He also cried during sex, which Neal secretly admired.

"S&M is not a big deal," Neal said, reaching a hand out then drawing it back. "I used to punch a guy in the nuts."

Nick turned and pulled out a pink pocket square and rubbed his nose.

"Well, put that in your stupid column," Nick said.

The hail had stopped, the moon was out. People were moving out to the pool area. Neal glanced inside again. The model boy, now nude, stood alone in the living room. He looked disoriented, lost. He gingerly picked up his discarded swimsuit and paused for a moment, glancing out through the beveled glass doorway at Neal. Then he turned and left the house, not bothering to dress.

The two blond twins, who had adored Neal's column, ran naked past them and dove into the water. Trudy Pratte was coming their way.

"Can we do lunch in the city?" Nick said. "The beast known as Trudy is coming this way."

"Bergdorf's, Café III," Neal said. "Then you'll owe me one."

Nick smirked, then took off his shirt, revealing stunning abdominals, as he followed the twins into the pool before Trudy could reach them.

Chapter 23

THE SUMMER STORM vanished, replaced by a clear night sky. The pool was jammed with nude bodies, and both floors of the house vibrated with the island's elite and debauched. Neal who'd seen all the booze and pretty boy ass he could take, proposed an escape. Annie led the group out of the house. As they hit the boardwalk, Neal caught whiffs of scotch as Dewalt nuzzled his neck. Malice and Denny, both drunk, were arguing about the legacy of Coco Chanel. Annie and Laird walked down the plank path streaming a roll of toilet paper like a feathery banner in the wind. As they neared the Sip & Twirl disco, the young couple darted off alone to the beach before they reached the ferry dock. Neal wondered if this was Annie's moment. First sex on a summer night by the ocean would make for a nice memory. He wished, for her sake, that Annie hadn't taken ecstasy. As he reached the dock, he spied a stack of *Pop* magazines, poised on a ledge near a signpost. Dewalt grabbed an issue and gave Neal's shoulder a squeeze.

"Damn famous kid," he said.

Neal flushed. His column, the steam room, all that flippant

sexual cattiness, was right there in black and white. It was a side of himself he had planned to keep under wraps for awhile and was hoping rap-loving Dewalt wouldn't read *Pop*. Honesty was not necessarily the best policy, at least at this stage of the game. Dewalt shoved the magazine into the back of his shorts. The Sip and Twirl sat poised like a sparkling nightlife gem at the edge of the water. It had been completely overhauled. Gone were the nautical details, sea conch knick-knacks and beer-stained wooden bar. A design team from Manhattan had gut-renovated the joint, turning out a slick, neo-modern, stream-lined club complete with under lit glass top bar, lean leather seating and floor to ceiling windows looking out onto the bay. Go-Go boys swayed and balanced precariously on tiny glass cubes, looking more like agile circus performers than dancers. Neal spotted his swim shoot models dancing in the center of the room, amidst a gaggle of half nude boys. Malice and Denny headed into the fray as Neal grabbed a window table for him and Dewalt.

"You like it?" Neal said loudly, over the ferocious dance beat.

"It ain't how we party uptown," Dewalt said as loudly.

Dewalt sat up as if to go, then slumped down again with a thump. He was moving a little more slowly. Neal noticed a dumb, clumsy oafishness.

"So what's the party like uptown?" Neal said, irritated at the mild criticism.

There was a lull in the music and Dewalt grinned. It was a leading question. Now was the time to reveal his late nights with the Harlem boys. He imagined Dewalt may be a bit intimidated by the money and glamour.

"This is all…" Dewalt said, searching, then turned and watched the dance floor. "Fake. Uptown's real."

Neal flinched. This was his life, high gloss, silly but not fake. It was authentic in its own way. And suddenly, in the smoky dim swirl of the club, he felt a need to defend his world, his choices, and more deeply, who he was. He wanted Dewalt to understand why he was part of the scene. Dewalt rapped his knuckles on the table.

"They're a buncha posers," Dewalt said.

Neal stiffened his shoulders, clenched his teeth. He scanned the floor, watching the models dancing, waving their arms in the air to a new summer anthem. A drag queen with a mile high pink wig joined the cluster, and across the room, Candy Pinkerton held court. Neal folded his arms tightly.

"You mean the clothes, the attitude?" he said.

Dewalt shrugged and nodded, raising one arm out toward the crowd in a motion that Neal considered regal.

"Come on, you know they're stupid," Dewalt said. "It ain't real."

Neal's chin trembled as he took a breath.

"And you with all the 'yo yo nigga what's up' that's all true realness, is that it?" Neal said, his cheeks flushed. "Bullshit."

Dewalt gave Neal a deep stare. He looked about to speak several times, then he abruptly got up and left. Neal sat alone, his body shivering with a rush of rage. In a moment, what had felt soft and wonderful had turned jagged and mean. Dewalt was a stranger, and the lushness of his touch, the coolness of the night had vanished. Neal got up and went after him. He wasn't through. Outside on the boardwalk, he took in a gush of night air then stopped under the wide black sky. Dewalt stood on the dock, staring at him. Neal moved cautiously, aware of a growing shift that seemed to have come from nowhere, hidden but now rising. He stopped in front of Dewalt. He wanted to fight.

"I got a temper," Dewalt said. "I didn't want to say nothing mad stupid."

"So do I," Neal said.

Dewalt turned to the water.

"I read that column. That's what this is," Dewalt said. "I don't give a shit about your friends. Fuck 'em. It's you and me."

Neal froze, as a breeze blew in off the water and the moon slid out from behind a cloud. The column. He felt himself sinking. He hadn't prepared for this. He'd naively hoped it would never emerge, that Dewalt would somehow never take an interest, never read it, never know.

"I feel pretty stupid, sitting next to you, everybody reading that shit," Dewalt said. "It all for real, right? You just fuck around a lot? That guy really get a bloody nose while you fucked?"

This is a moment, Neal thought, an important moment, similar to the moment when his mother asked him if he could ever be happy being gay, or when a professor had confronted him about cheating, or when a friend had asked him if he knew how terribly cruel he acted when he was drunk. This was one of those moments when truth was there on the tip of his tongue, but fear, always fear, overwhelmed him. He did not want to lose Dewalt. That terrified him. He suddenly thought that Dewalt may be his only real chance at love.

"It's not really me," Neal said, choosing his words carefully. "Not me anymore. I make a lot of it up, or use stories friends tell me. Or use things I did long before I met you. It's all fake."

He took a deep breath, but the air got caught in his throat. The lie was alive.

"It's shit you did back when you partied bad, yeah?" Dewalt said, looking at Neal with concern and a strange innocence. "I done some shit too in the past."

Neal couldn't bring himself to say another word, knowing it would be a set of carefully shaded lies. He wanted to get past this. He couldn't stand how he was feeling. Dewalt smiled, then came at him in that way he did, like a reckless boy, wanting to grab something deeper than it could be grabbed. He lifted Neal and spun him, moving dangerously close to the boardwalk's edge.

"Let's get to the ocean," he said, setting Neal down.

Neal paused and watched Dewalt walk toward the ocean. The back of his legs were ashy looking, and he was swaying a little. His neck looked thick from behind, and his shoulders were broad but sloped, almost gnarled-looking and heavy in the moonlight. Neal suddenly thought he'd never seen a sadder looking back, a more pitiful slump, a more lumbering walk. He hurried ahead and stayed pace as they headed to the beach. Dewalt put an arm across Neal's shoulder. He was leaning on him, and Neal felt his weight. Dewalt was a much bigger man than he was.

"Dinner with my boys next week?" Dewalt said. "Time you met 'em."

Neal glanced up at the clearing night sky for reassurance but faced only black sky, stars in a wild emptiness. They paused at an intersection where an abandoned cottage met a raised path going out to the beach. The cottage was what Neal called the "Mockingbird" house, a deteriorated relic from the 1970's. It was the only abandoned house on the island, owned by a lazy, drunken realtor.

"Let's see the waves," Dewalt said, leaning heavily into Neal. "I ain't gonna be back here."

"Go ahead, I gotta pee," Neal said.

Dewalt kissed him, then stumbled up the dune path to the beach. Neal got off the boardwalk, looking for a semi-private spot at the side of the grey Mockingbird house. He took a breath, hoping a few minutes alone would clear his head, center him again, bring him back to that sweet place with Dewalt. The Mockingbird house had always intrigued him, so ugly and lost, like a rural shack abandoned on a long stretch of Missouri highway. He wondered what the little place cost, and he wondered for the first time if Dewalt had any real money. Standing in thigh-high weeds at the edge of the cottage, he swatted at a swarm of flies that were darting in and out of a gash in a side window screen. They had a blaring buzz like the greenback flies he'd battled during childhood camp-outs in Missouri. Nasty little things. Glancing into the cottage, he saw shadows. Someone was in the house. He heard voices and imagined it was trashy Long Island day-trippers squatting for the night. He stood on his tiptoes and pressed his face to the bottom edge of the screen, feeling like a nosy neighbor lady. There were two figures embracing. There was no breeze, the biting flies were circling. There was the sound of laughter from a group passing at the front of the cottage. Neal pressed against the wall, robber like, as the ocean thrashed in the distance. Overhead, the moon pressed out from the edge of a cloud, and a portion of the cottage was lit. Neal swore he heard moaning and he wanted to see exactly what was going on. Pulling a half-ripped piece of stone from the ground, he stood on it like a wobbly stool to get a better vantage point.

They were kissing, biting one another while the flies bit. It was Rovvie and Caz, kneeling, then lying down, pressing into the floor boards that bowed with rain. Rovvie's ass pushed into the thin wood as Caz lolled his tongue down Rovvie's stomach, going for his cock, swallowing it and rising again. Neal stifled a gasp. Rovvie moaned and bounced, and Neal was afraid the floor under him might snap and thrust the couple into some dirty raccoon hideout. From the sidewalk, Neal heard another burst of laughter and he toppled off of his stone shelf and stood, flies nibbling at him, half wanting to burst into the cottage and yank Rovvie away by the hair and put a stop to—what he didn't know. He pressed himself tighter against the edge of the cottage, remembering what Caz did for Andreas, the dirty violent jobs, the mean ugly messes. Caz probably carried a gun. Neal stepped gently away, back up onto the boardwalk and made his way out to the beach, trying to comprehend the deeper meaning of what he'd just glimpsed.

THE SCENE ON the sand, which he had hoped would comfort him, did not. Laird was passing a joint to Dewalt, and Annie was running topless toward the ocean screeching gibberish. He paused, wondering if he should head back to the beach house alone, but instead strode ahead through the moonlit sand. He stood near the two men, who were sharing a stupid joke.

"Hey sexy," Dewalt said, lolling on his side.

Dewalt had removed his shirt, as if he were preparing to swim. Laird was sucking the last of the joint, which he pressed between his fingers to extinguish, then stood unsteadily and ran toward the water and Annie. Dewalt, eyes slits, mouth gaping like a fool, pulled Neal toward him. He could smell the pot, that rank stink he'd never liked even when he was getting high. Neal did not want to lean in for Dewalt's kiss. He pulled away and sat huddled, looking out at Annie and Laird, embracing in the rushing surf. The copy of *Pop* Dewalt picked up lie near him in the sand, rumpled and wet. Neal sighed, and wanted to say something, but couldn't find the words. He felt a welling up in his chest, a sudden fear that his past, his damaged heart, would never really let anyone in. He thought of telling Dewalt the truth about his column, letting everything go. Neal looked directly at Dewalt, listening to the crash of the waves, and realized how radically different they were. He also was a bit disgusted by Dewalt's sleepy, stoned gaze.

"Let's get wet," Dewalt said.

Not waiting for Neal's answer, Dewalt hooted like a boy and ran toward the ocean. Neal leaned back in the sand, breathing deeply, remembering his yoga class and vaguely rehab and then, lying there looking up at a swarm of stars, brilliant rugged little slivers, he thought of how he had laid on his parent's driveway in Missouri, clutching that constellation map his father had given him, trying to figure out Orion's belt. He first remembered that night like he always had, how he got up and went in, but now, under this sky, in the sand, he scrounged for a forgotten detail that emerged like an ugly misshapen pearl and in a gentle way, he realized how deeply he relied on half-truths to survive. He hadn't gotten up that night, but had waited there, on the hot summer blacktop, looking up at the sky patterns for a long time, hoping his father would appear. He waited for hours and finally shut his eyes and fell asleep until at last came the footsteps, up through the sand, across the blacktop driveway, but it was not his father, rather a concerned neighbor, Mr.

Hensel, whose wife taught Neal piano lessons. Mr. Hensel gently urged him to go inside, and it was now, not Dewalt walking through the sand, but Annie, wearing a strange cape of seaweed on her shoulders, her eyes glistening as she bent drunkenly and told Neal it was time to go. Both times, he got up, silently, and followed.

Chapter 24

THE SUBWAY TRAIN was steamy, crowded and sluggish, which stoked a fire under Neal's rising morning anxiety. He'd returned to the city the night before riddled with fear and anxiety over the lies he had told Dewalt about his column, wishing he could run to Bergdorf's and hide. His head was throbbing, so he did what he always did on a hot, crowded morning commute to work. He distracted himself by studying men, bottom to top. Neal started with their feet, which on trains, for some reason, felt very sexual. Across from him was a barely middle-aged Wall Streeter in an expensive suit. The man wore a lace up, and his feet were large. A touch of an argyle sock peeked out from the cuffed edge of his pants. Neal imagined the length of the nude foot, the wideness of it. Typically, he did not have a foot fetish, but on the train, long elegant feet made his mind swim.

He roved up the pinstriped pant, to the crotch. There was a pant-bubble when men sat, legs just apart, slouching. It was a hollowed-out circle of fabric that could indicate well hung, or may just be loose space. He had to squint to decipher this one. There seemed to be the bare press of a cock head, indicating he was wearing no underwear and was well endowed, though the folds of material could be deceptive. Neal never lingered on the waist, rather moved quickly to the face, and the nose. Again, on the train, noses, then cheeks, then lips and eyes took on a strange importance. This man, who had his eyes shut, had a classic face, large flaring nostrils, no beard, fairly thin lips (minor turn off) and wide set eyes. The train was speeding express, nearing Chinatown. He scanned the drowsing man again, this time imagining him undressing for his lover at their country estate after the two had gone horseback riding. They would bathe together, rubbing one another's necks gently. A muscular black butler would serve them boysenberries with cream in flutes. The train halted, Neal's stop. He brushed the drowsing man's leg as he rushed to exit before the doors nipped shut.

ANNIE WAS STANDING at her desk, smiling wide, hands on her hips, wearing cuffed black jeans and a tight scoop-neck shirt. The press was running loudly in the distance, voices drifted from the back, and there was a stack of *Pop* magazines on Neal's desk. Neal gave Annie a hug.

"You are officially a woman," he said, noticing how busty she looked in that tight top.

Annie let slip one of her squeaky little bursts of feeling and hugged him tightly, whispering in his ear.

"Not really," she said. "Laird's a virgin too."

Neal stepped back, trying to summon an image of that super-skinny, stoned youth in his ragged shorts. He perched on the edge of Annie's desk and folded his arms. Annie blushed and began.

"We tried but we both sort of, well, it just didn't work," Annie said. "But he's amazing. We both get migraines, isn't that weird?"

A match, hatched in Fire Island, made in heaven. Neal felt parentally proud, and also a bit relieved that Annie hadn't lost her virtue in a drugged haze. They embraced again and Annie scurried back to her computer to fire up that week's big splashy swimsuit issue. Neal went to his desk. He paged through the current issue. He hadn't had time to admire his work, and with a weekly magazine, it was always about the next trend, the next bar, the next it-boy. He felt an urgency, a warm desire to hold tight to success, a success he had finally created. With this light rising, this pride, he suddenly glimpsed in his memory the eye watching him, the bit of white iris and delicate lash curling up from the tattoo on Dewalt's ankle, the design he'd studied on the beach. They had spoken little during the trip back from the Island, and hadn't made a plan to meet, just separated at Penn Station. Neal was aware of those potent little lies he'd told. He wanted to call Dewalt, and more, he wanted to reach out and touch his shoulders, wide, sloping and dark, and feel Dewalt's callused fingers drifting across his temple. He wanted to pull Dewalt into his excitement, and share this success and open up to him, but as he envisioned it all—the column, the gossip, the sometimes quiet but always running current of sexual obsession—the eye on Dewalt's ankle snaked open and became probing, turning red with rage. He felt a rising panic, a sense of looming loss. He wanted to run to and away from Dewalt. His forehead ached.

Andreas rushed in from the press area, his eyes ablaze. He was wearing a linen suit and a paisley patterned shirt. He stopped at Neal's desk and placed his palms wide on its edge. Neal felt very uncomfortable, until Andreas began to grin, his eyes brightened and he launched.

"I've got a meeting with Marty Zukerman, the owner of Splash Bar. He wants a full page ad every week opposite your column," Andreas said. "I have calls from four boutiques for ad space after I showed them a few of Denny's shots from this weekend. And that sports club. They want to sue you for the sex in the steam room crap. It's notoriety. I'd put it in your column."

At that, Andreas threw his head back and laughed like Neal

had never seen. It was a deep resonating laugh. His entire body moved with it, and the man looked more human, less beastly. Andreas was always so cool, a little cruel. As his laughter peaked, he clapped his hands together, then took a chair and sat.

"This is what we need Neal, exactly what we need. It's why I started *Pop*," Andreas said. "Once the swimsuit issue is out, come up with another fashion soon. Use Denny again. And keep that column hot and sexy."

Andreas stood, adjusted his jacket and slapped Neal on the back. He smiled again, turned to go, then nearing the elevator he stopped.

"Have you seen Rovvie?" he said, his face stern again.

Neal shook his head, and Annie did the same. Neal felt a chill run up his back. Caz was not around. He imaged the two together, screwing, and for the first time since he'd met him, as Andreas turned slowly, his shoulders tight, moving to the elevator, he actually felt sorry for the man and a little angry with Rovvie. As the elevator doors drew shut, Andreas smiled and waved to Neal, the look of victory returning. Neal dialed Rovvie's cell and headed back towards the clattering press area, so as not to involve Annie. The sound of the press, the smell of ink, reminded him he had a second column to pull out of his ass. Rovvie answered, sounding groggy, maybe a little drunk.

"Yeah," Rovvie said.

There was the sound of voices in the background, and Neal tried to figure out who it was, listening for Caz. There was laughter, music.

"Where are you?" Neal said.

"Neal…Call ya right back sweetie," Rovvie drawled and hung up.

The press was slowing down, growling now, getting ready to shut down. He headed back to his desk feeling a strange sense of defeat amongst the success. His phone rang.

"Hey sexy, wassup?" Dewalt said.

Neal tried to imagine where Dewalt was, and saw him lying,

long, elegant and naked, arms overhead. Annie smiled at Neal from across the room. She winked, which he found incredibly irritating.

"I've been thinking about you," Neal said.

There was a deep, long sound of air releasing, like a satisfied hum from Dewalt.

"Dinner tonight uptown? Meet my boys?" Dewalt said.

Caught in his own lingering rush, Neal nodded in agreement, then realized he'd said nothing, and in the long pause Dewalt spoke more gently, more clearly.

"Neal, are you okay?" he said.

"Tonight is good," Neal said.

Dewalt gave him the details, a rib joint called Mama Ruby's up in Harlem, then ended with a light promise.

"Then you and me after," Dewalt said, hanging up.

Annie, who had followed the orchestration of the call, was grinning madly. She began to clap and honk with laughter. *She looks like a manic seal,* Neal thought.

"You are so in love," she said.

Neal smiled, but felt a deep gnawing sadness. He was committed to his lies, certain they could only multiply and grow, that they were an integral part of this growing relationship with Dewalt, that he couldn't go forward without them, yet also that they could be his ruin. He glanced out the window, down at the churning Canal Street. An elderly Asian woman, wiry and tough, stood alone, waiting for a bus. She was rubbing one hand against the other, massaging a finger, and Neal imagined it was her ring finger, her connection to a long lost lover. She spat, and Neal knew he did not want to be alone. He did not want to grow old single. Not in this city. He sat and thought of his column, and then Dewalt and then sex. Just the act, the physical grabbing, the gyrations that he felt compelled to do over and over and over. Neal glanced out the window again. The old Asian woman had disappeared. It would be easy to write week after week about cocks, asses, cute boys, hustlers, new innovative ways to meet and pick up men. He considered a few notes he'd recently jotted down about gay dating and wondered if he could add a tiny hint of depth to the column. Would *Pop* readers go for the ride?

"What do you think of gay marriage?" he asked Annie.

Her head, hovering close to the blue computer screen, snapped up.

"Did he ask?" she said. "Oh my gosh, say yes Neal."

Neal had felt an immediate rush of excitement at the very mention of a Neal/Dewalt wedding. He didn't like the unexpected surge, or the sudden, random image of himself in white moving angelically down an aisle of strewn petals toward Dewalt.

"Not me. I'm working on my column. Why would you think that?" he said.

Annie rubbed her chin. She frowned and seemed stumped by the question. Neal looked down at his pad and doodled, the shape turned into a skin and bones dove. He decided suddenly that he wanted a tattoo. He'd get a symbol, something to connect him to Dewalt. It came to him like that, in a snap, which he saw as a good omen. The lies, the big mess of nonsense that he was trying to control and configure would work itself out. He'd *do* something instead of think about something for once in his fucking life. He'd tell Dewalt that night and together they would go get him a tattoo. And then things would start to change. He was sure of it.

The elevator rumbled, rising, and he imagined a flash of cameras, a stampede of well-wishers, congratulating him on finally finding a path toward what the world called love. As the doors slid open Caz emerged, stepping out uncertainly, hot and greasy, wearing a tight white tank top and blue-jean shorts. His shorts were unbuttoned at the top and he stood unsteadily, rubbing his tight belly. He looked sexy, like a tough blue-collar guy stepping onto a porn set. He shouted at Neal.

"Is my brother here?" Caz said.

"No," Neal said.

"Good. Come to the office," Caz said swaggering to the back.

Annie shrugged as Neal followed. As he went through the doors, Annie mouthed "he's so weird" and blew Neal a kiss. The press area was quiet, the door to the boss' office ajar. Neal thought of this trio of men—Andreas, Caz, Rovvie—and wondered how Rovvie had let himself get stuck in the center of such a volatile situation. From inside, he heard Caz.

"Come on, I ain't gonna bite," Caz said.

Caz sat at Andreas' desk. He'd taken off his shoes and his dirty feet were heaved up and onto the desk. He was rocking back in Andreas' leather chair, looking like a deranged bandit ready to shoot hostages.

"Shut the door," Caz said, flexing his naked feet.

Neal thought of running. His instinct told him to go. But his rational mind held tight. This was his job, this was the boss' brother. This may all add up to nothing. He shut the door.

"Rovvie says you know, says he knows you know," Caz said, stretching his arms over his head, a light tuft of hair popping out at his belly button, the top of his crotch hair showing.

Neal wanted to touch Caz's flat stomach.

"Know what?" Neal said.

Caz laughed, then put a finger in his mouth and swam it around in there, as if looking for a piece of something lodged in a tooth. Neal imagined this was the type of man Rovvie had grown up with. Dumb, dirty, uneducated men that picked their teeth and relied on physical intimidation to get their way. Neal had fantasized about a grease monkey, a blue-collar lover, but had never had one.

"You better tell me now," Caz said, placing his hands lazily in his crotch, which Neal swore was puffing forward with a semi hard-on.

Neal was silent. He knew better than to offer anything. This was all too vague. The silence was broken by a screech, then a clank, as the press came on for another run. The noise of the press made it easier for Neal to hold still. He could just stand there dumbly, waiting, as if he were utterly confused. The rising noise seemed to irritate Caz. He pulled something red out of his mouth, studied it, then threw it on the floor and pitched his head back looking as mean as a viper.

"Whatever you think you know, you keep your mouth shut," Caz said. "My dumb-fuck brother trusts me. I'm Blood. He'd fire your ass in a second. Stupid shit trusts me."

Neal waited for a dismissal as Caz sighed deeply then ran a finger along his stomach, his eyes shut. Neal thought of Caz and Rovvie together, like a back-woods couple, and he thought of his column, and Dewalt, and love and sex and gay men mingling, and sex always sex. He wondered what Caz's crotch smelled like, all sweaty and angry. It all pitched around in his nervous brain as he waited, then finally Caz raised his hand.

"Go on, get out," he said.

Neal stepped into the press area. Manny, one of the straight middle-aged machinists waved and smiled. Manny lived in Queens with his wife Martha and two kids. He'd worked for the press before Andreas bought it, and happily stayed once they started publishing *Pop*. Neal saw him once a week to check the magazine's color separations. He'd need to work closely with him to make sure that week's swimsuit issue was flawless. Manny always had something nice to say, and liked to talk about his family. Neal wondered if Manny told his wife Martha the type of magazine he printed, or if he lied, or if she would even care. He wondered what they talked about at night. Manny turned back to the press, and Neal went back to his desk, anxious to write his column, to get the swimsuit layout going, and that night, to see Dewalt.

Draft Column Two/BB

BB here after a dizzy weekend on Fire Island. Creaming over Pop's very first, very frisky swimsuit issue, then stay tuned for more of the same soon. I could tell you about the lawsuit threatened by that nasty muscle-runt gym owner who insists nobody ever has sex in his gym's steam room. Or I could reveal dirty details about the bald-headed Project Runway contestant I saw giving a blow job at the West Side Club. But I'd rather talk about gay dating and ask, what is a 21-century gay date? Everyone I know desperately wants to date, but why? What's the true agenda, boys? It comes down to one of two greedy goals: great frivolous fuck or future husband? The true goal of dating is to land a man, right? Fact is, we gay men cannot keep our pingas in our pants. The most committed couple I know."J" a former 5th Avenue shop boy and "C" a successful surgeon who enjoys Botox, still track down an occasional three way, and each go on regular solo hunts to squeeze out a bit of relief in the steam room. Is that gay commitment? I'm ready to grab my red pen and delete the word "dating" from Webster's and replace it with Prowling. Dates are bullshit, all we men really want is self pleasure.

Neal paused and shuddered at that last line, rereading it. He thought of his boyhood dreams, imagining Starsky truly loving Hutch on television or of Elton John writing his songs for a secret gorgeous lover. Neal wondered if he had become terminally jaded. He deleted that last line and shifted gears.

Speaking of prowling, get your ass to Bergdorf's. Fashionista tidbit of the week: A luscious Gucci leather lace-up in light brown and white with metal Gucci crest and perforations. BB trick of the week: Tall, muscled Italian, in my bedroom, hot and sultry. He pulls out a pair of nylons. Drag anyone? Then he puts the nylons over his head and wants to kiss me. Mugger chic? Truth is, I did it and it was sort of...hot. His tongue pushing through all that naughty nylon. Try it boys.

Until next week. BB.

Chapter 25

RUBY'S WAS BIG, dark and smoky. There was a heavy scent of chicory and BBQ sauce in the air. A fat man smoking a chubby cigar sat in the back singing along with Bessie Smith on the jukebox. Everyone was black, except for Neal. The floors were uneven, the walls covered with a mish-mash of artwork of black leaders and athletes. The tables were big, round and shiny and people shouted across the room to one another. Dewalt stood and waved from a back corner, not too far from the cigar smoker. Billie replaced Bessie on the jukebox and Neal wanted to run out the door. As he approached the table, he began to think of excuses: work just called, Annie had an emergency, the press blew up.

"This is Jimmy and Boney," Dewalt said pointing to the two young men at the table. "My boys, this is Neal. Be nice."

The boys flashed toothy grins and held up clenched fists in greeting as Neal awkwardly pulled back his open-palm hand-shake. The two men were tall and thin, drinking beer and wearing low-hanging baggy jeans, gold chains and T-shirts. Jimmy's head was shaved and he was wearing brass knuckles which spelled the word 'PEACE'. Neal wore a sailor-striped Paul Smith pull-over, skinny jeans and floral flip-flops. Boney, who was very tall and thin, came around the table and squeezed Neal in a tight hug and said, "Crazy fucka." As they sat Dewalt grabbed Neal's hand under the table. Dewalt's hand felt clammy, a tad greasy, like the place itself. Neal wondered if the boys were gay, or knew he and Dewalt was a couple. This suddenly bothered him, the mystery of it all. Neal tried to pull Dewalt's hand up and in view but Dewalt pulled away and slammed his fist on the table in response to a joke Boney had just told. The lingo was littered with 'was up, nigga, you know what I'm saying, mad crazy, aright, that ain't right.' Neal tried to keep up, and desperately wanted clarification. Why wasn't anyone talking to him? He spoke up.

"Did Dewalt tell you how we met?" Neal said, realizing his fatal error.

The table went abruptly silent. They met at a gay bathhouse. He tried to recover.

"...Or that he swam at Fire Island," Neal said, feeling desperate.

He winced at the hyper-gay Fire Island reference. Boney hooted.

"Get the fuck out, Sticky swam, that's the shit. What this kid doing to you Sticky?" Boney said reaching a high five palm to Dewalt.

Neal flinched at Dewalt's nickname.

"Sticky?" Neal said.

"Cause he always stick by you. You gotta know that right?" Boney said, smiling in Dewalt's direction. "My man's solid."

Neal glanced at Dewalt, who had lowered his head. He wondered what sort of nickname they'd give him. White lie?

"So when's the fucking wedding, fudge packer," Jimmy said, guzzling his beer.

Dewalt stood swiftly and wrapped an arm around Jimmy's neck, yanking him up from the table, the beer spilling. He rubbed his fist briskly back and forth on Jimmy's skull. Boney was in hysterics.

"Give, give, give," Dewalt said, his face a tight mask of glee.

Jimmy flailed and screamed and finally Dewalt set him back down, then waved for more drinks. Neal sat still. Boney winked at him.

"Apologize," Dewalt said softly.

Jimmy grimaced and nodded to Neal.

"No harm kid," he said. "I give him the shit, ya know? It's cool."

Neal wanted to cry, feeling like a total idiot, but he nodded at Jimmy with fake thanks. Dewalt took his hand again under the table. On the jukebox, someone sang about pig's feet. Neal wondered if anyone really ate a pig's foot. Disgusting.

"So where you live?" Boney said.

"Hell's Kitchen," Neal said.

"Why don't he move in with you, Sticky? Shit, if this white boy got you to swim in da fucking ocean, that's it man," Boney said.

Jimmy nodded in agreement, looking bored. Dewalt said 'shit' through a long hiss, then drained his beer. Boney started talking about a new song he liked by Rap Master Maurice. They soon switched to a story about 'the kid, his nigga, her part in it, the store security and that shit ain't right'. Neal gave up trying to follow. The food came, though nobody had seemed to order. Plates of ribs, a platter filled with greasy fried potatoes and a bowl brimming with beans swimming in a deep red sauce. Dewalt plated it up and everybody ate. Neal asked for a Diet Coke, and nibbled at things, afraid to get grease on his expensive shirt, hunting for a wet nap. He got water in a paper cup and a napkin. The boys shut up while they ate, smiled every once in a while at Neal then looked away. Dewalt leaned close, again gripping his date's sweaty hand under the table. Jimmy was talking loudly, a little riled up by his third beer. Something about a girl named Pam and then the word crack. He turned to Dewalt.

"She's yours right, fucking crack whore right, but she pays good right, she called today, right?" he said.

Dewalt let go of Neal's hand.

“Shut the fuck up, nigga,” he said. “Ain’t your business.”

The boys got quiet and went back to eating, and Neal realized Dewalt must be the ringleader. Nobody said much after that and Neal decided he’d ask Dewalt about the crack whore named Pam. A banana cream pie landed on the table with plates and they ate it. In the lull, mouths gobbling whipped cream, Neal tried again to chat.

“I thought I might get a tattoo, like Dewalt’s,” Neal said.

“Of what?” Dewalt said between bites.

“An anchor. I like sailors, that sea theme,” Neal said.

“Bet you do,” Jimmy said.

Dewalt let rip one of his long hissing ‘shits’ between bites of pie and just shook his head. Neal didn’t know if he was being insulted or included.

“Anchor on your arm. You got a good build,” Boney said.

Jimmy laughed and made a face.

“Shut the fuck up J, shit, we ain’t in school,” Boney said. “Don’t mind him. Sticky ain’t brought nobody round before so this ass don’t know what to think.”

Dewalt blushed.

“I never had nobody to bring around,” he said, squeezing Neal’s hand, and this time, lifting it up and onto the table in clear view.

Jimmy stared at their twined fists and rolled his eyes and Boney smiled.

“So, like I said, when’s the fucking wedding?” Jimmy said.

Neal took a cue to jump in.

“I’m writing a column about gay marriage,” he said.

The table was quiet. Dewalt rubbed his chin and turned slowly to look at Neal.

“You’d do that?” he said.

Neal met Dewalt’s gaze and as he stared at him, into his wide dark eyes, he forgot the table, the three men. This was about him and Dewalt. He realized this was one of those topics that could unite or separate a couple. Dewalt’s face was expressionless, and Neal saw soft creases at his eyes and realized he had a very kind face. He had not looked at Dewalt that way often. He hadn't thought of him as a friend, or a man with a mind. He thought of him naked, his black skin shiny, his body lean and hard. He realized he'd considered Dewalt a bit stupid, limited, a brute. Dewalt's eyes softened further.

"I'd like to do that someday. Get married. I like the idea," Neal said softly.

The jukebox went silent and the boys slumped in their seats, waiting, looking uncomfortable like they were part of a secret they didn't want any part of. Dewalt gently caressed Neal's wrist.

"I like that idea too," he said.

The waiter dropped a check and rolls of money came out, closed fist hand touches were exchanged, peace was uttered multiple times, and the dinner was over. Before he left, Boney touched Neal's shoulder and looked at Dewalt.

"Bring him to Kofi's house party," he said. "He family now. He met Big Lou?"

Neal recalled the mention of Big Lou, Dewalt's Aunt who'd raised him. Dewalt shook his head, grunted, sent them all off, then lead Neal away from Ruby's. They were back on the street, alone as night fell. Neal felt like he'd gone through a rushing set of doors leading somewhere new, like Alice in a dim and foreign wonderland. For a brief second, he thought of the column he'd just written that day. Catty, pessimistic, all cock and fashion, his slick persona. He thought of Dewalt reading it, and suddenly felt deeply vacant.

Chapter 26

SINCE IT WAS early and a warm summer night, Dewalt suggested they head down to Central Park and sit by the fountain bordering the Time Warner building after dinner. Neal had a better idea. The train deposited them at 59th Street, and Dewalt grudgingly followed Neal's lead past Central Park and toward Fifth Avenue. They trailed the Park's edge, past the elite Paris Cinema and the Pulitzer Fountain with its gape-mouthed granite fish spewing water, then stopped at the doorway to Bergdorf Goodman's Men's store.

"You wanna go to a store?" Dewalt said.

"It's not just a store. You'll see," Neal said moving toward the door.

Dewalt didn't budge.

"I'll wait over there," he said, moving away.

It was near closing time. Neal caught up and touched Dewalt's arm.

"This is my favorite place in the city," he said.

Dewalt followed Neal into Bergdorf's, grunting. Inside, Neal looked around with pride like he owned the place. He started his guided tour, curling past the Ralph Lauren shop back toward the staircase to three. As they passed a counter of alligator wallets, Neal noticed something different. The sales woman, a Botoxed blond in silk, eyed them disapprovingly. Neal kept going, glancing for a second at Dewalt's jeans with the knee-holes, faded T-shirt featuring a picture of rapper Big B, and dirty high-top sneakers. Dewalt smiled, flashing a gold tooth at the sales woman. As they hit the back stairs, an elderly gentleman in a white linen suit was coming down. He stopped and turned his head, as if not seeing them, then hurried past. Neal bounded up the stairs to three, anxious to get to 'his' floor. Things would be nice there. As they walked, Dewalt heaved a sigh and asked why they didn't use the elevator. Neal noticed a smudge on the carpet he'd never seen before. Also, one of the etchings of London was tilted on the wall. At three, Neal breathed easier. The floor was empty, music played softly, things were immaculate. He took Dewalt's hand and walked him past designer chambers: Etro, Diesel and Sander, past the beautiful striped side chair he had noticed last week. The Libertine shirt he mentioned in his column hung on a hanger, set off alone like an exhibit. It was a variation on a tuxedo shirt, with swirling blue and red chunky fabric replacing the traditional front ruffle.

"I love this," Neal said.

As he studied the shirt, delicately testing the thick ruffle on the front he turned to see Dewalt flopped in the striped side chair, playing with his phone. Neal held the shirt up to his chest and moved toward Dewalt, noticing a silver-haired sales woman heading their way. Neal landed first and the woman turned away. Neal was ready to launch into details about the hot new designer when Dewalt fingered the hidden price tag and whistled.

"Shit, six hundred bucks, you fucking nuts?" he said.

The shirt felt heavy in Neal's hand. Dewalt was drumming his fingers on the chair. Neal turned away, hung the beautiful shirt back on its rod. He wanted to tell Dewalt that the clothing pieces were like art, that the seam work was impeccable, that this was more than a store, it was an experience, but instead he said nothing and waved his date to the back stairs, realizing for the first time that they were, in essence, taking a rear staircase which could be seen long ago as a servant's exit.

Dewalt stayed in his chair.

"Why'd you bring me here?" Dewalt said.

Neal stopped, scanning the empty selling floor. They were alone.

"I told you, it's my favorite store," Neal said.

"You write that column here," Dewalt said. "I'm not stupid."

Just beyond them, beyond a curving wall, was the entrance to Café III, which was closed. Neal felt trapped. He stepped away, wanting to go into a chamber, hide amidst cashmere and silk, or laugh and tell a joke and guide them in a new direction. He felt aimless, uncertain, sad. Dewalt was holding his palms up, his eyes wide, looking like he was getting angry. Neal could not deal with anger. Dewalt reached for him and pulled Neal into his lap. Neal resisted, wondering what the sales woman might think.

"Come on, cut da shit," Dewalt said.

He sighed as Neal slouched in his lap like an errant boy. Dewalt started again, more gently.

"This is it, arright," Dewalt said, still holding Neal on his lap. "I'm into you. I want to take it up a step. Just us. Like you was saying at dinner."

Neal knew what he meant. Going steady, getting exclusive. They were propped on the chair Neal had fantasized about, the elegant side chair they could buy for their country home. That's what he had safely fantasized last week, alone. That's what he'd fantasized about safely alone all his life. He was surrounded by unreachable clothing and untouchable things, and glancing into Dewalt's eyes, he saw something real and terrifying that had nothing to do with the store, and was not at all tied up neatly with rich silk. There was a gentle bell ringing overhead, indicating the store was closing, and he thought of his mother's wind chimes, on the back porch back home, and the dreams he'd had as a boy on that porch, of shopping at this store, living in New York and falling deeply and madly in love. He knew, back then, they would all mix perfectly together, but here on this black man's knee, he felt absolutely lost. Dewalt breathed into the pause.

"Tell me the truth Neal, it's all right," Dewalt said softly. "I'm a big boy. Better now than later."

Neal sat very still, thinking again of the nights on the porch, and the hundreds of lies he'd told, about his sexuality, his hidden lovers, what he thought of his family, all of it, all shaded, all hidden, nothing ever really revealed. He felt Dewalt's muscular leg beneath him, hot now, sinking with the pressure of his body. He had no idea if he could curb his anonymous sex, or go deeper, but he knew he dreamed to someday, as if he were someone else, and he knew he would have to lie about the column, and his sex life, to tell Dewalt what he thought he wanted to hear, because that is what he knew how to do, and that had to be enough.

He whispered, "I love you," in Dewalt's ear and leaned his lips into his hot black neck for as long as he possibly could, until the store lights gently dimmed and the night ended, at last.

Chapter 27

COPPER, A SUCCESSFUL full-service men's salon in London, had recently launched its flagship Manhattan store in a massive and elegant old bank at the edge of the West Village. A rumor had quickly spread amidst the sex-savvy steam room set that you could get a facial "with sensual release" at the spa. Neal was there to find out if it was true and to see if it was a column worthy tidbit. The design of the spa, by Laurence Tangiers, simulated a submarine with chrome walls, accessories of ocean blue and silver, and soft azure lighting. The front desk, manned with athletic youths in yachting gear, bristled with attitude. Neal checked in anonymously, wondering why anyone would pay such outlandish prices to be treated with disdain by a blond boy in faux sailor gear. He'd requested Sebastian (the "release" facialist) but half expected it to be a bust, another rumor as fake as a starlet's rehab commitment. He also half hoped it fell flat, having just last night gazed into Dewalt's eyes agreeing to take their relationship to the next level. He had committed, quietly to himself, to only have anonymous sex, no names and even eventually to let go of that and be faithful once they were…married?

That was as far as he could go at this point. Standing at the desk, he hated the fact that, deep down, his soft, soft voice was telling him that anonymous or not, he was being a real shit.

He was getting a Youth Refresh treatment, featuring Copper's secret hydrating serum and sea algae glaze. Neal was guided to a private facial chamber on the second floor, past a gigantic floor to ceiling black and white photo of a shirtless, grinning brute wearing a dirt-smudged sailor cap. The 'facial chamber' was dimly lit and smelled of lavender and mint. He sat on a reclining table. There was a tie-dye robe hanging on a hook. He made a mental note of the overall atmosphere for potential use in a future column, and considered writing about it 'as if' this experience had been reported to him by a friend. While he had hoped to hide out in his column, to get away from himself, he felt it was forcing him to look inward, which was totally disarming. He felt increasingly conflicted about which direction to go in the column: flighty and frivolous cock and fashion tips, or simmering thoughts about dating and gay marriage. The evolution of this weekly column both thrilled him and made him feel a touch psychotic. He was keenly aware that Dewalt would likely read it.

Sebastian stepped in clad in a tight nautical outfit. He was tall, early thirties, thick dark hair and a warm smile. He gripped Neal's hand and suggested he change into the robe. As he left, he dimmed the lights further and added a footnote.

"If you'd like a touch of massage after, strip. It's more effective," he said with a wink.

Neal was quickly aroused, piecing together the answers to his own questions, knowing now how a facial became sensual. He undressed, put on the robe and rested on the table, tingling with excitement, shaded with guilt, reminding himself he was simply doing his job, writing his column, not cheating on his boyfriend. It was anonymous. It was nothing. It wasn't even him, really. It was Bergdorf Boy. He shut his eyes and drifted, then felt warm hands on his neck. Sebastian had slipped in like a cat.

"You're having the Youth Refresh," Sebastian said so softly Neal could barely hear him. "Did you want to add the after massage for another fifty in tip?"

Neal nodded in agreement, aware that his arousal must be obvious under the thin robe. As Sebastian rubbed a warm liquid into his cheeks and forehead, Neal sighed, and thought of Dewalt's fingers caressing his brow. He'd never thought so often of a man, during so many different pieces of his day. The scents of lavender, and the feel of Sebastian's strong hands massaging his temples led Neal deeper toward a place of resting, and he sank easily, giving up resistance, then envisioned the ocean and Dewalt, and that eye tattoo on Dewalt's black ankle and that gold tooth. Things were slipping away from him. He didn't struggle to stay alert, rather let himself float off, giving up the details needed for his column, until within the depth of it, he felt a hand exploring his crotch, delicately caressing, and a tickling sensation. He didn't open his eyes, or protest, or move. He just let it all happen, thinking of the black of the ocean at night on Fire Island, and Sebastian's masculine beauty, and Dewalt waving at him from the dark sandy beach, afraid to swim at night, and Neal afraid to go to him.

Chapter 28

NEAL WAS STRUGGLING at his computer, wondering if he could really layer in the details of the sensual facial release in a column, or if it would trigger a valid slander suit. He also wondered if the whole 'gay dating angle' he explored in his current column was a good one or would fall flat. Again, he felt torn between being flaky or thoughtful in his writing. He paused at the computer, recalling the facial experience, which had been surreal. Sebastian had actually delivered both a top rate pore cleansing and an elegant little hand job. *New York*, Neal thought, *really is bizarre*. Reporting it all could cause a stir, good for the magazine, but could he honestly tell Dewalt it was yet another adventure from his past, or "told" to him by a friend? He had nagging doubts. And Annie wasn't helping. After reading that week's "dating" themed column, she had gone unusually somber.

"I don't know about the end," she'd said, "What about Dewalt?"

"It's just a column," Neal had said. "It doesn't mean I did all that. It's Bergdorf Boy."

She sighed and read aloud the last section.

BB trick of the week: Tall, muscled Italian, in my bedroom, hot and sultry. He pulls out a pair of nylons. Drag anyone? Then he puts the ny-

lons over his head and wants to kiss me. Mugger chic?

She'd handed him the pages and asked him to be careful, then smiling, gave him a long tight hug which he'd found a bit condescending and strange. Now, writing, he wondered what he was doing. He was not single, yet he was writing as if there was no one he could injure. He realized these things, but as he sat to write, he felt reckless, almost angry, and wanted to tell everything, to purge. He wondered if he was bent on sabotaging a good thing, like Annie hinted at. Was he too afraid to let things move forward for once in a positive and…loving way? He sat back, stuck, recalling a dream he had that morning. He had woke stiff and restless with the residue of twin matadors, two beauties who were so colorful and vibrant that he thought they stood, side by side, at the end his pull-out couch. Of course he was alone, but he had felt the dreamy breath, the mirror image of identical Spaniards in pants tight like paint on muscle. In the dream, this extreme masculinity was accented by bull gashes and scars visible through rips in the pants cutting their thighs and calves, scars won in the ring, reds and purples mixing with the elaborate brocade in their bullfighting vests. As the grip of sleep faded that morning, he'd sat up and considered doing something about his raging sexual compulsions. The twins, he had thought, must be his two conflicted sides. They were his insatiable sexual urges, but their scars were the mystery of Dewalt's tattooed and cut up body. Now, recalling the dream, he decided it was time to act. He would go to a twelve-step meeting for sex addicts.

During his month stint in rehab, a perky cherub faced woman with deep black hair had spoken to his group about "other" addictions beyond drugs and booze. Fran (from Alabama, now a Manhattanite) was a dyed in the wool member of Sex and Love Addicts Anonymous and told the group it had saved her life. Neal struggled to believe Fran's southern-fried debauchery tales involving Vern's pick-up truck and a trio of truckers balling her at a Motel 6, but there was something solid in the way she shook his hand at the end of the group. She'd mentioned a daily meeting at the Gay Center in the West Village. Sitting at his desk, he whispered to himself: "Hi I'm Neal and I'm a sex and love addict." The phone's ring saved him from going further.

"Meet me after work, it's important," Nick said.

Neal took a deep breath. He'd told Nick they could meet and he'd help him out with sex tips, but he didn't expect it so soon.

"It's important. Wear black," Nick said. "Meet me at the Tom Ford cologne boutique on Madison."

Nick hung up. He considered calling him back and telling him to go screw himself, but as he headed to the press area to review the final layout for the swim spread he decided better to get this done with. Give the queen a few lessons on being a slut and go back to being cool to one another. Maybe this whole thing with Nick was another signal to get his ass to the Sex and Love Addicts meeting. He didn't really want to be seen as the city's gay sex-pert. He could make it to the Center's meeting before he met Nick.

As he studied the color separations in the swim issue, he decided he would ring Dewalt and tell him Nick needed to meet to discuss a writing project (small lie). Dewalt's friend Boney was spinning as a guest DJ at La Noche, a midtown dance club for the first time that night. Maybe he could meet up with Dewalt later. A little guilty about the whole facial experience, and confused over the fate of his column, he wasn't looking forward to staring Dewalt in the eye, at least not so soon. Maybe the sex meeting would give him a boost, or some clarity.

THE LGBT CENTER had been renovated a few years back, the drab lobby spiffed up with a granite greeting counter, elevators, new sofas and a brass rail on the curling staircase sweeping to the upper floors. The SLA (sex love addicts) meeting was on the 4th floor. Neal was wearing loose faded jeans, which he thought were appropriate. Nothing too tight. There was a hole in one knee, but who lusted after knees? He wore a brown straw hat to give the look flair.

The room was bright with huge windows at one end, and a long table in the center. Half a dozen people sat at the table and gave him an up and down as he entered. He smiled and sat, wishing the clock would rush from 4:57 to 5 P.M. when the meeting was scheduled to begin. The concept of attending was invigorating, but actually sitting in the meeting was awful. With each of the three passing minutes, he felt increasingly paranoid. What if someone saw him here, sitting with a bunch of love addicts. He could handle being a drug and booze hound (like Liza and Lindsay), but felt oddly shamed about having sexual issues. Also, two of the men sitting around the table were model-hot. There was a Brazilian with thick wavy hair and a skintight tank top. He was wearing headphones and bobbing his head back and forth, mouthing to music. Near him was a thirty-something guy with a crew cut, huge green eyes, and arms the size of melons. Finally the meeting began, and Neal breathed a sigh of relief. The group leader's name was Gemini, and she looked mildly insane. She appeared to be about sixty, wore a man's fedora, tons of blue eye shadow and had deep orange rogue slathered on her tan, wrinkled cheeks. She was dressed in clownish shades of turquoise, green and yellow. She identified herself as a sex and love addict, then added that she was a survivor of ritualistic satanic abuse. Neal eyed the door. It was only a few feet away. He could start coughing, and act as if he needed to run for water. If she was the leader of the group, what did that say about SLA as a whole? He decided he was the sanest one in the room. They were going around the table now, identifying themselves. The Brazilian's name was Benito and he spoke with a heavy accent. The crew cut fellow, Bob, spoke softly and giggled a little as he said it was his first time attending. There was a pause, and Neal caught his breath.

"I'm Neal and I have sex issues," he said, the words tumbling out of his mouth.

The group shouted, "Welcome, Neal," in unison and for a moment, he did feel welcome. Gemini was also the group's featured speaker. Neal hoped her story would encourage him, similar to Fanny's warm smile in rehab. It did not. She spoke quickly, using bright language, speeding up at spots and shutting her eyes, waving her hands for emphasis. She had been a successful corporate lawyer, married for years, discovering her sexual addiction and desire for young flat-chested women late in life after her husband's death. Her late blooming addiction, she said, was fully realized after a recent stint in psychotherapy when she had summoned dormant memories of abuse as a child. Neal was listening, but his eyes kept roving to the Brazilian, who was nodding with her every word, pursing his big elegant red lips, hugging himself in his tight tank top, his nipples pressing forward and his arm muscles popping. Neal wanted to leap over the table and nibble on his delicious looking chest, then strip and fuck his hard rump. Why would anyone wear such a hot little outfit to an SLA meeting? Strike two for this group.

Finally Gemini ended with a flourish and passed her funny little hat for people to contribute a dollar. They began around the table with sharing. Neal panicked. He was not telling these nuts his story. The cute man with the crew cut had laid his head on the table like he was taking a nap, and the Brazilian was rattling on about his life as a model and hooker, looking like he would soon burst into tears. Gemini raised her hands and shut her eyes then began humming as if she was summoning spirits to heal him. As much as he wanted to lick the Brazilian's chest, he had to get out. This group was insane. He stood abruptly, started to cough, and darted out the door. Leaving the center, he decided he wasn't so bad after all. He'd come a long way being sober, and with a little determination, he'd figure his sex issues out on his own. He had no room in his life for SLA.

Chapter 29

TOM FORD. SUPER sexy, gay, masculine, successful, married to former editor in chief of Vogue Hommes International, Richard Buckley. A role model for the millennium, Neal decided, thinking of his youth, when he was reaching for something, anything to aspire to other than Liberace. The Ford flagship store at Madison and 70th was more an über-bachelor pad than a spot to shop. The frosted double door entrance swung into a penthouse-like foyer, with a large metalwork sculpture. There were doorways left and right. Neal went left, toward a room set up like a Lord's sitting area. An armoire revealed velvet slippers and a dressing gown ($3,900). On the sofa two men sat chatting in low voices and sipping cocktails served by a butler in traditional uniform. The place was surreal, complete with beaver rugs, oversized lamps and sumptuous wall art. Beyond the sofa, a hall led to the Tom Ford scent boutique where Nick stood alone. The cologne chamber had a long center table lined with crystal bottles. Nick was sniffing Black Orchid. He held it to Neal's nose. It was oddly addictive, earthy and rich. A small white card read: *Sensuous top notes of Black Truffle and Ylang mingled with fresh Bergamot and delectable Black Currant.* Nick turned, a sales person magically appeared, and he handed her the black bottle that looked a bit like a whiskey flask.

"My gift to you," Nick said. "Let's go."

Neal stayed at the scent bar. He wasn't' going to be lead by Nick Sands, and couldn't be bought for a bottle of Black Orchid, despite its delicious allure. For a fleeting moment, he wished it was Dewalt at his side, buying him cologne. He reached for his phone, wanting to call Dewalt, but a rush of anxiety and remorse over the sensual facial overwhelmed him. He hesitated.

"Go where?" Neal said.

Nick stepped back and glanced around the elegant chamber.

"It won't cost you a thing. Brandon gave me the car and driver for the night, just go with it," Nick said. "Trust me."

Neal took a long hard look at Nick, dapper as always in black pants, black silk shirt, perfectly sculpted brows, high cheekbones. He recalled why he and Nick had initially been friends in college. Beyond his money and sense of style, Nick was a risk taker and he was fun to run with. Maybe a "girls" night out would clear his head and help him move past the lingering guilt. He'd shake off this angst and by the time he met Dewalt at the club, he'd be feeling good again. Nick was dousing himself with cologne, the remnants wafting past Neal. The lush mix of earthy scents made Neal a little dizzy as he imagined himself rushing to Dewalt and suddenly telling him the truth, spilling it all, revealing his authentic self. He would finally tell someone who he really was and things would get clear. Neal was hit with a hard sense of urgency and a feeling that everything was going to change for him that night. His lips were dry, his throat tight.

"All right, but you have to go with me afterwards to meet Dewalt," Neal said.

Nick nodded, then raised a tweezed eyebrow, took Neal's hand and led him to the waiting limo.

Chapter 30

THE HELL FIRE Club sat at the far edge of the trendy meat-packing district, hidden in a block-long cellar below a shuttered tobacco store. A steep and cracked set of concrete stairs lead to a wood slat door that looked like it had been beaten down and put back up again piece by piece. Neal and Nick stood side by side at the top of the staircase, both in black, glancing down into the dimness.

"It looks like a shit pit," Nick said.

"This is the S&M club Brandon likes?" Neal said in dismay.

Nick shuddered and nodded. The door at the foot of the dreary staircase swung and a drunken leather queen stumbled out, bending over and looking like he was about to vomit. In a dizzy flash, Neal saw himself in the exact spot, bent over, throwing up two years ago. The shady edges of a forgotten three-day binge came rushing back to him. He had been there, falling on his knees, dirt mixing into a jagged cut as he threw up stale beer. A stranger had yanked him up and they'd gone to a disgusting West Side Highway transient hotel (was it called the B-Line Inn?) They had holed up there for days. Confronted with the blacked-out memory, Neal had deep reservations about visiting Hell Fire. The leather man straightened up and climbed toward them. Nick covered his mouth and stepped aside, letting the old drunk pass.

"Charming," Nick said.

"Maybe we should just go?" Neal said.

Nick hesitated, then turned to Neal.

"Brandon will leave me if I don't go along with it. I don't know if I can survive without him," Nick said, heading down the grimy staircase.

Neal followed and pressed into the club's entry hall. A burly man sat in a booth looking like a cheap carnival ticket taker.

"Clothes check available inside to the right," he said, in an unexpectedly high-pitched voice.

A set of floor to ceiling plastic flaps, similar to those shielding the entrance to a meat refrigerator spread apart as they moved into the main club. An emaciated man wearing nothing but a leather jock strap waved them over to a coat check and motioned to a sign above: "Nudity Encouraged." The thin man smiled, revealing missing front teeth.

"Ain't seen you in awhile," he said.

Neal realized he knew the toothless man. He had a fuzzy memory of sitting on the derelict's lap, smoking something, wearing nothing but bikini briefs. Pieces of other doped-up nights at this club rushed forward, things he had no desire to remember. He was angry with Nick for dragging him here and dredging up the past. He wanted to bury it all. Thinking of that afternoon's SLA meeting, he again told himself he was still much improved over his booze-soaked trampy former self. He hurried into the club, as if being pursued by a ghost. Luckily, the scene inside became increasingly attractive. At the front was a long bar and small tables occupied by male couples and a few single men, all fairly good looking. The bartenders, wearing leather jocks, caps and bracelets, were sexy. Nick and Neal faced the bar, taking in a row of several firm asses mixed with a few flabby messes. A young, square-jawed bartender with a mass of chest hair smiled and set down two napkins.

"First time?" the bartender said, as if they were attending a cocktail mixer at the Metropolitan Museum of Art.

"Vodka on ice and a Red Bull," Nick said.

Next to him at the bar, a cotton-haired European fashion designer smiled. The man was famous for his early work with Chanel and his outrageous couture. He nodded his fluffy white head at them. Nick grabbed the drinks and Neal's arm and led them toward the back.

"Dear God, what will I say to him at his tent show this fall?" Nick said.

They stopped at a decrepit looking bench and Neal caught a bright flash of fear in Nick's eyes. The place, which had been eerily quiet, came alive with a Tiesto dance anthem. The floor was coated with something sticky, and Neal thought of the run-down double feature movie theatre he used to hide out in as a kid. His tiny sneakers would get stuck to melted candy and soda stained floors there in the dark. These floors, he knew, were not covered with spilt cherry coke and JuJu Bee candy. The club stunk of cheap draft beer and cigarette smoke.

"This is unreal," Nick said, moving tentatively into the space.

Neal recalled telling someone in a drunken ramble how "real" places like this were. He used to swear these dives brought out the hard, gritty honest sides of people. He suddenly realized how full of shit he'd been, for so long. Nick looked pale and was wilting fast. Neal wanted to tell Nick how there was an awful, desperate surrendering in letting strangers lie you on a sofa, slowly undress you, not caring who they were or what they did because you never remembered it anyway. He wanted to confess there was no responsibility, back then, no sense of owing anything to anyone. Looking at Nick, he reminded himself that back then there was also no respect. Nick walked deeper into the club.

Beyond the bar, the wide center area was painted black, even the concrete floor. Glancing back, Neal noticed the cotton-haired fashion designer trailing them. In a dim corner, a very tall, wide-shouldered black man was bent over, gripping his ankles while a thin white boy with a huge mound of red hair gently pushed his gloved fist up his ass. Neal gripped Nick's shoulder and whispered in his ear.

"Let's go."

Nick pulled away and moved on with determination. The booths were all taken. As they moved slowly past, Neal made out couples and sometimes threesomes crammed into the door-less squares; reaching, grabbing, mouths on feet, hands, bobbing cocks. Finally, at the back, they came to a small group shielding a very young man who was facing the wall, wearing a hood. He was strung up to the ceiling by his wrists with leather bracelets. The music was loud, but his muffled, ragged groans hinted at both agony and thrill as the men took turns lightly lashing his ass and the backs of his legs with a whip.

Neal wondered if he had ever let anyone do that to him. He hated the fact that he couldn't be sure. The young man hanging on the wall called out and finally, Nick turned and fled. Neal sighed in relief, and followed his friend.

NICK WAS SITTING on a stoop across the street from Hell Fire, head in his hands, feet flat on a cobble-stoned patch. Neal gingerly sat next to him. Before he could whip out a witty line about Nick allowing his D&G pants to touch the scummy sidewalk, he looked out toward a faded sign hawking the long ago shuttered S&G Meats. They'd been there. The memory was muddled but he felt that odd déjà vu. There was another after-hour's club, and a drunken moment with Nick on this very corner.

"We were here," Neal said.

Nick looked up to reveal mascara running down one cheek. Neal was shocked both by the tears, and the subtle application of makeup that had slipped his radar.

"You threw up across the street," Nick said, wiping his

face. "It was that first year in the city when we were still talking. You threw up all over town."

Neal was silent. He was glad to be here again, after all the lost years, to rediscover a friendship that he'd had a major role in shattering.

"I can't do it," Nick said. "And he'll leave me."

Neal took in the straight-forward statement, and knew in gay terms what it meant. There was often something beyond compromise, more like surrender, that came with committing to an extremely rich or powerful man. There also was no protection, no marriage agreement, no divorce settlement. Brandon could leave and offer nothing to Nick. Things could come apart quickly with men like Brandon, if they were deeply challenged. Sex was often an unraveling element. Neal knew that. He wrapped his arm around Nick.

"Couldn't he do it on his own?" Neal said.

Nick drew a deep, shuddering breath, and let his head rest on Neal's shoulder.

"A few years ago, we both had a week free, and Brandon wanted to go to the Paris apartment," Nick said. "I work in Paris so I told him I didn't want to go. In so many words, he told me I didn't have a choice. I have very little that's mine. My salary goes to clothes. He owns the rest."

Neal held his friend there, in the heat, on the grimy sidewalk. Across the street, a tranny hooker emerged from an idling limousine, then stumbled into a dark corner, flaring up a pipe.

"What do you want?" Neal said.

Nick pulled away and faced Neal, a touch of mascara staining his pretty cheek. He burst out laughing, lowered his head, snorted a little, then turned back to face Neal.

"I want to design swimsuits," Nick said. "Isn't that fucked up?"

Across the street the S&G Meats sign looked a little less ugly as the moon high beyond it glowed over the West Side River. Neal put his arm across Nick's shoulder and for awhile, they sat silently, taking in the moon, friends again.

Chapter 31

THEY ARRIVED AT midnight, *the witching hour*, Neal thought. Nick took in the La Noche club's dreary store-front façade and rolled his eyes.

"You owe me. I went to Hell Fire, you can do La Noche," Neal said, swinging open the ugly black door.

The interior was dark, crowded and loud. Dewalt's friend, Boney, was revving the crowd from the DJ booth.

"You punks in da back, yo hoods on the side, I said get up and dance all you fucking nappy headed niggas," Boney yelled over the sound system.

Nick froze, as did Neal. Neal decided they must look like waspy match sticks draped in Bergdorf silk and expensive shoes. Nick was carrying a petite alligator man-bag. He leaned close to Neal as a Wu Tang Clan song ripped forth.

"We are going to die here," Nick said.

Neal punched him in the arm and scanned the crowd for Dewalt. The dance floor took up most of the club, with a few booths and beat-up couches at the edges. There was a second floor with a dark balcony circling the place. A long bar lined one far wall. Neal guessed Dewalt would be in a booth, so he started forward, Nick holding tight to his back belt loop. While

Neal had intended to curve around the edge of the dance floor, the duo somehow got shoved and thrust with rolling bodies into the fray, forcing them to snake through a cluster of riled-up dancers. The rap music thumped harshly as they forced themselves across the floor. Neal saw Dewalt, lounging, legs spread wide, wearing a black tank top and an oversized ball cap. He sat with friends in a booth. In the dark, spread out like that, he looked dangerous and alien. He saw Neal and sat up, then shot a gold-toothed smile. Neal and Nick maneuvered toward the edge of the booth as Boney's voice boomed.

"Come on mothafuckas this is Boney saying get up and get stuuuuuu-pid."

There was the sound of a gunshot. Nick screamed and ducked. Dewalt's booth fell out laughing. The shot was the punctuated end of a rap song. Nick straightened and tried to regain his composure.

"Is there room for our skinny white asses?" Nick said.

The group scooted around until both Nick and Neal were seated. Neal thought it was odd Dewalt hadn't gotten up and moved so they could sit together side by side. He recognized Jimmy from their dinner at Mama Ruby's, but the other guys were strangers. Jimmy again had on his brass knuckles spelling out 'PEACE'. They all had their eyes on the dance floor and were drinking. Dewalt was in the center and there was an empty shot glass lying on its side before him. Neal tried to get Dewalt's attention but he wouldn't look his way, which Neal found rude and irritating. Two black girls were approaching the booth. The first, wide hipped with a huge afro was dragging along a mutt of a girl, rail thin, wearing a kerchief and a spaghetti string tank-top with a picture of a black version of Tweetie Bird on the front. Neal couldn't be sure in the dark, but thought the Tweetie girl might be barefoot. Jimmy jammed his fingers into Neal's side and spoke loudly.

"Come on, you and your friend, let's dance," he said.

Before Neal could react, Jimmy pushed him to his feet,

waved Nick along and took the angry afro girl with them to the dance floor, leaving Tweetie girl behind. Jimmy aggressively pushed the little group to the center of the floor, as Neal lamely resisted, staying close to Nick. Boney was playing a scratchy mix of Beyoncé spliced with rapper Big B, and the crowd was eating it up. Neal felt he was being swallowed alive and was angry that Dewalt hadn't interceded with this dance floor hijack. He pulled away from Jimmy in time to see Dewalt leaving the booth with the Tweetie girl. Nudging Nick, he took a deep breath and rammed his way off the floor, despite Jimmy's protests. Afro girl had her fat arms around Jimmy, which kept him at bay.

Following Dewalt through the crowd, Neal was repeatedly banged and pushed by aggressive partiers. Two big girls squashed him into a ratty couch, a man stepped on his foot. The music made Neal's head throb and he cursed loudly. His resolve to confront Dewalt and tell him his "soul" truth was evolving into an angry crusade. As he fought his way through the club, his mind raced. Dewalt, he realized, was not so perfect. It was time to get clear. Neal's heart was racing. He caught sight of Tweetie girl going into the men's room near the bar. He moved steadily, sweating now, seething, pushing back at the crowd, shouting curses over the music, not caring. He entered the men's room which had three stalls, two urinals, a cracked mirror, graffiti covered walls and a group of three men passing a joint. They gave Neal a stare as he went to the last stall. He pushed the paint smeared door. Dewalt was holding cash, Tweetie a small bag of powder which Neal guessed was heroin. The girl, her kerchief gone and her eyes blazing, pushed past Neal out of the stall. Neal stared at Dewalt. He looked stoned, stupid and at that moment, ugly. He was wavering as if he may fall, his lips curling in an asinine grin, his eyes beaded black stones staring ahead at nothing. The cubicle stank of piss, pot smoke and bad cologne, and Neal recalled moments like this, facing derelicts in crap crusted bathrooms, accepting the disgust of it all in a drug and sex starved haze. Dewalt looked back at him, then stuck the cash in his pocket and reached for Neal, pulling him into the stall and shutting the door with his foot.

"Come on," Dewalt slurred.

He held Neal tight, pressing into him, stinking of sweet liquor and smoke, pushing his stiffening crotch at Neal and rubbing his lips on Neal's cheek. At once turned on and disgusted, Neal tried to pull away but Dewalt held firm. Nick was knocking on the stall door.

"Are you ok?" Nick said.

Neal wanted to return Dewalt's kiss, to slide into the drugged-up sexual rush, to do what he'd done so many nights in the past, to let Dewalt be another hot, late-night screw, but he could not. He realized, in a totally fucked up way, that he loved Dewalt but that he was also terribly afraid of him and of his own feelings for this man. He stirred something in Neal he'd never felt before. He pushed Dewalt away with a hard thrust. Dewalt slipped back and flopped into the toilet, his ass sinking down into the bowl's dingy water. Dewalt, eyes slits, began to laugh first softly then louder and uncontrollably, struggling to wrench himself free of the bowl, his legs sprouting out of the nasty toilet like flailing sticks, his arms waving. Frozen there, Neal saw not Dewalt, but himself, his reckless stupid drunken self that had sex with anyone, who cheated on his boyfriend because it was easy, who lied to everyone and hated something deep inside, something so indefinable, something so reckless and self-hating.

"You suck," was all Neal could muster, as he pushed open the stall door and grabbed Nick's hand.

As they fled, the three pot smokers at the sink snickered and muttered "fags". Neal turned just outside the bathroom door near the exit, shaking and screamed at them in a high, ragged voice.

"Oh, shut up, nigga," he said, then yelled louder as Nick dragged him away. "You know what I'm saying, nigga! Nigga nigga nigga."

As he screamed, a petrified Nick yanked him away from the club before the stoned trio could register what had happened. The two fled to Nick's car, chased by the sluggish hollering of the men in the bathroom, the dim shouts of Dewalt, and the sound of Boney revving the crowd into a rap-inspired frenzy.

Chapter 32

IN THE LIMO, weaving through traffic, Neal saw over and over the image of Dewalt, ass sinking in the ugly toilet bowl, heroin dust on his fingers. It was meant to be a night of change, of secrets revealed. Now it all seemed impossibly cruel. He couldn't see through the smoky glass out of the limo's window. It suddenly became very important to him to know exactly where they were in the city.

"I can't see," he said, pushing his face close to the glass, knocking his forehead gently against the window.

Nick, who had sat quietly at his side, touched his arm to quiet his panic.

"It's gonna be all right. He's really fucked up," Nick said. "You haven't known him that long."

For a moment, Neal forgot his anger at Dewalt and wanted to lash out at Nick. He felt a welling sense of pride at what he and Dewalt had created thus far. He realized it was more than just the weeks they had known each other. There was something more, a deeper connection, a mingling between them that couldn't be defined and that Nick would never understand. Shutting his eyes again as the limo stopped at a light, he again saw the image of Dewalt in the stall, stoned and stupid. He couldn't reconcile his mixed feelings, couldn't stand the conflict he felt. Near his knee, a shelf was stocked with fine liquor. As the limo pulled into traffic again, Neal reached for a bottle of Vodka and held it in his lap. It was sealed, untouched. It was Russian and the glass felt cool against his palm. He stared at the pretty silver logo, which looked like the wing of a bird to him. In a swift movement, he twisted the top and broke the seal. As he lifted the bottle to his face, smelling the pungent aroma, Nick slapped his arm.

"You quit drinking, what are you doing?" he said.

Neal held the bottle and for a split second he met Nick's eyes. They were probing and gentle, and he imagined that his friend had told him many times before to stop, to put a bottle down and Neal imagined he told him to go fuck himself. But then, in the past, he was already stoned. Tonight, looking into Nick's warm eyes, he was sober and he was lost, and Dewalt was somewhere far away. Nick took the bottle from him, then pulled Neal's head onto his shoulder as Neal began to cry.

"How did this happen?" Neal said between sobs.

His cell phone rang. It was Rovvie. Neal listened, sighed deeply, then hung up the phone and shut his eyes.

"Can you drop me at the Pierre Hotel," Neal said. "It's Rovvie. Something has happened. He said he has to see me now."

Nick alerted the driver, and they made their way toward Central Park.

"That bitch has impeccable timing," Nick said, rocking Neal in his arms, petting him. "It always has to be about him, doesn't it?"

Neal sat back, glad Rovvie had called with a dramatic distraction, glad to do anything other than sit feeling so lost, thinking about Dewalt.

WHAT WAS SO utterly strange was the calm and the beauty of

the tableau. The Pierre Hotel was dead quiet. Riding up in the deserted elevator, Neal had expected chaos. Opening the door to the grand suite, he saw, sitting near a broad window looking out onto a softly lit Central Park, an impeccably dressed man, hands resting on the arms of a lovely silk chair. It was Rovvie, his hair pulled away from his face. Near him sat two large steamer trunks and several Louis Vuitton suitcases. Rovvie wore a pale linen suit, a diamond tennis bracelet, and the two-tone Gucci lace-up shoes Neal had just written about in his Bergdorf Boy column. Rovvie looked very much the elegant man off to discover the world. He turned to Neal but stayed still, in the chair. Caz was nowhere to be seen.

"Come in," Rovvie said softly.

Neal moved into the sumptuous suite, from the entry hall into the living room. The chair Rovvie sat in was cream with wood accents. There was a tall, willowy orchid near him. He motioned Neal to the sofa.

"I wanted to see you before I left," Rovvie said, a touch of his drawl coming through, a flash back to the wild party boy.

Neal sat and waited. Rovvie was still gazing out the window and over his shoulder, Neal could see the barely lit park, trees lilting in a hot summer night's breeze. His entire body softened, and he forgot for the moment all that horror with Dewalt. It was terribly quiet in the suite.

"We're leaving tonight, Caz and me," Rovvie said, then stood and walked to the bar.

He moved slowly, more gracefully than Neal remembered. It was as if he'd gone through a transformation since Neal had last seen him. He looked much older, his shoulders sat lower, his walk was almost a drift. Rovvie poured a drink into a glass, and leaned against the wall. Watching him, Neal thought not of Rovvie, of craziness and nonsense, but of the hero in *The Great Gatsby* a lost and elegant man.

"I'm so full of shit," Rovvie said. "I ain't been straight with you, Neal."

Downing his drink, Rovvie moved toward the sofa.

"We got into it, Caz and me, right after I moved in with Andreas. I couldn't tell anyone," Rovvie said, and instead of continuing toward the sofa, he turned and went to the window. "Once you found out I knew we had to go. It's not safe. We've been reckless."

Neal watched his friend moving, but he did not recognize him and he thought, *This is a man who knows exactly what he's doing. I am not at all like him, not at all.* Still, he asked the question.

"Do you know what you're doing, Rovvie?" Neal said.

Rovvie stayed with his back to Neal, at the window, poised.

"I'm in love. You know what that's like, right?" Rovvie said.

Neal sunk into the sofa, and realized Rovvie—dumb, backwoods, drunken, former call-boy Rovvie—was traveling far past him, floating off and away, reaching out for something that at this moment, Neal felt was impossible for him. *This is not how it's supposed to be working,* Neal thought. *I was going to fall in love and that was going to be beautiful.*

"Caz has been planning this for months. He's always resented his brother. He invested money on his own, and has been saving it. We're going to some awful place in Asia first," Rovvie said, turning back toward the bar. "He'll probably get rid of me some day. Trusting Caz is pretty stupid. I imagine he's really doing this to get back at Andreas for some long ago hate."

Rovvie stopped again at the bar, and started to laugh. He laughed loudly, his hand shaking, as he filled his glass.

"But love is insane, rrrright," he said, looking into Neal's eyes for the first time, as if he were expecting a clear answer.

Neal held his gaze, and saw a depth and sadness in Rovvie's eyes he'd had no idea existed. He considered the fact that he had judged Rovvie harshly, pegged him as stupid, but had not been sharp enough to realize it was an act, that Rovvie was a gutsy survivor who played the game to win, and took chances like this if his heart lead him. He also felt incapable of answering Rovvie's question about the insanity of love, and as he thought of his column, his advice on sex and dating that would run that weekend, his feelings for Dewalt, he wanted to sleep, just sleep for days. He had to get away. He had turned his cell phone off after a call came from Dewalt during the limo ride to the Pierre. He couldn't speak to him.

Neal got up and went to Rovvie, embraced his friend, and held him tight. He realized he may never see him again, and that he had never taken the proper time to get to know this man who was really the only friend he had in the city. He knew he took many things for granted, and let many things slip by. Thoughts of Dewalt kept racing toward him with incredible speed and force, but he could not bear to embrace them, he could only focus on the idea of flight. They stood there together, he and Rovvie, like a dancing couple at the end of a party, holding onto one another, neither wanting to let go, both afraid of what the next step would be once the movement ended.

Chapter 33

NEAL FELT DELIRIOUS from heat and fatigue. He was scrunched down in the back of a Missouri County Cab with its broken windows at half-mast. The sun was blazing through the window. As the cab approached the house, he sent Annie a text, so he wouldn't have to speak with her.

Run my column as is. Have to be away for few days at my parents in Missouri. Swim issue design will be great.

Approaching, he could see the house's sloping lawn, meticulous and bright. Shorn hedges lined the big front picture window. A sweet gumball tree, prickly fruit on its branches, stood proud and alone near the edge of the yard bordering the blacktop driveway. Neal noticed a new pinkish flowering bush at the far end of the grand lawn. It was mid afternoon, the temperature searing, making tiny tar bubbles at the edge of the street. On the red shingled roof stood Neal's father, wearing blue knee-length shorts, a white undershirt, black knee socks and lace-up shoes. The look was strangely close to what they had shot for *Pop* magazine's swimsuit issue. He smiled, wondering what his father would think of the photos. His mother stood in the wide front window, arms folded tightly. Neal paid the cabbie and set his weekend bag on the driveway, which seemed to be melting in the heat.

"I could use a hand," his father said. "The ladder's in back."

The front door swung open, and his mother dipped her head out.

"Tell him to get down," she said to Neal, then shut the door abruptly.

Neal recalled childhood, and his mother's insistence that opening the front door let precious cool air slide out, straining the central AC system. She loved air conditioning. His father hated it, preferring wide-open windows and the hallway attic fan circulating air through the house. His mother, at home all summer while Dad was at work, had won that debate. Carrying his chic black-and-white striped bag, Neal went up the driveway to the backyard where he imagined the ladder was propped. His father had built the house, all done before he was born. Dad still did all repairs. His mother had a wrought-iron fence and gate put in around the small back yard, another fight she had won. His father did not like fences. At one point Sandra, a neighborhood sheep dog, had taken to lying in front of their back door, petrifying his mother. The fence kept Sandra out, though she'd gotten run over by a car soon after.

The ladder was leaning up the back of the house, into the roof's gutter. Neal kicked off his cream leather flip-flops, set down his bag and climbed. It was easier to walk barefoot on the sloping roof. He ignored his mother's knocking on the back set of latticed windows. He'd never been on the roof with his father, he'd only gone up alone to do chores. They would send him up to clean debris from the gutters after a storm. He liked the task, being above it all, feeling the sun on his back. It was also the only thing his father trusted him to do. Dad was a carpenter, brick layer and amazing handyman, while Neal was baffled by the contents of a tool box. He'd once snuck into his father's workshop and tried to build a bird house. He'd given up after slamming a hammer on his thumb, and never told a soul about it. Climbing the ladder, he remembered how as a teen he used to sneak beer up with him and sit for hours. He gingerly placed one foot, then another onto the scratchy roof shingles. The first few steps were the scariest. After that, it was easy. He steadied himself, pulled his weight up and maneuvered his way. The tiles were hot. He moved swiftly up the slope to the other side, where his father stood waiting. He was chewing a toothpick, pointing to an obstruction in the center of the front roof's gutter.

"It's a branch," he said. "I can't bend."

Neal squatted and scooted his ass down to the edge. This was also scary, being so near the precipice, losing a bit of equilibrium, then having to reach in and scoop out wet leaves, mud from a past rain storm and today, a gnarled branch blocking the flow of water. He nabbed it and tossed it to the lawn below.

"Good," his father said, moving back up the slope toward the ladder in back.

"Dad?" Neal said.

His father turned, and Neal could see strain in his face. His eyes were still sparkling and blue, but his jaw was lean and flabby, and he wore uncharacteristic stubble. Neal wanted to say something, to ask advice about the terrible pitiful ache he felt over Dewalt. He'd never spoken to his father about anything personal but always secretly considered him very wise. His father looked strange and tired today and he wondered why. He realized he'd never taken much time to even look at his father, or notice whether he looked tired or not. He couldn't find the words to ask what he wanted to ask.

"It's good to be here, Francis," Neal said, suddenly wanting to address his father by his given name.

Neal's father frowned, scratched his nose, then seemed to brush off his son's abrupt use of his proper name.

"I hope you didn't take off too much from work," his father said.

Neal was silent, watching his father go up and over the peaked top of the roof, disappearing to the other side. He sat on the hot shingles, and felt the intense Missouri sun on his face. It always felt hotter here. He wanted to take off his shirt, and lie quietly in the heat, but he knew his mother was fretting, wondering what was going on, so he got up, and followed. His cell phone rang. It was Annie. He hesitated, then answered.

"Are you okay?" she said.

He could hear the press running in the background. The issue, with his second column about dating and the much-touted swimsuit shoot, would be circulating soon.

"Dewalt is calling non-stop," she said. "I think you should talk to him."

"No," Neal said. "I'll be back in a few days. I can't deal with him, Annie."

"He sounds so sad," she said.

Neal felt the tears welling up, but he pressed one palm roughly into the hot shingled roof as he bit his lip and reached for justified anger. He would not feel anything now, not at his parents' house. Annie spoke up.

"And there's something else," she said.

"Go on," Neal said.

"Rovvie's gone and Caz. I'm all alone here," Annie said. "What's going on?"

He sighed, not wanting to involve her in the messy drama of Rovvie.

"Give it a day. I'll get a hold of Rovvie," he said.

He hung up before she could ask him any questions, then headed back to the ladder, making his way down, wishing he could leave everything from New York behind, at least for a few days. He knew, somehow, that he could not.

Chapter 34

THE SOUND OF the crickets and cicadas was loud, constant and melodic. Neal had always loved the brutal buzz, reminding him that it was deep summer and the nights were long and full of stray sounds from dark insects and rambunctious children on neighboring lawns. He sat on the back porch, looking out at a row of bridal wreath bushes, round and filled with blooming flowers. The line of bushes set a border in front of the yard's back fence, their round and tall fountain-like branches arching up, covered with pearl white flower tufts. Near these were tulips and stray gardenias. His father did all of the planting, though his mother asked every year if they could hire a gardener. That night, they'd had grilled strip steaks for dinner along with ripe tomatoes from a local woman who grew and sold them five pounds for two dollars. They'd finished eating and his mother was busy loading the dishwasher, having promised ice cream soon. Dewalt had called twelve times since he'd arrived and he'd answered none of the calls, then finally shut off the ringer on his cell phone. He was afraid to speak to Dewalt, and felt very muddled with conflicting feelings of yearning and distaste.

He had a very odd and unsettling rush of emotion when he thought of Dewalt. It reminded him of his fear of extreme heights. Whenever he got close to the roof edge of a very high building, his body tingled and he felt a wind would knock him to his death at any moment.

His father emerged, martini in hand, and took a seat with Neal on the porch, in the dark, under a slowly rotating ceiling fan. Neal resented his father's ability to drink sensibly, like a gentleman. He secretly believed that his father saw his inability to "hold his liquor" as one more disappointment in the "loser son" log. Neal guessed that his father must have at some time hoped for a boy he could consider his equal.

"Doesn't get any better than this," his father said, sipping the gin and vermouth in its cut glass tumbler.

This was the phrase Neal had heard all of his life and this was the only place he really witnessed his father being still. Dad liked to sit at day's end, surveying the grounds, sipping gin and reminding anyone who would listen that he had exactly what he wanted in life. Neal normally found it infuriating, though tonight, he was oddly moved. He glanced at his father, and knew this was the time, the still moment to speak, if he were ever going to speak this weekend. He searched for the right phrase, the way to engage this man, to step a tiny bit closer, but his mind was empty, and he blurted out a catch all, weak little utterance.

"I'm lost about something," Neal said softly.

His father made a snaky hissing sound through his lips, something he did when he disagreed with someone or wanted to emphasize a point. Neal realized the sound was identical to the hiss Dewalt made, usually tied to the S in uttering, "oh shit" when he disagreed with someone. Neal glanced at his father who was staring out into the night, wearing a polka dot short sleeve shirt, and his blue knee-length shorts. He looked peaceful, listening to the rising cacophony of crickets and cicadas.

"Don't live in regret son," Francis said. "How's that Dewalt fellow?"

Neal sunk into his chair, and knew his father knew or sensed something, and also realized he'd find little comfort here. His father had always been pragmatic, to the point and steady. Neal was silent, and his father continued the conversation as if the pause were Neal's response.

"Drama, you and your mother," Francis said, drinking. "Too much of that. It's useless, son."

Neal had always sided with his mother in arguments and enjoyed her often silly logic.

"You don't get it," Neal said softly.

He felt an old anger rising, a desire to get up and go, but he suddenly recalled a long ago instance when his father had taken his side. He was seventeen and he'd come out to his mother (in reality, she'd caught him making out with a boy in his bedroom). The family was having dinner one evening soon after his mother's discovery. Neal was headed out to a very "gay" little party at a friend's house that night and he made the error of mentioning it. His mother, still stung from the revelation of him and the boy, stated that it sounded dangerous and illegal to have a group of men "congregating" like that. His father had come to his defense.

"I congregate with my golf buddies every Saturday. Don't be dramatic, Catherine," his father had said.

Neal glanced now at his father, wanting to say something. There was a loud rising rush from the cicadas, a slow building screech. The rise happened every twenty minutes or so. The insects rallied together in the night's heat and took over. It was difficult to be heard until they reached their peak, and arced back down again. They rose and fell, and then his father began.

"I ever tell you about the summer recital?" he said.

Neal shrugged, expecting another story about his Aunt Bet, who'd won a number of dance championships before settling down with a mechanic in a nearby town.

"I was tapping," Francis said. "I was good. Your Aunt Bet taught me. There was a cash prize."

The cicadas had leveled off and Neal realized this was one of those rare and unexpected revelations that came from his father. He never even knew his father danced. There seemed to be a huge trunk of stories his parents kept hidden, and decided to reveal spontaneously as they pleased. He also realized he asked them few questions, and never probed into their past. His father sipped his drink.

"I was back stage and saw the Italian kid, the one who won," he said. "He was tapping, and doing flips. They cheered really loud. I couldn't do a flip. Never even tried. So I walked out. Didn't want second place. I made a choice."

His father drained his martini, set his glass down, and with one foot, did a soft little tap move.

"I never regretted that, I knew what I was doing," he said. "Whatever you do Neal, think it through."

With that, he got up, gave Neal a soft pat on the shoulder, then went inside, passing Neal's mother on the way out. Neal sat quietly, shaken by his father's brief moment of sharing. She balanced two bowls of ice cream on a tray. The tray was blue and decorated with bright white flowers, similar to the buds on the Wedding Bushes lining the lawn. Her summer dress was also blue with tiny white buds, and Neal wondered at her ability to coordinate so many elements so well. No matter what she was doing, she dressed as if she were attending a fashionable function.

"Dad's all about those martinis, but for me it's ice cream," she said. "I don't know which is worse for my waist line."

She moved to the chair near Neal, testing the air with a delicate step, as if it needed to drop a certain number of degrees to make it palatable for her to enter the evening. As she sat, he thought she looked like a fluttering bird, an elegant but fragile thing. As they ate, and the crickets raged on, Neal realized he was most like his mother, always looking out, always looking for solutions in changing the behavior of someone or something else. She ate her ice cream in tiny bites, holding the spoon like a quill pen, smiling at him between nibbles. They were silent.

Neal handed over his dish and bade his mother good night, and as she escaped back into the air conditioning, he realized that he did not regret as his father indicated, so much as he avoided. He did not reach high enough to truly regret. He also spent a lot of time blaming. He blamed his father for their lack of a relationship, he blamed drinking for wrecking his early life, he blamed Dewalt for ruining their budding love. He never had to take responsibility for anything, because it was always quite logically someone else's fault. He thought of his father, and realized he would never really reach him, and he thought of Dewalt, strangely again, of that eyeball tattoo on his ankle and the gold tooth in his smile, not the entire Dewalt, just those details. His mother shut off the lights inside, letting him know she was off to bed. Alone under the cool ceiling fan with the cicadas and the night, he finally, slowly, easily let himself cry, sure that no one inside could hear him. Then he dialed Dewalt's number, but overwhelmed with fear, he hung up crying at the hollow sound of Dewalt's voice on the recorded message.

Chapter 35

THE PINK BEDROOM had changed since he stayed there as a child. It had been white back then. He wondered if his mother's re-styling the small room into a confection of pink walls, a flower petal floor board trim, a window seat covered in a pattern of salmon colored swirls, was a subtle nod to his gayness. The smallest bedroom in the house, it bordered his father's. Dad had taken over the master suite, his mother had taken a third bedroom a few years back to get away from Dad's snoring. It was near dawn, and Neal was only half dozing, having slept fitfully, his father's guttural roar pulsing through the wall. He thought at one point, deep in the center of sleep, that he heard his father cry out with anger. Neal got up and crept into his father's room. It was silent, his father lying on his side. He'd whispered his name a few times, but there was no response so he went back to bed. He hadn't slept much since then, but was finally drifting, back on the beach, seeing the ocean from being within its waves, ready to turn, when he awoke again, angry at his father's snoring, then realizing it was his cell phone. He snatched it, hoping not to wake his insomniac mother. It was Dewalt.

"Neal," Dewalt said, his voice a ragged cry.

Neal sat up, very groggy. The room's window let in the rising morning sun. In utter confusion, he snapped the phone shut then quickly turned it off. He'd forgotten to do so after his weeping call to Dewalt. He heard his father's snore begin anew, and in the distance, the patter of water beating against a neighbor's house, indicating the start up of an auto sprinkling system. In Missouri, people watered their lawns and flower beds either at dawn or dusk, to avoid the intense heat. Three yards down, he heard Mrs. Droctor, a sad, misshapen and wealthy widow (she drinks her breakfast, his mother said) turn on the hose to water her roses. Somehow, listening to all of that, surrounded by sounds and memories as they can only appear after a sleepless night, Neal felt he had to speak to Dewalt. At the same time he was still terrified to do so. He got up and crept out of the house, then across their front lawn to the blacktop driveway. He laid down, watching Mrs. Droctor in her pink housecoat bring the morning to life. He was wearing a nightshirt, a stiff cotton thing his mother had picked up and kept for his visits. It fell to his knee and he was naked underneath it and barefoot. The air was sweet and very warm. There was a voice snaking through the grass, a calling. Neal turned his cheek onto the warm, dirty black top and saw his mother, in the doorway of the house, her nightgown brilliant white with tiny pink bows at each shoulder. She tentatively stepped out toward him.

"What in the world are you doing out here?" she said.

In his fantasy, of course, it was his father who entered this scene, but as he sat up, he was glad it was his mother because she rarely expected anything from him.

"I couldn't sleep," he said.

She sighed, wrapped her arms around herself as if chilly.

"Oh me too. I don't like taking those sleeping pills Doctor Leinheart gave me, so sometimes I just lie still," she said. "I'm afraid you got the sleepless thing from me. Lord knows Dad can sleep through a tornado. That man."

For a moment, Neal thought she looked as if she wanted to sit down, just plop on the lawn. Instead she turned her hips to and fro and stood, ever the lady. The sky was gradating, a far off light milking its way into the fading night's black. His mother bent to pick up a gumball which had fallen from the sweet gum tree near them.

"I'll get this thing cut down, I've always hated it," his mother said, feeling the prickly ball in her hand and glancing at the willowy tree. "It drops these sticky little things. Someone has to rake them up. Dad's getting on."

Neal imagined the yard without the tree, and thought it would be awfully ugly, a stump, brutalized. He wondered if she would really do it.

"I'll start some coffee," she said and went in. "Then we'll go to church."

Neal waited, thinking the sun would creep up over the hill or something, brighten the lawn a generous green and start the day. It did not. His back felt stiff on the blacktop, so he got up, going in for his mother's coffee, wondering if he had anything to wear to St. Dominic Savio's Church Service. Attending mass with his mother was one tradition he had chosen not to break, mostly because he found the atmosphere, the incense, the art-work, peaceful and alluring.

Chapter 36

HE'D BROUGHT A pair of white flannel pants, and paired it with one of his father's short-sleeved button ups. The shirt was a deep emerald green, which brought out Neal's eyes, and was only slightly too large. He wore his Roman sandals from Bergdorf's, despite his mother's worried look. As they approached Father Conrad, a loud oafish Irish priest who was on visit from a mission in India, Neal's mother glanced at his feet, as if she wanted to sneak through a side exit. Neal would have none of it moving briskly toward the front entrance of the church.

"These are from Bergdorf Goodman and cost more than most of these people's entire summer wardrobe," Neal said.

Father Conrad was attractive in a big, red-headed and burly way. Neal recalled his mother stating that he gave "scandalous" sermons since arriving last spring. The priest was surrounded by three elderly women, who were clawing at his purple robe and white sash. Neal held the big oak door open for his mother to enter the church, glancing back at Father Conrad, who smiled broadly and waved. Neal blushed. The lobby of the building separated the church proper from the grade school, which Neal had attended. A long hall snaked away from the lobby. The hall had classrooms on either side, in a row, grades one through eight. Another set of big wooden doors opened from the lobby into the church itself.

Inside the church, things were dim. The place was simple with oak pews, a cry room for children in back, an organ up front and the altar featuring a tastefully carved life-sized savior on the cross. Little had changed since his years there as a boy. As they moved up the aisle, Neal recalled how the students were required to attend services daily during school until grade eight, when they were given a choice to go to mass or read. Neal always read, sneaking Harold Robbins novels past the prying eyes of the nuns.

They sat in a center pew. Neal found the church calming—the hint of incense, soft purring organ and light sifting through rows of stained glass windows. They were sitting near a window depicting Jesus during the final stages of his brutal crucifixion.

He glanced around at the backs of heads, hairstyles and younger men's necks. Most of the local men kept their hair cut very short, and quite a few high school and college boys had that soft, tanned elegant arch to their naked necks. Neal studied a boy two rows up, noticing one tiny mole at the nape of his smooth hairless neck. The service began, and he quickly recalled the prayers, the format and rhythm of the thing. A reading, a response, a song. His mind drifted. He tried to make out the body shape of the stained-glass Jesus in the third station of the cross hanging near them, then snapped his head away, feeling odd and perverse. The homily was coming, which marked the second half of the mass and a slow resolve of the service. The pretty-necked boy with the tiny mole had stretched an arm across the back of his pew, his bicep plumping in a cheap cotton polo. Neal could see the strain in the boy's muscular shoulder, a slight pulling at the side. He probably wrestled, Neal thought, or was a budding gymnast. Father Conrad came down from the altar, standing at the front of the pews.

"He's very modern," Neal's mother whispered at the priest's casual demeanor. "Our monsignor would never leave the altar."

A woman in the pew ahead of them with a terrible red dye job and a bold summer dress turned and smiled at Neal's mother in acknowledgement. The two women nodded at one another, sharing a secret like school girls. Father Conrad spoke loudly.

"There's an article here in the *New Yorker* magazine," Father Conrad said.

Excited, Neal's mother nudged him as if the priest had planned his homily for Neal's visit. The red head turned again to glance their way, but rolled her eyes.

"We play bridge together," Neal's mother said, whispering and nodding toward the red head.

"It's by a respectable writer, and it's a pretty good article, but it worries me deeply," Father Conrad said, rolling the magazine up into a cone, then speaking through it like a megaphone. "We are at war. The sanctity of marriage is being attacked."

Neal felt his breath stop for a moment. He did not look toward his mother, nor at the red head that was turning again with her eye rolls. He kept his gaze on the boy with the mole on his lovely tanned neck. Then Neal forced himself to breath and shuddered as subtly as he could in disbelief.

"Our nation wants to tarnish morality, that is exactly what is happening, my friends," Father Conrad said, still speaking though the rolled up magazine. "We preach tolerance, we preach inclusion, but the sanctity of this most sacred act must be kept alive. Let's face facts, people. I will tell it like it is in terms we can all understand."

At this, the priest pounded the rolled up magazine on his lavender cloaked knee to punctuate his phrases.

"Marriage is radically threatened by our nation's so called high courts and lawmakers intent on legalizing gay marriage," he said, his face going crimson. "Today's Gospel, Ezekiel 33, states clearly that we must raise our voices. Ezekiel said that if you warn the wicked, trying to turn him from his way, and he refuses to turn from his way, he shall die for his guilt, but you shall save yourself. We must save ourselves and save our children and save the sacrament of marriage."

The mole boy was tilting his neck back now, casting his eyes to the eaved ceiling of the church, twisting the muscles in his neck left, then right, obviously bored and restless. Neal thought of how the boy's neck might taste. Salty, or maybe there would be residue from some cheap pale green soap he'd used to shower with that morning. He wanted to taste that cheap perfumed soap on his tongue.

"This is not an argument," Father Conrad said as he trolled the aisle, turning to address individuals and pressing for an air of camaraderie. "It is not a concept. It's a fact. Marriage in God's eyes is sacred and between one man, one woman. And I leave you with this, my friends. You, me, all of us must boldly take up the defense of marriage for it is an urgent necessity to ensure the flourishing of persons, the well-being of children and the common good of society. Amen."

The boy straightened his neck again and Neal thought he saw a single bead of sweat. He wanted to go touch it, and lick it off. Neal did not turn away from the boy's neck nor glance in the aisle as Father Conrad passed and headed back to the altar. The sermon was coming to a close and his mother smiled, seemingly oblivious to the deeper meaning for Neal. Like him, she hated conflict and was able to blot it out completely. He imagined that somewhere, deep down, she had to be aware that her local priest had just disturbed him.

"Thank goodness he's brief, the one saving grace," she said, as the red headed woman turned and nodded her head vigorously in agreement.

The rest of the service was a long glide to communion, and Neal kept fighting the urge to get up and leave, to tell his mother he felt a little ill. He stayed in his pew as his mother scooted out and joined the line for the holy wafer at communion. As people drifted past him on their way back to their seats, he recalled a habit he had developed as a boy, something he'd done for years, and forgotten. He closely studied the men as they turned the corner from communion at the altar, and approached him. It was similar to the way he scrutinized men in New York on a crowded subway, their feet and hands and crotches. He'd never connected the two. The men walked slowly now toward him, hands folded in prayer, mouths shut chewing the wafers, and Neal had plenty of time to check the fit of their shirt, whether their chests were tight and if they had firm stomachs. Then of course their often ill-fitting pants might reveal, in the best cases, a fluffy puff of cock, hiding and bored. The boy with the mole was headed his way, and was moving like a panther. His crew cut set off his features, big bright eyes, a tanned face and hard lips. He wore a cotton polo and Neal could make out stiff nipples. He wore khakis that pulled at the crotch and Neal shut his eyes, shutting down all arousal as he saw his mother making her way up the aisle. As she knelt, he spoke.

"I have to use the restroom, I'll meet you out at the car," he said and fled.

He stopped in the empty lobby wondering for a second if that asshole of a priest had spoken directly to him. At the curve of the hall, just leading toward the classrooms was the boy's room. Neal headed there, curious. It was very large and dark, and exactly as he'd remember it. He'd hidden in the boys' room nearly every day during recess, to avoid having to play dodge ball. The walls were painted dark red, the stalls were brown, and the urinals were short and small for boys. A row of white sinks was the only bit of lightness, other than a dirty old window at the end of the bathroom. Neal stepped up to the sink, but shrunk back, not wanting to see his reflection. He'd sat often, as a boy, on the cold tile floor and waited for the recess bell to clang, so he could slip out and meet the lines of children coming back inside. He'd imagined so many things happening to him in the bathroom. Someone yanking him into a stall, a priest he'd admired coming to find him and ask him why he was hiding, or one of the athletic Grade Eight boys coming and forcing him to kiss them on the lips.

His mother was calling lightly from the hall, and the sound of organ music was drifting in with her voice. He recalled a nun, calling him out of the bathroom. He'd been caught hiding there once. She'd had kind eyes, that nun, and he'd lied and said he was throwing up. She'd given him a warm hug. He was sure she did not believe him. He searched for her name, for the shape of her eyes. Were they like almonds, or round like bright balls? Blue or green? He was angry that he couldn't remember. His mother called again.

"Neal, are you all right," she said.

He turned the sink on and off, then went out to meet her. The lobby was crowded and Father Conrad stood surrounded by the same cluster of older women pulling at his purple robes. Neal turned and led his mother out of the awful place just as Father Conrad shot him a friendly wave.

Chapter 37

BB HERE ON *a Midwest pit stop, asking…*

Neal sat in the pink bedroom's window seat and reached for something sexy, cutting and salty to say, something about country cock and ridiculous mall fashion. He had to get a column back to New York. Staring out the window, he felt as if the things he had experienced the past several weeks and months had happened just an instant before—the cluttered, clawing whirl of his column, the revelation of Dewalt and of sobriety and the endless obsessive sexcapades—they were somehow only a few seconds old. Looking out past the delicate salmon-colored window shade at the blazing summer sun and the hissing metal lawn sprinklers, he felt he hadn't ever really left this sad little boyhood window seat. He started the column over.

BB here, begging the question—what is gay marriage? What does it mean for two men to join hands in union, to commit to monogamy to share a home, a bank account and every last chatty choice?

Again, Neal tried for a witty line, a neatly packaged phrase about dull sex and who wears the veil, who buys the condoms, who picks the china pattern…but he slumped as he heard his mother's delicate footsteps pause in the hall, under the attic fan, near his room, as she checked for noise, to spy, as she did on summer nights when he'd taken to bed early because he just couldn't stand the tougher boys in the front yard. He kept writing, challenged now to come up with something. He ignored her subtle creeping in the hall.

Gay marriage, says BB, involves a loss of sanity and really, of self. It's about giving up the essential YOU and making room for another's manly madness. It seems like an utter release, girls, but it's a trap and for gay men, it's practically impossible.

Neal shut his eye and wanted to stop, but he could not and he felt the door sway behind him, felt his mother creep near because she couldn't stand the suspense of his aloneness, and he kept writing.

If you're still determined to marry that man, BB says, you have to grow up first.

He wrote faster and felt a surge of words and feeling.

To grow up in depth and understanding because you have to see the wild world from inside this other man's shoes. So get ready to get loopy and lose yourself boys, I know, I mean really lose it, lose it all like… the breath in his arms, and pieces of myself to make room for him. Compromise to see his humanity and I reveal mine and I let my ugliness come though and we find our way ahead…Because it is a union, and it's four balls not two swinging in all my selfish drama.

He knew she was directly behind him, reading, which made her a part of it, which was fine because she was and always had been. He wouldn't acknowledge her and he would not stop and he would not hide anymore. His fingers fled from him, on fire, like a piano playing itself.

Men want to fuck and to be left alone and then I am alone and empty and empty men find emptier men out of that terrible place. It is impossible to reveal anything other than the fake self, the sex self. Because men loving men, is a sacred and beautiful thing and it is delicate and easily broken, and BB knows because I glimpsed it and then snapped it into pieces before it had the slightest chance to bloom.

Neal sat up and could see, out of the corner of his eye, his mother's deep wandering eyes prying, reading, and he did not care. He was lost to the surreal veil of this whole thing.

BB says go and marry him. Do it. And please keep him close, and yourself closer, don't let the BB types in, don't let them scoff at your happiness or blow you in the steam room and say it doesn't matter because it does, it demeans what you have with that one you love, and don't let BB tell you it's all a ridiculous scam. Don't listen, don't...because BB really is just full of so much shit and soft pink sawdust.

Neal stopped. He turned and she was gone, like a ghost, and he knew she would never speak of the secret he had just written to her and himself, and he wouldn't press nor would she. He felt it was over now with Dewalt. Maybe with New York. He would send the column, untouched, to Annie and tell her to print it. And he didn't care who read it or if it sounded like utter nonsense or if he lost his job over it. He may never go back to that city, those people, the men, Bergdorf. Because he felt what he'd been doing, and writing and buying and fucking and claiming for years was utter nonsense. He lay down on the tiny pink bed, and shut his eyes, and thought of nobody, and went to sleep, listening to the distant sound of the sprinklers and imagining it was an endless, lifeless rain.

HE WOKE FACING forgotten boys he'd had sex with—buck-toothed Johnnie and fat neighbor Tom—long ago nude collidings that were more acrobatic than sensual. He sat up and saw her perched on the edge of his bed hands folded, hair swept back and he thought she may have been crying but then decided it was only the new morning light on her face. He'd slept through the night. She didn't look at him, and moved very little and spoke so softly he had to strain to hear. He wondered if he were still dreaming.

"There's a lot you give up. I don't think young people see

that," she raised her head to the ceiling and sighed and he felt he didn't know her at that moment. "There is just no other way. Everyone gives up a lot to make things work. Dad gave up the dancing. I didn't even think about going to college."

At this, his mother laughed and covered her face like a girl caught in a prank.

"Oh, I lie like a rug, of course I thought of it," she said. "But I chose us, you and Dad. I just wanted you to know. You seem so…"

She didn't finish the sentence though she seemed to finish the thought and with that she stood up and patted a hand through her hair and left the room.

Neal lay on the bed and thought of New York, knowing that despite his recent rush of feeling, he'd go back. He had to. He had nowhere else to go. It was his city. And he'd go straight to Bergdorf's and things would be all right. He felt that the ghost he'd seen, his mother, had been only a dream, and the whole thing, his horrid marriage column and this long sad trip was just a mirage. He would find his way back and he would drink lots of coffee and he would have lots of sex and he would be okay again and all memory of Dewalt would fade completely. He sat up and went to wash his face.

Chapter 38

HIS FATHER SAT reading the paper on the back porch under the ceiling fan. The morning heat was ferocious. Neal stepped out. His mother was at the grocery store. He planned to dart away for a walk with a nod to his Dad, but instead he sat, drawn in for a moment.

"Nice to have you visit son, always makes your mother happy," he said, flipping through the real estate section.

His father set the paper down and turned to look at him directly. The phone rang. They both sat still. Annie had been trying to reach him ceaselessly.

"That young girl has been calling all morning," his father said, referring to Annie. "Your friend Dewalt called three times last night when you were knocked out. We spoke. What's going on there?"

Neal was agitated that Annie had found his parent's phone number and likely given it to Dewalt, but more than that, he was angry at his father's intimate mention of Dewalt.

"What do you mean you spoke?" Neal said, flushing with a jolt of rage. "Why this sudden interest in my personal life?"

His father did not look up, and calmly read his paper.

"I'm interested in your success, Neal. You tell me what you chose," he said.

He'd always complained that his father was distant and unconcerned, but realized now that the liked it that way. It was safer. He had no intention of opening up. He found his father's nonchalant attitude infuriating.

"I'm going for a walk," Neal said.

Francis looked up from the paper and gave Neal a short smile. He went back to reading as Neal headed out across the neighbor's yard, out of the secluded neighborhood and toward a nearby field.

The field stretched up toward a set of railroad tracks where Neal used to hide out as a kid. He wanted to see if anything had changed. He also liked the feeling of blazing sun on the metal tracks, and the rumble of an approaching train. He entered the field, pressing through a patch of tall purple wild flowers. He wore a pair of plaid linen shorts, his Bergdorf Goodman woven sandals and a Jil Sander tank top. The high field grass was itchy, licking at his bare legs. Gnats nipped his ankles. His sandals felt heavy, and he realized he must look odd traipsing through the field dressed like he was going to a Hampton's pool party. The two-lane highway near the field was quiet. In the distance, he saw a mound of a hill, wild and overgrown with a twisted sea of colorful weeds and sticky spiked flowers rising up to the railroad tracks. It had seemed huge as a child, he recalled, like climbing a rugged mountain. Getting closer, he realized it was little more than a mound. The rail tracks were elevated, and cargo trains still ran through St. Louis several times a day. At the foot of the hill, he felt something bite his ankle and he swatted, then stumbled back onto his ass. From the ground, the hill looked higher, and he thought of long ago childhood summer afternoons sitting alone on the tracks, writing poems, fantasizing, wishing someone would come along and scoop him up, or come along and rape him with passionate abandon, or kidnap and marry him. He'd masturbated on those tracks a few times, in the heat, feeling absolutely deviant, like a child convict defiling the entire state of Missouri with his lewdness.

He took off his heavy sandals, giving into the biting insects and hot grass, then got up and climbed the ragged little hill. At its top, he could see the blacktop highway below, and not so far off the edge of his parent's neighborhood. He sat down onto the metal rail, feeling the burning heat rush up onto his thighs and ass. He'd always wanted to fry an egg on the searing train tracks, to find out if it was possible. He pressed a finger to the rail, and pulled back, as if from a stove. In the moment of contact though, he felt a tiny tremble. Somewhere in the distance, a train was coming. The tracks scooted up and onto a little bridge over the two-lane highway, then dipped down out of sight. Neal knelt and pressed his ear to the ground, listening. He'd read as a boy that you could hear the rumble of the train coming up through the earth. He heard nothing, just a hollow muffle. His hand back on the rail, he again felt the tremble, wondering how long until the locomotive would creep over the hill and race toward him. In the distance, a pickup truck sped across the two-lane highway, and near that, a black man approached. For a second he wished it was Dewalt, rushing to find him. For once, someone rushing to find him. St. Louis was truly changing, become more diverse. Diversity when he was a kid was the Italian family moving into an otherwise Irish neighborhood. He knew no black children, no Asians, no Latins.

Neal sat balancing on the track, placing both hands on the rail to sense the slowly approaching vibration. He could feel the blazing morning sun on his face. He knew he needed to call Annie. The swimsuit issue was out. He wondered what she thought of his nutty column and he wondered if he ever really thought he could follow through on any of his late night insanity about never going back to New York, quitting the magazine, leaving the life he'd spent years building. And he thought of Dewalt, the impossibility of that, and he shut his eyes tight and felt the trembling rail on his ass and he saw in his black eyes, the eyes of himself as a boy, with long unkempt hair and pale pale skin and a naked urge to have sex, to be touched, to make contact, and he saw that tiny little elf of a kid here alone on these tracks reaching for something that he now knew would never come. He felt the rails shaking and he realized he needed to move because he wasn't prepared to be smashed by a train. He had too much to do. There was still a chance. The rail shook and he felt a movement, something pressing into the rail, something hard. He opened his eyes quickly and stood, dizzy in the sun, half expecting to be sliced open by a speeding train. In the sunlight, he saw Dewalt. He stood before him, sweaty, one hand cocked on his forehead. It was not a mirage.

"I found you," Dewalt said.

The tracks under his bare feet now began to shake, and Neal realized the train was approaching. He stepped away from the track, off to one side, followed by Dewalt. Over the near hill, a locomotive approached loud and angry, clanging. Dewalt spoke, but Neal heard only bits of words against the rush of the train. The engine slid past, car by dirty car, rattling and screeching on metal rails.

"Annie sent…your column…sent me," Dewalt's voice came in and out, staccato with the rushing noise of the train.

Dewalt kept speaking, then quit, and reached out and grabbed Neal harshly, he held him by the shoulders and shook him like a child, just shook him and Neal thought Dewalt might throw him into the rushing train, but instead he pulled him roughly to him. He kissed him, buried his tongue, that gold tooth tasting like the metal rail tracks, pushed into his mouth and rushed his tongue all through Neal's mouth, saying something as he kissed, all this too blotted out by that monster relic of a train screeching past. Finally the train, all its cars, passed, its sounds fading, and Dewalt, still holding tight to Neal spoke.

"I don't give a shit about nothing, it's us," Dewalt said. "I been mad nuts, I had to get at you. You fuck who you want, or just me, just be with me. Don't be stupid."

Neal looked into Dewalt's eyes.

"Why?" Neal said.

Dewalt again shook him, violently now, like a loose little rag doll.

"I love you asshole, all right, come with me, stay with me, marry me, what the fuck," he said. "Ssssshit."

Neal took it in, under the hot sun, seeing beyond Dewalt the boy naked in the field, masturbating alone, fantasizing angry little desires and never believing anything, never thinking anyone would ever come to him. Dewalt released him and sat in the dirt. Neal sat down next to him. The train blew its whistle in the distance and the sun blazed as Neal leaned into Dewalt, and shut his eyes, and smiled back at the smiling boy in his mind, and it felt right for the first time in a long time, felt right the first time in forever. He pressed his lips to Dewalt's ear and said it, said it over and over, yes, yes, yes.

Chapter 39

IT WAS A crisp and unusually bright May day in the city, which Malice took credit for, insisting it was part of his master orchestration of the "hottest gay wedding since Ellen and Portia tumbled down the aisle." Neal nursed a Diet Coke in bed, surveying his studio apartment which was a messy mix of nuptial chaos. A teetering tower of Wedding Issue magazines hovered over three dozen color fabric "day theme" samples, a slew of discarded invitation envelopes, DJ audition sampler CDs and seven wilted bunches of flowers. There was a yellowing *New York Times* article about Campillo de Ranas, a small village in Spain where chic gay couples were tying the knot. Neal had nixed that Malice-inspired brainstorm. The buzzer blared. It was Nick on his way up with one of the bridesboys. Originally planning a simple procession with Annie as Best Woman, Neal had agreed to four sexy bridesboys in what was becoming a mini-runway show for Nick's new swimwear line.

Dewalt gave Neal full reign to dream and "knock it out of the park, cause you ain't ever doing it again kid." Dewalt's only stipulation: "I ain't wearing no fucking dress and neither are you." With Malice at the helm as wedding planner, what began as a simple affair edged toward an event promising to eclipse Andreas' annual summer Oracle Orgy—in spirit if not in numbers. Neal wrapped himself in an oversized robe as Nick burst in, Toby and Annie in tow. Toby, who had been appearing regularly in *Pop* fashion spreads since his splashy debut the previous summer in the swimsuit issue, wore a belted raincoat over bare legs. Annie wore huge black headphones, gym shorts and a hoodie.

"This is all so outlandish. I gotta pee," she said in a high-pitched voice, giving Neal a hug then dashing to the studio's tiny bathroom.

Neal smiled, grateful for Annie's constant enthusiasm, which had kept his spirits high during the sometimes arduous wedding planning process. Nick's cheeks were flushed. The three men stood in the center of Neal's cramped little studio. A row of shoeboxes lined one wall, and yellow sticky notes papered the wall with reminders from Malice. Neal was moving into Dewalt's Harlem apartment after the wedding.

"I know you said no last second changes, but I was inspired watching *Querelle*," Nick said. "Consider this."

Toby dropped the coat. Nick had designed a navy trunk with a chunky woven rope waist tie and an anchor detail on one side. The top was new and much more revealing than what they had discussed. It was sheer and cream colored, connecting from the waist of the swimsuit and jutting up Toby's lean chest like a narrow tongue, leaving the sides very bare, his ribs showing. Nick pulled out the crowning touch and perched it on Toby's head. It was a white French Legion style sailor's hat with a red fluffy pom pom on top.

"It's hot," Neal said. "Go for it."

Nick threw his arms around Neal's neck and held him tight, his body shuddering a tiny bit as if he were holding back tears. Ever since Nick had left Brandon, with an unexpected hefty "divorce" nest egg to create his small "dreamed about" swimwear line he'd become increasingly emotional. Neal hugged Nick and smiled at Toby who stood stock still, as if he expected runway cameras to flash at any second.

"It's my wedding day not yours, why are you crying," Neal said.

As Nick pulled away, laughing and rattling off details about the other bridesboys looks, Neal thought briefly of Rovvie, and missed him, wishing he were there. He would have been his Best Man. He'd gotten one postcard from Rovvie, with an opaque note "doing ok…in ugly Burma, love R". Neal worried about his friend. Andreas had recovered quickly, and Neal suspected he was doing a lot more than just escorting young Toby to the event that day. Andreas never mentioned Caz, and Neal suspected the loss of his kid brother was the greatest pain for Andreas. The door buzzer blared three times in a row, the rapid-fire designator of Malice. He refused to speak into intercom boxes, rather announced his arrival with a triplet buzz.

"I'm going, I can't take her right now," Nick said, also aware of Malice's entry code. "See you this afternoon."

He gave Neal an alternating triple cheek kiss—the two cheek kiss was as over as Chelsea—and darted out with a wide-eyed Toby. Malice swept in, arms full of deep purple calla lilies, nearly colliding with Annie as she came out of the bathroom. Malice threw the flowers on Neal's pullout couch, which was still open and disheveled, then threw himself dramatically onto the couch next to the flowers, eyes shut, hand on forehead.

"This is what the bitches gave me," he said. "I said pale purple, these are as dark as cow dung."

Neal plucked a flower off the bed and handed it to Annie. The deep purple was strange and alluring. Annie held it to her cheek, attempting drama.

"These are perfect," Neal said.

As if poked with an electric prod, Malice bound off the bed, hands on hips. He wore bell-bottom white lounge pants, a form fitting white nylon top and a huge paisley patterned bandana wrapped around his forehead. He eyed the flowers, then sighed.

"Well, you're the bride. Dark purple it is," he said.

A voice trailed from the hall.

"A deep deep hue is always, as they say in the naughtiest

spots in Berlin, what one needs to keep…is it an eye out for or something about the bum's rush?"

Albert stood at the doorway, gasping for breath after the three-floor walk up, looking like a flouncier version of Malice in bell bottoms and wide bandana but covered with jewels. He stood still, gazing at Neal, and very softly began to hum "here comes the bride" then put his hand to his mouth as if overcome with emotion. Glancing across the room, Malice screamed. He'd spotted Neal's tuxedo, which was meant to be a secret reveal. Nick had helped him pick it out, and spent hours convincing him that it was a "very worthy attire investment." Luckily, in a wildly uncharacteristic move, his father had granted him a big advance on his trust fund to finance the wedding. Perhaps it assuaged Dad's guilt for not attending, Neal thought. Both Neal's parents had declined his expertly designed, cream-colored invitation with the silver blue stenciling. The invite was thumb tacked to the wall, next to the Tuxedo.

Neal Tate & Dewalt Johnston
Invite you to celebrate with them as they join in loving union
On the twenty-fifth day of May
At half past three
At the home of Madame Gingerleen Winderfeld
New York, New York

Malice eyed Neal's tux, D&G's spring line from Bergdorf, a single-button lean silhouette high sheen white tuxedo with tar black lapels and front pocket detail. The bow tie was white with black stripes. The shoes were Gucci. He bought the opposite look—black tux, white lapel, black tie with white polka dots—for Dewalt. Nick had urged him to do the whole black and white theme though initially Neal had balked at the crass obviousness of it all. Nick had won that argument, insisting that it was best to boldly emphasize rather than hide. Neal went with it for a reason that had nothing to do with fashion. He liked the idea of embracing, instead of hiding. He'd lived with so many secrets for so long. The tux choice, he vowed, would be a symbolic beginning to a new, more honest Neal. Listening to Malice's gushing gasps, he wondered if he could ever really change that much.

"This is so fucking classy," Malice said, spinning back toward Neal. "My baby is all grown up."

Neal smiled, taking applause from Malice and Annie, and Albert's warm embrace. He did feel grown up, or at least headed in that direction. He was taking more stake in his life. His parents had sent a beautiful antique writing desk as a gift, and had it delivered to Dewalt's apartment. Neal wondered what big, red-headed Father Conrad with his anti-gay marriage homily would say about the whole affair. He felt, deep down, that his mother would have thoroughly enjoyed the day, though her commitment to the Catholic church made it impossible. A big, black lesbian preacher, Reverend Alexis Sasha Cantrall, was performing the civil ceremony that day.

Neal missed his mother's input, though Malice had been amazing. He'd pulled out every favor, every connection, and taken on the wedding as a hell-bent crusade. He'd even secured the divinely hot Sylvia Weinstock, lauded by New York Magazine as the 'da Vinci of wedding cake chefs', to construct a towering, six-tiered, cream and blue shaded creation. Sweeping up the calla lilies, Malice twirled out of the house, followed by a chattering Albert. Though he'd never been asked, he'd taken on the role of Malice's assistant.

"I'm going to pick up Laird and we're heading to the mansion," Annie said.

Neal gripped her hand tightly, not wanting to let go. He saw a swimming swirl of joy in her eyes that he wanted to steal away. She gave him a kiss and darted off. Alone in his robe, Neal nursed his soda, realizing that, in a few short hours, he would be a married man. For a moment he had a rush of something like terror, but as he had done during many restless and sexless nights alone over the past few months, he brushed it away and focused on the joy of planning, and the sense of calm and happiness he had seen in Annie's eyes. It was the same feeling of calm he got when he shut his eyes and pictured Dewalt.

NEAL STOOD IN the wide, cool entryway of the Winderfeld mansion. The place was as quiet as a church. The mansion, built in the late 1800's, was four floors of massive, old world glam on the city's Upper East Side, and it had been unoccupied for years. It was owned by condiment heiress Gingerleen Winderfeld (just Gin to friends) who'd never stepped foot in the place. Gin was an 'ancient morphine addict' living in Paris, Albert had explained. Albert had spent boyhood summers with the heiress in Venice. She 'adored' the idea of a naughty gay wedding in her home, but vanished three months before the event. After weeks of absolute chaos, she resurfaced with a note of blessing to Neal scrawled in French, promising twenty of her staff to "dust up" the place. Albert made a pre-wedding gift of a diamond ring—the one Neal had recovered from Andreas' party last May—to defray costs.

Standing alone in the cool entryway, Neal recalled, a year ago, lingering at the door to Andreas' Oracle Orgy summer party. He shut his eyes and sighed, thinking of melting Greek ice sculptures, servant boys in white bikinis, and Trudy Pratte, then opened them, wanting now to take in every single second of *this* miraculous day. As Malice explained, guests would enter the mansion's double front doors and follow a path toward the grand staircase where a string quartet played. The base of the staircase was decorated with two eight-foot, circular sculptures of blue hydrangea flowers, this setting the cream and blue color theme. The second floor had a large garden area where the ceremony would take place. The reception was on the rooftop terrace, which spanned the length and width of the entire mansion.

As Neal opened his eyes, he noticed, in the distance, on the staircase, the back of a beautiful black boy. The fellow turned slowly, as if he sensed Neal's presence. He stared down a bit regally. He was tall, lean, muscular in a sinewy athletic way and dressed in bright tennis whites. His skin was a warm brown, his jaw square. He was striking, both masculine yet boyish. His head was shaved, save for one Mohawk style strip which had been dyed pale blonde. He put a hand on his hip and stood still, and Neal felt as if he were being confronted. The moment passed, and the boy moved swiftly and elegantly down the stairs toward Neal, reaching his hand out.

"I'm Justin, Dewalt's friend," he said. "It's great to finally meet you."

Neal had asked Dewalt if he wanted any of his friends to participate. Dewalt, who started calling the wedding 'a mad hot circus', had laughed out loud and told Neal he'd check it out, then came back with the news that Boney had volunteered to DJ and an old high school buddy (Justin) was up to being a bridesboy.

"We gotta represent, I got a few dudes in my past who are all out and shit," Dewalt said.

Justin took Neal's hand and shook it slowly.

"You're a lucky man," Justin said, revealing a perfect set of teeth and a subtle glint in his eye that frightened Neal for a moment.

A light and fragrant May breeze blew as the front door opened and Malice rushed in followed by three chattering boys and Albert who was wearing a short and sassy black wig for the occasion. Nick swept in just behind them. Barely acknowledging Neal beyond a swift kiss, Malice led his troop up the grand staircase, shouting orders the entire way while speaking rapidly into his cell phone.

"We're mere hours to curtain, what do you mean the shrimp is delayed, God save the queen," Malice screamed as he ran up the staircase.

Knowing that things would soon fly into overdrive with the

arrival of the catering staff, flowers, champagne and more, Neal grabbed Nick and retreated to his third floor bedroom suite to begin his prep process. Justin, for the moment, had vanished.

THE 'BRIDES' BEDROOM in the Winderfeld mansion was about five times the size of Neal's studio apartment. There was a seating area with two sofas, a dressing room, and a canopy bed set off against one wall. Three sets of double windows looked out onto the garden below, where the ceremony set-up was being completed. The bedroom's floor was marble, the walls covered with a tiny blue bud wallpaper pattern. Nick kept yanking Neal away from the window, terrified that Dewalt might see him.

"I didn't know you were so traditional," Neal said.

There was little for Neal to do. He'd had a lengthy shower, shaved and primped his hair. All he had to do was slip on his tux. Malice had set up a bar stocked with champagne, Diet Coke and Red Bull. Neal was on his third Diet Coke, afraid the Red Bull may get him so riled he'd run down the aisle and leap into Dewalt's arms. Toby and 'C' the Swedish model from last May's swimsuit shoot, were chatting on the sofa, already done up in their bridesboy attire. Nick had a few fashion magazine editor friends attending, a nice way to get attention for his upcoming swimsuit line launch.

The door opened and Nick ran toward it in a panic, afraid it was Dewalt. It was Andreas. As he entered, Toby stood up. Andreas paused at the door. He wore a simple Armani Tux. Neal held his gaze. Toby moved swiftly, his red trunks and matching sheer red T-top showing off every sleek and muscled curve. He stopped in front of Andreas, who reached out a hand to the boy's cheek, stroked it, then gently kissed him. He took Toby's hand and led him toward Neal.

"I wanted to wish you the best today," Andreas said.

Neal, wrapped in only a plush robe, felt a little vulnerable in front of his boss.

"You can still change your mind about the column," Andreas said.

Neal smiled. The Bergdorf Boy column he'd written in St. Louis and sent to Annie had never made it in print, but had made it into Dewalt's hands, which triggered Dewalt's dramatic flight to Missouri. He'd let Andreas know last month that he was abandoning the Bergdorf Boy column after the wedding. The column had always been a big hit, along with two subsequent fashion shoots. Andreas said that while he could never replace Neal, the column would continue to run weekly.

"Did you find someone to take over as Bergdorf Boy?" Neal said.

Andreas squeezed Toby's hand and nodded. The boy's eyes lit up and Neal wondered what may lie beneath Toby's deep Southern drawl and over the top enthusiasm. Again, he thought of Rovvie.

"I'm scared to death, but Andreas has faith in me," Toby said. "I'd love your feedback when my first column comes out. I went and sat at Café III in Bergdorf's like you did."

The door swung and Malice swirled in with Albert at his side.

"Everybody out. We're nearly there. Give Neal his space," Malice screamed. "Annie will come to get you momentarily."

The room emptied, and Neal found himself alone in his robe, with a soda, and a lingering memory of Rovvie. He wondered where his friend was at that very moment. In Burma, Asia, Peru, Paris? He dropped his robe, and went for his tux.

THE GARDEN WAS in full bloom, a wash of spring flowers in blue, purple and white. Guests were seated and, from his perch at the bedroom window, Neal could see their heads. Hatted, styled, sprayed, coiffed, bald spots and three veils. Up front, Albert's black wig glistened in the mid-day sun. Neal stepped away and took a final look at himself. He couldn't quite meet his own pale blue eyes, but he took in his outfit.

He'd had the tux fitted. The pants hung just above the ankle, a nod to designer Thom Browne. On Neal's right ankle was an eyeball tattoo, wide and staring, his with lashes to differentiate it from the twin tattoo on Dewalt's ankle. He was sockless. The Gucci shoes hurt a bit, but the look was right for May. He'd had his eyes tweezed, his hair lightened, his face peeled. He looked as good as he possibly could, and yet he had a sudden desire to flee. There was a soft knock at the door. He imagined it was news. Dewalt had vanished. The wedding was off. Malice had slit his wrists.

Justin crept in, moving toward Neal, hesitating. Neal turned to the boy. They'd added a gold shimmer to his eyelids and something pink and glistening to his lips. His trunks were white, his sheer T-top also white with a very thin blue stripe up the center.

"I couldn't find Nick. Could you check my seam in back," Justin said.

The boy slowly turned, offering his ass to Neal. There was a slip of a seam up the center, setting off his perfect, high, toned beefy ass. Justin flexed slightly and Neal felt dizzy, ill, wanting to reach out and touch what could be the most beautiful ass he'd ever seen. He felt his hand moving, felt his lips moving and one knee bending, but he shut his eyes and did not move and did not cry out and told himself to stop shaking. Things were going to be different now.

"Dewalt likes it," Justin said softly.

Neal opened his eyes and Justin was facing him, looking triumphant.

"What did you say?" Neal said.

Justin smirked, gave Neal a full up and down look, then turned to go. There was a voice at the door.

"Neal, you ready?" Annie said.

She stepped into the room wearing an adorable boy's-sized black tuxedo, a bow tie and black leather high-top sneakers.

Neal paused and thought of his desires, his deepest desires, beyond the asses and cocks and bathhouses, beyond Bergdorf and success and really, beyond what he could even imagine. Annie's eyes were soft as she smiled broadly.

"This is it," she said.

"Justin," Neal said. "One more thing."

Justin turned and Neal moved to him quickly, directly, raised his hand as if to touch the boy's cheek, then pulled back.

"Stay away from my husband," Neal said.

Justin smirked and turned, giving Annie a look.

"Now," Neal said. "Now, I'm ready.

NEAL STOOD IN a shrouded spot just beyond the back row of seats. Toby, the last bridesboy, was scattering blue and cream flower petals as he moved up the aisle, pausing for photographs and a smattering of applause. The music was energetic, high pitched and clubby. Annie squeezed Neal's arm as he stared up the aisle toward the front. Malice had placed a row of large potted Brides' Wreath bushes, the same his mother had in her backyard, near the altar.

Neal saw, first, the eyeball on Dewalt's naked ankle, then slowly, in the distance, he met his lover's eyes. He breathed deeply, and was glad there was a mysterious little Justin and glad there was a tiny hint of doubt in Dewalt's eyes mixed with a light and an honest calling. He imagined Dewalt having as many secrets as he did and he wanted them, all of them, they would unravel each other slowly, revealing. A gust of wind blew as the music shifted to a traditional march. As the wind scattered the petals up and over the guests, Neal took in one very long deep breath, and then, Neal took a step.

About the Author

AN AWARD-WINNING WRITER, Scott Alexander Hess has written fiction which has appeared in the *Thema Literary Journal* and *Omnia Revitas Review*. Richard Labonte of Bookmarks called his gritty debut novel *Diary of a Sex Addict* "relentlessly erotic and divinely written."

Scott is working on his new novel, *The Jockey*, set in rural Arkansas and New York City circa 1918, and his screenplay, *Tom in America*, is being produced by Queens Pictures in 2012. Scott has contributed to various national magazines, including *Genre*, *OutTraveler*, and *Instinct*. His essay on male intimacy will be part of Leslie Smith's book to be published in 2012.

He is a MFA graduate of The New School. For more information, please visit scottalexanderhess.com.

Made in United States
North Haven, CT
25 February 2024